A Love Reborn

A Love Reborn

DANA LYONS

Black Lyon Publishing, LLC

A LOVE REBORN
Copyright © 2013 by Dana McEndree

Our books may be ordered through your local bookstore or by visiting the publisher:

BlackLyonPublishing.com

Black Lyon Publishing, LLC
PO Box 567
Baker City, OR 97814

This is a work of fiction. All of the characters, names, events, organizations and conversations in this novel are either the products of the author's vivid imagination or are used in a fictitious way for the purposes of this story.

ISBN-10:   1-934912-52-2
ISBN-13:   978-1-934912-52-2
Library of Congress Control Number: 2013930319

Published and printed in
the United States of America.

Black Lyon Paranormal Romance

For
Faby

CHAPTER ONE

Byrgamon, Queen of the Amenti, reached for Kedare, running her fingers across the warm skin and hard muscles of his chest. "Our marriage and this plan of yours will turn the world upside down," she said. "Two lands, two rulers, one country. This means I can finally bury my Journal of War."

Contentment overwhelmed her being, fed by their recent love-making. Kedare brought a new life to her tired world, and she was suddenly free. Free from battle and death, free of the loneliness of a queen at constant war. Free to experience love.

"Bahk-ir will not like our arrangement," Kedare said.

His words spoke a sharp and brittle truth, intruding on her happiness. A shudder came snaking down her spine, for she dreaded the day she must inform Bahk-ir of her and Kedare's union.

Kedare stroked her shoulders and pulled her close. When he held her tight, he rolled until he covered her, heart to heart, hip to hip. "We should take your Journal of War and close the Temple at Gebel together. Come with me to Cyrenaica, where we will announce to the world our plans. Summon Bahk-ir there and we will meet with him together." Nose to nose, he peered deep into her eyes. "My love, I do not trust Bahk-ir. Please do not meet with him alone."

"Calling him to Cyrenaica would be a great insult to such a powerful man," Byrgamon protested weakly. "He is a mighty warrior who has fought many battles for his country—for this he deserves a measure of respect. The retirement I offer will be too sweet for him to re—"

"The General," he insisted, cutting short her words, "is a mighty and powerful man who desires much beyond what he is due."

Deep in her heart, Byrgamon agreed. Lately, Bahk-ir had come to speak of the Magic of War as their power, and he watched her with bright possessive eyes. While he had come to repulse her, he was commander of her army. She could not ignore him.

Outside, the wind howled, jerking at the tent ropes, making them hum. Byrgamon cocked her head, detecting a faint song of loneliness out on the distant plains. She strained to hear more, her gaze fixed on a point beyond Kedare's face. In her peripheral vision, the tent flaps fluttered angrily, allowing a foreign, dusty odor to invade the tent. She inhaled.

Ancient and dry—the smell of vast time ... and sadness.

She stiffened with alarm, feeling the cold of eternity at her toes.

"Gamon, my love," Kedare said, hugging her tight, rubbing warmth back into her rigid body. He turned her chin, reclaiming her eyes and attention. "You are not alone in this battle."

"I am not ... threatened by anyone. I am Queen," she stated with finality. She shook off the morbid mood that had grabbed her and turned her thoughts to their bright future.

"This great kingdom of ours will be born, not from an act of aggression, but from an act of love." She moved her hips suggestively, drawing his quick response, lightening her mood. His love always made her feel invincible.

"I am a great queen, accomplished in the Magic of War," she declared. "I am a woman in love, eager to begin life with my true heart. With these two forces behind me, what could possibly stop me?"

The Eastern Frontier, Two Days Ride from Gebel

General Omon Bahk-ir swirled the goblet of wine, feeling the future fall right into his hands. "Byrgamon, my Queen, we will unite into a power the world has never known." He strode to the tent opening. Before him, as far as the eye could see, was the army of Amenti.

I am the Lord of War. My army is the greatest fighting force on the northern plains.

Next, the queen would be his—and then her power. Once he took control of her power, he could command the battleground from the comfort of the palace. The Lord of War would then take the world.

He threw his head back and smacked his lips, savoring the exhilaration, for he was on the brink of attaining his life's dream. The years of sacrifice and his long career of mean living conditions were at last going to yield him what he deserved. When he possessed the secret of the magic symbols in the Journal of War ... gold, power—the world would be his.

The sound of an approaching horse intruded. A rider bearing the General's banner came from the direction of Gebel. Bahk-ir recognized Tareq, his man in the queen's household.

The rider came up to the General's tent and swung off a horse lathered dark with sweat. He offered a salute. "General."

Bahk-ir commanded his young slave. "Take the horse and walk him cool before you water him."

The boy sprang from out of the darkness and took the horse.

With Tareq following, Bahk-ir strode into his tent. After sitting at his desk, he motioned for the rider to help himself to a water skin.

"My Lord," the rider said as he took the skin. "Forgive me for arriving at such an hour. Matters of interest to you have developed in Gebel."

"Go on," the General encouraged after the man drank.

"Of late, the Queen has been restless. Since she returned from Cyrenaica, I have seen her stare with longing across the mountains toward the great sea. In the early mornings she often times will appear in an instant, as she does with her magic, and I see the hem of her cloak wet with dew, as though she had just walked the plain. So I rode down the mountain in the direction of her longing. There, about a day's ride out on the plain, I found a cluster of tents with one great tent some distance off alone. I waited and watched. In the heart of night, I saw Queen Byrgamon meet a man there, then she returns to the city before the sun rises." The rider paused to drink again.

General Bahk-ir slowly absorbed Tareq's words, his mind

stunned by this report of the queen's betrayal. A chill began ebbing into his heart. "What else?"

"After observing their behavior for many nights, I knew I could approach quietly under cover of their lovemaking. I was able to move near enough to the tent to listen for some time while they repeatedly—"

As Byrgamon's full betrayal became clear, Bahk-ir felt his face grow hard with anger. A cold wave of resentment fanned outward from his heart, smothering the hot fires of his ambition. Pressure grew within his head as a great roaring wind battered his ears, even though the walls of the tent lay quiet.

The rider rushed on. "They would talk, afterward. The queen intends to dispose of her journal and consort with this man, Kedare, after she has bought your compliance. There is talk of combining the two armies."

Bahk-ir's toes curled within his sandals, gripping an earth suddenly rolling in chaos. His fingers squeezed the hardwood arms of his chair, longing instead to wrap around the traitorous neck of his queen. Rage filled his throat, defeating any words.

In the lengthening silence, the rider anxiously moved from foot to foot, looking at the tent opening. "Shall I go, sir?"

Bahk-ir looked up, having forgotten the rider even existed. He stared at the man intently, reviewing all he said. "Did the queen say how she intended to dispose of the magic book?"

"No, my Lord. She gave no such details."

"Huh," Bahk-ir grunted. He reached for a small chest on his desk and counted out several gold pieces. As he walked past the tent opening, he glanced out and saw the servant boy walking the rider's horse some distance away, barely visible beyond a small dip in the terrain. "Does anyone else know what you have shared with me?" Bahk-ir asked.

"I always acted alone, as you instructed."

"Excellent," the General said. "You deserve to be rewarded handsomely." He handed the gold pieces to the rider, who took them eagerly. As Tareq inspected his treasure, Bahk-ir smoothly stepped behind him and slipped a sharp dagger into the man's ribs. Tareq cried out with pain, but Bahk-ir already had a hand over his mouth. The rider sagged to the floor, scattering his gold pieces across the carpet.

General Bahk-ir wiped his dagger clean on the rider's robes and set the dying man on his side so the bleeding would spill internally and not onto the carpeted floor. As the man moaned through his last breath, Bahk-ir's brown eyes turned westward toward Gebel and the queen.

The rider's shocking news initially brought a cold feeling to swell in Bahk-ir's heart, reaching to chill his mind. But his thoughts were on fire now. He dragged Tareq's body from the tent and pitched it down an incline where it disappeared into the shadows. He returned to his tent and collected the fallen gold pieces.

"My Lord, he is cool," called the servant boy from outside. He held the reins to the now rider-less horse.

Bahk-ir walked out and tossed the boy one of the gold pieces. "Bring me a fresh horse," he commanded. "One I can ride hard."

•

Byrgamon walked down the Temple, past the spoils of war, so abundant since she became queen. She passed the jewelry and the furniture in exotic woods from lands far to the south. Even the life-like statues of the cheetah and gazelle and the crocodile did not sway her.

"This will be my final and lasting contribution to the art of death and destruction," she said. "I will put the Journal of War out of commission."

At the end of the corridor she stopped and reached out her right hand, waving her fingers in strange contortions. She materialized on the opposite side of the stone in a small chamber she had created with her magic.

She gestured again and flame lit the wick of a lamp she left on her last visit. The wick ignited immediately, sending a warm glow to drive back the utter darkness of the chamber. At the far wall she set the lamp on a zebrawood table next to a niche carved in the rock. She picked up the journal and held it to her forehead. "For a long time, you were all I had," she said softly.

A tear ran down her cheek. 'How lonely I was with only war and the General to sustain me. But now I have love—and there is no room for war." She carefully placed the journal in the niche.

"No one shall ever use you again, for I am the last to know your secrets. My hands are the last to rouse the power from your symbols. You are forbidden to reveal your presence and knowledge to any soul's hands but mine." She moved her fingers as she spoke. With her last gesture, the journal disappeared.

A special ironwood panel was carved to fit in grooves cut into the rock, sealing the niche. She poured water from a pitcher into a bowl filled with dried clay and stirred the concoction. A layer was applied, and while the clay was still wet, she collected a handful of small rocks and commanded them to break apart. She tossed the rubble at the wet clay where it stuck and joined with the wall of rock.

"It is done!" she whispered. In a life without the Magic of War and the General, perhaps she could make up for the death and destruction delivered by her hands. "The journal is laid to rest, never to see the light of day nor the darkness of man's heart."

She set the lamp down and extinguished the flame. A quick move of her fingers and she was once again at the rear wall of the Temple. She walked down the corridor and stood at the rock precipice perched over the mountain valley.

The lush expanse of the distant plains brought moisture to the Oweinat Mountains, feeding the springs that kept Gebel alive. The night air was crisp and cool, and a full moon hung suspended, witness to all man's actions. The rich smell of fertile earth filled her nose, reminding her of her secret. She cupped her flat belly and closed her eyes with simple joy.

He will be so surprised.

As much as she desired this new life with Kedare, she could never leave her people in Bahk-ir's ruthless hands. "Tomorrow I will summon the General and pray he comes on the wings of the gods. The sooner he arrives, the sooner I leave."

A last look at the Temple, and she felt satisfaction in her deeds. With the journal buried, her new life awaited. She made a subtle movement with her fingers and appeared in her chambers.

"Bahk-ir!" she exclaimed.

He stood alone with no servants, and just off his horse from the look of him. When she called his name, he jumped and turned her way.

"My Queen, there you are."

"How are you here?" Byrgamon asked. She stepped away from him and removed her cloak. His appearance roaming alone in her chambers was disturbing. The hairs on the back of her neck rose as she contemplated his reason for taking such liberty. "I thought you were on the frontier. What matter brings you here like this?"

He stepped toward her, seeming to expand, towering over her with a searing hate-filled look. The fanatic light in his eye turned her cold. She stepped back.

Could he have learned about Kedare?

Fear turned her mouth dry. She took another step back.

Bahk-ir glared at her and pointed to the hem of her cloak. "Where have you been?"

Byrgamon didn't like his tone. She lifted her chin and spoke in a stilted, commanding tone. "You were telling me your cause for being in my chambers."

His hesitation was fleeting. She saw rebellion flash in his eyes before his demeanor changed completely. His face became worried, his brow wrinkled with concern. He went to one knee and bowed his head, exposing his neck in the ultimate submission.

"Forgive me, my Queen. I received word your life was in danger and came immediately. I have ridden two days straight to arrive," he mumbled to the floor. "When you could not be found, I came to look for you myself. If I go beyond my boundaries, you know I do so out of loyalty and dedication."

Instinct told her he lied. "What threat on my life do you speak of?" She stretched her fingers and felt the power respond, ready for her command. Knowing such power was at her fingertips, she could not conceive a mortal threat.

"We heard of an attempt to poison you." He peered up at her from his bended knee position. "I am getting too old for a two-day ride," he groaned. "May I stand?"

Byrgamon saw he looked tired. "Rise," she commanded. "Obviously, your information was wrong. But your sudden arrival saves me from calling you in from the frontier."

"I apologize for the travel clothes," he explained, struggling to his feet. "I came straight to your quarters, fearing for your safety. We did not learn who planned the assassination, or when."

He drew a fist to his chest in a sign of fealty. His attitude, his stance and bearing—even the tone of his voice were all subservient and respectful. "May I pour a drink?" he asked.

Byrgamon, unconvinced of his sincerity, nodded for him to proceed. "I have just come from the Temple," she said. "Please, pour for us." She gestured to a table bearing wine and goblets.

Bahk-ir stood at the side table, taking time to wash his hands in the basin before touching the wine. Byrgamon sat on a cushioned couch with a matching side table. Bahk-ir's back obscured most of her view. When he picked up a towel to dry his hands, she said, "I am glad you are here, General."

When she called him General, he stiffened.

"I was planning to call you home, for I have an announcement. You shall be the first to hear my news."

He looked over his shoulder. "What announcement?"

Byrgamon saw his forearm muscles bunch as he tightened his hand around one goblet. She spoke slowly, and gave her fingers a cautionary flick, touching the power for confidence. "After so many difficult years of war and toil for the Amenti, the time has come for peace and prosperity. Bahk-ir, I have committed my heart to Prince Kedare of Cyrenaica. We are to be married. We will unite our kingdoms."

Bahk-ir continued pouring the wine. She watched closely. When he turned, he presented her with a smiling face, but she heard the strain in his voice. "If you have found love, I am happy for you." He offered a goblet, holding it from the bowl.

She took the goblet by the stem. While she spoke, she examined the wine for any sign of treachery. "You do not seem too surprised," she added lightly.

"Women are not meant for war," Bahk-ir responded. He shot a quick glance at her hands. "At least not most women. I know the long campaign has been hard on you. You must desire children, as all women do. If this man, Prince Kedare, brings you your dreams, then I wish you the life, happiness and future you deserve."

He lifted his goblet to her and drank.

Byrgamon brought her goblet up and tilted it to her lips. The golden fluid was clear and gave no suspicious odor. While she detected nothing amiss, she did not touch the wine. "We will combine our armies under Kedare's command. As I do not expect you to follow another commander, I am prepared to offer you a handsome settlement for your retirement. Lands, gold, slaves—"

A creeping numbness invaded her hands. She looked askance at her goblet. Her fingers were suddenly stiff and unresponsive. Alarmed, she looked at Bahk-ir.

He lifted his chin, looking at her down the thin blade of his nose. His eyes, dark, flat and immovable, held no hint of concern for her distress. One lip rose in a self-satisfied sneer. Shocked, she saw he enjoyed her difficulty. She tried to lift her arms, but found them too heavy. "Bahk-ir, what have you done?" Her goblet clattered to the floor.

"You believe you can make these decisions over my life just because you are queen? Did you think you would buy me off as though I were little more than a whore?" He moved to stand over her, his voice hot and scathing. "Without your magic, you are nothing but a woman. I would have made you Empress of all the lands. Together with the power we could have ruled the entire world—"

He paused to look at her with disgust and pity, his sneer now a grimace of distaste. "No matter—you have betrayed me with your plans. But I have killed you. You are feeling the venom from a small snake in the Nile swampland. You absorbed the poison from the stem of your goblet." He kicked the tainted vessel across the room.

"Where is the journal, Byrgamon? Tell me, and I may give you the antidote." He pulled a small vial from a pocket in his robes.

She knew he would never give her the antidote.

My hands! I cannot move my hands ... my body—

Her fear swelled, growing into total panic. Breathing was difficult. She slid from the couch to the floor with a thump.

"You ... will never ... have the power," she whispered.

Bahk-ir grabbed her by the shoulders and shook, flinging her head wildly. "Where did you put the journal, witch? The Temple?"

She struggled to speak these last words while she could, wanting him to know he had lost. "The Journal ... of War ... is gone. You will never ... find it. Only my hands ... can find the journal."

He drew her close. In spite of the desperate fury in his eyes, she feared he was going to kiss her. "You are nothing without your hands," he snarled. "You are even less without magic. As the warrior who has killed your body, I curse your soul."

Helpless, she could not recoil, could not flee from his damnation. The curse he used was a weapon she gave her army, to be used against those vanquished on the battlefield. Never did she imagine her own magic used against her like this. How could such a betrayal happen?

"Queen Byrgamon, I curse your soul in all its future incarnations," he declared.

Unable to speak, her mind cried out, pleading with the gods.

Please, not now, not with this life I bear—

Rage and hysteria tortured Bahk-ir's face. His teeth were bared, his eyebrows slanted and feral. "I take from you all memories of magic. I curse you blind of magic through eternity." He spit his damning words at her like chunks of hate ground between loss and despair.

She cried, but could not feel the tears. He had taken everything—her entire existence, her life, her future, her child ... magic, and her soul. Her breath came in little gasps as she fought to remain alive. Unable to turn her head, his hate-consumed face was all she could see.

"I damn your soul, Byrgamon. Let bitter betrayal follow you through all your lives, for you do not deserve life, love or magic."

Her gasps came farther apart. Blackness swarmed her vision, thankfully blotting out Bahk-ir's face. In a brief moment, she mourned Kedare and the baby she would never hold, before darkness took sight from her eyes.

The venom stopped her heart, and Bahk-ir's curse consumed her soul.

•

Kedare stood at the rear of the crowd surrounded by his squad of armed guards. They wore common robes, to blend in with the Amenti attending the funeral of their sovereign.

Gamon, what did he do to you?

"I will see him pay for this, if it takes me all eternity," Kedare mumbled.

The grieving crowd marched the long way to the Temple. Byrgamon's body was dressed and laid out in preparation for her soul's journey through eternity. Her sarcophagus, instead of occupying a private chamber, was placed against the rear wall of the main hallway.

Kedare and his men worked their way to the front. When he saw General Bahk-ir, Kedare reached for his dagger. He stopped, only because such an action would produce not the General's death, but his.

The Amenti, like the Cyrenaicans, believed the soul followed the sun, and life began in the East at sunrise. The trip into darkness and back to light, represented by the path of the sun, was the soul's journey from body to body, allowing the soul to continue its journey with a new body and a new heart through reincarnation.

A soul's journey begins and ends in the same place, so Byrgamon's belongings filled the Temple in preparation for her eventual return.

"We mourn the loss of our queen," General Bahk-ir spoke to the gathered crowd.

At the sound of Bahk-ir's voice, Kedare stopped. He closed his eyes and tightened his lips. His jaws went rigid and his teeth came together in a growl, his breath shooting from his nostrils. He swallowed hard and opened his eyes, knowing his hatred for Bahk-ir was mirrored there.

"We curse the unknown mongrel who did this," Bahk-ir proclaimed. "When I find this murderer, he will be cut up and fed to the dogs, a fitting end for such a treacherous crime."

The crowd murmured their agreement of this punishment, but they were restless. Their queen was gone, their once rich future was now troubling and in doubt. Without a ruler, what would happen to them? They wanted answers.

"As I have done all my life, I will continue to care for the Amenti," Bahk-ir said. "Have no worry."

The unholy irony of Bahk-ir's words was more than Kedare could bear. He shouted, "I say you are the mongrel who killed her."

Kedare and his men threw their plain robes aside, revealing the Cyrenaica royal colors and insignia. He marched boldly up to the General. The two men came face-to-face. The air around them throbbed with primal animosity.

"Who are you to make such an accusation?" Bahk-ir challenged. He eyed the armed men accompanying the stranger, but they stood back, allowing the two men their confrontation.

"I am the man she was going to marry. I am Prince Kedare of Cyrenaica." He waved a rolled skin document. "Here is our contract with the queen's mark. There was no mongrel," Kedare shouted. "Only you."

The Priests would have cleaned Byrgamon's body, and in the process determine if foul play was involved. With no proclamation of her cause of death, Kedare wanted to know how Bahk-ir killed her. He grabbed the General's arm and loudly demanded, "How,

Bahk-ir? How did you kill her? How did you take the life from one so beautiful and powerful?"

Silence fell across the masses. They looked with questioning at their General. In the space of a breath, dozens of armed men, Amenti and Cyrenican alike, reached for their weapons.

"No," Bahk-ir shouted, throwing out his hand. "Let him speak. He is sick with grief, as we all are, and his words are heartfelt ... if inaccurate."

Barely a hand span kept them apart. The General's blasphemy in a holy place stunned Kedare. Clearly, the General bore no grief. Instead, Kedare saw only cold, hard hatred in Bahk-ir's eyes—hatred for Byrgamon and Kedare.

The need to kill this man seized Kedare, snatching his breath, spreading darkness across his vision. A growl started deep in his chest. He quivered on the edge of control.

Bahk-ir responded. One eyelid dropped into a threatening leer as he sucked on his teeth.

Kedare understood.

He wants the journal.

Kedare leaned close and whispered in the General's ear. "One day when the time is right, you will pay for this evil. One day, she will return to deliver justice upon you." He pulled back to look Bahk-ir in the eye. "Know this day will come. Know I will be there."

CHAPTER TWO

Santa Monica, California, Present

"Phoenix Donovan. I always liked Donovan better than Harper anyway," Phoenix said to herself. She snatched the *Harper* label from her mailbox slot with a jerk of authority and slipped in a new label with *Donovan.* "I'm just Phoenix now."

She walked back and went up the stairs to her small garage apartment. Inside, she took an assessing look. Boxes were still unpacked from her move-in ... how long ago? "Eight months," she said, shaking her head. "I need to get a life."

"Hey, are you in here?" called a female voice.

"Yeah. Come on in," Phoenix answered, glad for the interruption. If there was someone capable of cheering her up on this dismal day, her friend Lacey was the one.

Lacey stepped in, a slender and tanned, blue-eyed blonde. By comparison, Phoenix felt plain with her green eyes and short black hair, even though Lacey frequently complimented her on the exotic nature of her dark looks.

"Phoenix, I swear, if you don't open these boxes, I'm gonna haul them off to the Humane Society."

"As long as I've put off the chore, maybe that would be the most humane thing to do," Phoenix said. "Please, come in, I need saving today." She flopped down on her second-hand couch and poked a bare foot at a thick envelope on the table. "My divorce decree—arrived yesterday."

"Good riddance to bad baggage, I say," Lacey offered with a frown of distaste. "And a pox on him and his secretary."

Phoenix gave a quick burst of laughter before chiding Lacey. "Careful what you wish for, Lace." Still, Phoenix had to smother a smile. The quick image she got of her ex-husband and his big-boobed secretary covered in boils was quite satisfying.

Lacey picked up Phoenix's hand. "Come with me down to the boardwalk. You need some cheering up, and I feel like doing something adventurous."

Phoenix gave her friend a wary look. "And what form of adventure do you have in mind?"

"Come with me and you'll see."

They went in Lacey's Beetle. As usual, she found a perfect parking place exactly where she wanted. They got out and she dropped quarters into the parking meter. When they started walking, Phoenix commented slyly. "You always get a great parking place. How do you always manage that?"

"Before I leave, I just smile and see me pulling into the perfect spot. You should try positive thought more often," Lacey answered.

Phoenix grunted with a lack of conviction. Still, she made a mental note to give her ex-husband a call later to see if he and the soon-to-be Mrs. Harper were experiencing any unexplained dermatologic eruptions.

They wandered among the shops, booths and displays along the boardwalk. With no warning, Lacey drew Phoenix into a small shop off the alley behind a corner hotdog stand. Phoenix looked up in surprise. When she saw the shingle displaying a deck of Tarot cards, she read, "Faby Knows?" Instantly she objected. "You've got to be kidding."

"Come on," Lacey cajoled. "This won't take long. Just sit while she does a reading for me." She took Phoenix's hand and pulled her into the fortune-teller's shop.

In the waiting area Phoenix saw a rattan couch and table. A red box was on the table along with a *People* magazine, a coloring book and a well-used box of crayons.

Squelching her rising disdain, Phoenix sat reluctantly. As an archaeologist specializing in ancient pre-dynastic Egyptian culture, she dealt in facts and tangibles she could hold and see. Being this close to any mumbo-jumbo made her uncomfortable.

A fringed door hanging parted as a woman entered the room. "Ladies, good morning. I am Faby."

She spoke with an accent Phoenix couldn't place, in a soft, yet powerful voice. Petite with chestnut hair falling loose across her shoulders, she was dressed in capri pants and a soft cotton shirt, all of which did nothing to make her look like a fortune-teller. But

Phoenix noted the woman's brown eyes were anything but casual.

Faby gave Lacey a quick look before her sharp gaze came to rest on Phoenix. "What may I do for you?"

Phoenix squirmed under the woman's intense look. Those dark eyes seemed to see all too deeply, making Phoenix wonder, just what did Faby know? Phoenix put her hand up in guarded protest and waved off Faby's interest. "I'm just waiting." She pointed to Lacey. "She's the one here to see you, not me."

Faby continued to stare with a curious and speculative glint Phoenix found disturbing. At last Faby gave a nod of concession. "As you wish," she said, and ushered Lacey into the back room.

Phoenix drummed her fingers and shifted on the couch. She picked up the *People*, but tossed the magazine back on the table. The crayons caught her attention and she thumbed though the color book with interest, only to find the pages all filled. "Phooey," she grunted.

On the table, the red box waited. "Well, aren't you patient." She admired the enameled box and gently eased the lid from its latch. Inside was a deck of Tarot cards, exquisitely portrayed in an Egyptian style.

"Oh," she exclaimed with interest and pulled out the deck. She glanced at the card faces and saw lions, jackals, ankhs and an abundance of hieroglyphs. She flipped them over and admired the back design before spreading them on the table in an arc with practiced ease. Long, lonely nights playing solitaire over the last eight months had left her adept with cards. She pulled a few cards out of the arc at random and set them neatly aside.

She didn't know how long she was absorbed in studying the hieroglyphs on the cards when the silence in the room broke into her concentration. She looked up. Lacey and Faby stared at her. Faby's eyes went to Phoenix's hands and the Tarot cards. She came quickly and sat beside Phoenix.

"The art work is lovely," Phoenix stammered as a rising sense of "Aha! Gotcha!" flooded her. "I was surprised to read the hieroglyphs were accurate and not ... just for show." Her words faded as she ran out of nervous babble.

Faby stared at the cards Phoenix had selected. She pulled the first card forward. "The Tower, your future, speaks of transformation. Your life will be destroyed until all that remains is trust."

"Don't waste your breath" was on the tip of Phoenix's tongue as she recoiled—but she held back the words. Faby's voice, her posture, the rushing speech all worked to send a liberal dose of goose bumps down Phoenix's arms.

Another card now, The Lovers. Faby continued. "Two men of your past return. They have already entered your life. You must make a decision. Beware whom you trust. Deceit surrounds you."

Phoenix licked her lips. She wasn't amused.

Faby pointed to the next card. "The Empress." She tapped the card where a phoenix sat on the Empress's shield. "This is you. You have a talent. I see great power within you and around you."

Phoenix drew her lips together in a tight line. If there was proof this stuff was nonsense, here was exhibit A. Phoenix possessed no power, unless attracting men of dubious worth qualified. She shifted her feet to rise.

Faby grabbed Phoenix's wrist. She nodded toward the last card—The Emperor. "He is coming for you."

Chills took off down Phoenix's spine. She peered closer at the card. The Emperor had blue eyes, or were they brown? She couldn't tell. "Coming for me? Who? Why?"

"You must draw another card," Faby instructed.

Intellectually, Phoenix knew continuing with this farce was utterly preposterous. But a disorienting pressure filled her ears, swelling into a buzz that muted out Faby's voice. Cautiously, Phoenix looked up to see Lacey watching with interest.

They don't hear the buzz, the pressure—

Phoenix suddenly wanted to see the next card. She knew if she walked out and didn't do this, she would wonder for the rest of her life about the card she never drew. The instant she acknowledged this desire to know, the buzz and the pressure in her ears escalated. She licked her lips, surprised to feel them trembling, and cast her hand out over the spread. She picked a card. She turned it over.

Death!

Phoenix bolted to her feet. Her knees crashed into the table and sent it flying. The Tarot cards scattered and fell. She ran out the door.

Bright sun assaulted her eyes. She threw her hand up. A sudden slick of sweat broke across her back, trapping her blouse like a shroud. Her heart banged a little too fast, and a rising sense of nausea said lunch was long overdue. She stopped in the shade of a palm tree and fluttered her hand in front of her face.

Transformation. Betrayal. Power.

Someone coming for me.

"Let's not forget death," she whispered. She couldn't get that last card out of her mind.

"Are you all right?" Lacey asked.

Phoenix felt her cheeks flame with embarrassment. "Sorry to run like that. She was creeping me out."

Lacy peered at Phoenix with sympathy. "She says you should come back so she can do a more extensive reading."

"I know you think this stuff is entertaining, but I just don't believe in it," Phoenix protested. She snorted with derision and shook her head, condemning the so-called psychic for missing the obvious. "Huh. I'm no Empress."

A sudden raft of bumps flashed across her scalp and she stopped fanning mid-motion. "You told her my name, didn't you? When you were in the back room together."

"No, we didn't discuss you at all."

Fresh heat rose in Phoenix's face, contradicting the chills rising from the nape of her neck. "Faby pointed to a phoenix bird on the Empress card and said, 'This is you.' If you didn't tell her my name, how did she know?"

Lacy shrugged and offered, "Because she's a psychic?"

"Huh." Phoenix grunted, unwilling to concede anything.

They had lunch with Phoenix more subdued than usual. Lacey brought them back to Phoenix's apartment. "You'll do something about those boxes, won't you?" Lacey reminded.

Phoenix gave her the oh-I'll-get-right-on-that look.

Lacey laughed. "Tomorrow's a new day, a new week, and according to Faby, maybe a new life."

"Ha, ha. Easy for you to say," Phoenix replied, waving as Lacey drove off. Standing alone on the sidewalk, she repeated, "Yeah, ha, ha."

Having the unknown universe arranging a new life without her input wasn't funny to Phoenix. "No thanks," she muttered as she climbed the stairs to her apartment, grateful for this one stable aspect of her life.

She took a sweater and a glass of wine out onto the deck. The salty ocean tang tickled her nose. Moist air brought chill bumps to her arms. She pulled on the sweater and pondered Faby's words about transformation and two men entering her life.

"I don't see it," she argued. She couldn't think of any men of interest from her past. "See," she said, tilting her glass to the hazy night sky. "I told you that stuff was nonsense."

The next morning Phoenix pulled into the UCLA faculty parking lot and parked in the farthest corner. The disparity between associate professor pay and tenured pay was readily visible in the choice of vehicles present. Phoenix preferred to spare herself the indignity of parking next to a Porsche, choosing to walk the extra distance to her building.

Her office was a small room tucked into the archaeology department. Little more than a closet, the office was her haven, the one place where she felt supreme. No one knew pre-dynastic culture better than she did—except Professor Barnes, her mentor. He often said she had astounding insight and intuition in the field of pre-dynastic cultures. A couple of her theories were published, garnering peer respect and accolades from Barnes.

She walked to his spacious "study" as he liked to say, and peeked in the door. He sat behind his desk, hands behind his head, peering into the ether with a frown like Atlas holding up the weight of the world. She rapped lightly.

Prof. Barnes looked up and squinted. When he made out her identity, he motioned expansively. "Come in, Phoenix. I was just thinking about you."

"Please tell me I'm not responsible for this grave look on your face." She walked around the piles of books and shelves of artifacts, all assembled in a haphazard jumble.

"My dear, you could never give me the kind of grief I regularly receive from that man."

"That man" was the designation Prof. Barnes saved for the Head of the Archaeology Department, a sorry individual whose undignified job was to make decisions based on numbers. How the professor despised him.

Phoenix watched her mentor and felt a coil of tension unfold from the pit of her stomach. Department heads were well known for swinging the ax over little necks like hers. She cleared her throat in hopes she sounded more solid than she felt. "And what indignity has that man foisted upon you today?"

"I'm sorry, Phoenix, but I have bad news. However, let me say I also have good news."

The tension spread from Phoenix's stomach, speeding upward into a headache. She cleared a stack of textbooks from a chair and sat. "I'm let go, aren't I?"

"I'm afraid so. I bartered to keep you as long as I could, but the ax had your name on it." He reached into a desk drawer. "However, I have something—this came for you today. All things considered, I believe the timing of this missive to be quite interesting."

He passed her a thick envelope. "This letter came with an introduction from a mutual friend. I can, by association, vouch for the sender of this correspondence. While I have never met him, he keeps company with the elite of the archaeology world. He is a connoisseur of the pre-dynastic and wishes to make you a most interesting offer. I would consider this to be an exceptional opportunity for your talents."

My talents, Phoenix mused. Twice in twenty-four hours she was reminded of her talents. She took the letter and examined the return address. New York. Ultra heavy, cream-colored paper politely screamed wealth. She hefted the weighty envelope—it was almost as heavy as her divorce papers.

One door closes, another opens.

She stuffed the envelope in her bag. "Professor, I'm not one to stay where I'm not wanted. I would just as soon pack and leave today, if that's all right with you." She glanced at him and saw the moisture brighten his eyes.

"You are my best student. Whatever opportunities come your way, child, God be with you." They shook hands awkwardly when he said, "What the hell," and gave her a bear hug. "Correspond. Let me know how you're doing. When you become famous, I want to say I knew you when. Remember, I'm always here if you need a reference."

Phoenix packed her belongings from her tiny office and carried the boxes all the way to her car. She sat in her domestic-model vehicle surrounded by the trappings of a job she no longer had, and wondered what the future held. Three years she had been here, and like a rock with no inertia, the momentum to leave was hard to generate.

When Phoenix saw Prof. Barnes' worried face, Faby's words came to mind. The mysterious envelope in Phoenix's bag was a blatantly daring confirmation of the fortune-teller's words.

"And so transformation, as I was warned, appears on the horizon."

When she got home she lugged all the boxes up to join the other unopened compartments that represented what her life once was. She heaved the last box up the stairs and let it drop to the floor with a thud.

"There, you have lots of company," she told the box.

She changed into her favorite yoga pants and a T-shirt from Cozumel, needing something she could feel sorry for herself in, should a little self-pity become necessary. She poured a glass of wine even though it was barely lunchtime, and eased out onto the tiny perch they call a deck in Santa Monica.

The rich, fat envelope sat on a small wrought iron table, waiting patiently for her. She was reminded of the bright enameled box at the fortune-teller's that also waited so patiently. Had the turbulence rocking her life come from her opening that red enameled box?

If so, she wasn't sure she wanted to open this envelope.

"Who are you?" she queried the envelope. "Are you one of the two men? Are you the one coming for me?" Curiosity drove her to consider going back to Faby for more about the card of Death and the Lovers. She snorted, rejecting such a waste of time and money.

She picked up the envelope. The heavy custom stationery bore an embossed return address that began with the Feather of Maat.

Below that was *Gamon~Search Institute.*

The name Gamon was unknown to her. She wondered who he was, and what comprised his search. "Using the Feather of Maat? Mr. Gamon is looking for justice," she mused. "Well, good luck." She held the envelope.

On the front was her name hand-written with *c/o Professor Barnes, UCLA*. She ran her fingers over her name, admiring the firm, cursive letters. "Looks like a man's writing."

She tested the back flap—it was tightly sealed. The envelope was too beautiful to tear so she put it down and went to the kitchen for a sharp-edged tool. Just as she picked up a knife, a voice called from her open front door.

"Hello inside."

A man stood at her screen door. The lighting gave her no details of his features, but her body reacted to his voice, sending fear skittering down the back of her bare legs. She flinched, and the small knife opened a slice in her palm.

"Ow, dammit," she cried. "Just a minute." She shot a quick glance at the man, wondering what it was about him that spooked her.

"I'm looking for Phoenix Harper," he called out. "Do I have the right address?"

"Yeah, hold on." She grabbed a paper towel and wrapped her hand as she walked to the door. Through the screen, she evaluated her startling caller. He was tall and muscular, a good fifteen years her senior with short cropped hair and dark eyes.

"The last name is Donovan," she corrected. "It's not Harper anymore. I'm Phoenix. What can I do for you?"

When she stepped into the light, he seemed stunned at her appearance. Slowly, as if he had found the mystical end of the rainbow, his eyes brightened and he smiled broadly.

Phoenix wondered what he expected. Since he was clearly pleased to have found her and his smile so infectious, she smiled back. She was piqued with curiosity as to how she could be so important to this man. He must be Mr. Gamon.

"Miss Donovan, Phoenix Donovan, I have an offer I wish to discuss, if I may come in," he said.

Phoenix appreciated his obvious good humor, but still she asked, "Who are you? Do you have any identification?"

"Of course, excuse me." He fumbled as he set down his briefcase.

While he pulled his wallet and passport from an inside jacket pocket, Phoenix noticed his dove grey suit and royal burgundy shirt were custom made. The absence of a tie only made him appear all the more distinguished and powerful.

"Forgive me," he pleaded. "I was just so pleased to find you. I'm Asa Ducaine, and I wish to hire your archaeological talent for an expedition, Miss Donovan." He showed her an Egyptian passport and Egyptian National ID.

Phoenix eyed his documents through the screen door. His use of the word talent caused her breath to stall in her chest.

Talent.

There's that word again, three times in less than thirty-six hours.

The short hairs on the back of her neck stood up. Wildly, she wanted to tell him to wait while she ran over to the boardwalk to get the fortune-teller to remove the spell that had taken over her life.

She ran a hand across her neck, rubbing away her fear. "Come in, Mr. Ducaine, are you with the G—"

"I'm an independent researcher, Miss Donovan. May I call you Phoenix?"

His pleasure reached out to enfold her. His expression was boundless, open like a child's, yet he was charming. His zeal and excitement were infectious, causing her to wonder what had disturbed her when he spoke earlier. She smiled and offered him a seat on the couch. "Where is your expedition, Mr. Ducaine?"

"Please, call me Asa." He pierced her with a direct look. She saw he had brown eyes—eyes that looked as though they held their fair share of secrets. He seemed especially eager to share one of them with her today. His expression sparkled. "I would like you to supervise an excavation in the area of Gebel Oweinat."

Phoenix struggled to contain her disappointment as his statement killed the fizz from her excitement. How could this be exciting to him? "There is nothing there, Asa. Since the modern discovery of Gebel Oweinat in 1924, what's there to be seen is already well documented. The rock carvings are an enlightening view into life on a fertile northern plain, but—"

"No." His hand came up, stopping her.

Another transformation came over him, a mask or an alter ego, Phoenix thought. As he spoke, he looked like a man recalling an old lover. But something in his tone didn't match his words.

"There is a new find, a chamber discovered deep in the mountains of Oweinat. Preliminary dating confirms the site at 8,000 BCE—"

"I haven't heard of this. What university made the discovery?" Phoenix asked.

"As I said, I am an independent researcher. There is no university involved. Let me show you the coordinates. I have a map here."

He rummaged in his briefcase, bringing out a detailed topographic map of the Oweinat Mountains southwest of Egypt and the Nile—home of the ancient tribes who lived on the edge of the

African plains when the last intercontinental glacier still existed.

Phoenix pursed her lips in concentration. She placed a finger on the map. An immediate rapid rise in her heart rate shouted her desire to go on this expedition—no matter the cost.

"This is your location?" She pointed to a small mark. "This terrain is difficult to access for several reasons. I was not aware the Libyan government was favorable to outsiders." She passed a deep assessing look at him.

How did you manage to secure excavation rights from the Gadhafi government?

His face changed, sliding into a salesman's best pitch expression, his tone suggesting he was honest to a fault. "I have a great deal of wealth, and a great deal of connections in the Mid-East."

He withdrew an envelope with the official Gadhafi seal. Inside, on personal stationery from the Colonel, was hand-written permission to conduct an archaeological inspection at a given coordinate, complete with signature.

Phoenix felt the pressure of the moment swell. With keen determination she wanted to do this expedition, but something she couldn't place bothered her. Perversely, she sat back and dug in her heels.

He saw, and coaxed. "The pay is very good, the credits are all yours. Being recently unemployed—"

"How did you know I was unemployed?"

"I just spoke with Prof. Barnes this morning. It seems I arrived at the archaeology department just after you left. He gave me your address."

She teetered. This was an opportunity to garner prestige in the archaeology world and further her career. A solid, new discovery would cement the Donovan name to pre-dynastic studies. For these and other reasons, financial gain among them, she really wanted to participate.

So what was holding her back?

Ever so sly, his eyebrows went up as he reached into his briefcase. "A contract, generous, as you will see. Why don't you take a look?" He placed the many-paged document on the coffee table.

"Read this through, sleep on it, call me tomorrow. I'm ready to begin as soon as you can make arrangements here," he said, looking at the bare furnishings and stacked boxes. He rose.

Phoenix stood, feeling mentally paralyzed. Before she could speak, he was at the screen door. She followed him, wondering if he might think her suddenly impaired. "I—I will read … your offer," she stammered lamely.

What is the matter with me?

He pulled out a card and offered it. "Call me tomorrow. I look forward to working with you. You're the most talented specialist I could find."

He's coming for you!

The fortune-teller's words roared into Phoenix's ears, squashing any courteous response. She took his card and silently watched him walk down her stairs. After he left her line of sight, she went back in and set his card on top of his contract.

She stared at his paperwork for long moments. Finally, the sting of alarm that had stunned her into paralyzed silence suddenly let go. She rocked back on her heels. "Holy crap!" She darted out to her small deck and picked up the Gamon-Search envelope.

"Two men out of my past."

She put the unopened envelope and Asa's contract side-by-side, frowning when she saw blood from her small cut mar one corner of Asa's contract.

If, as the fortune-teller said, Asa was one of the two men from her past, how could that be when she was sure she'd never met him?

The other envelope from the Gamon-Search Institute presented just as much mystery.

And Mr. Gamon—why don't I know you either?

"This all started with that fortune-teller."

In the few hours since she met Faby, Phoenix's life had been taken over by interlopers. She pushed the coffee table back and stood with her hands propped on her hips. Her shoulders rose in exasperation as she cried out, "Who are you people?"

CHAPTER THREE

After a ten-day coma in the twenty-third year of his life, Max Parrish awoke. As the fog slowly cleared away and his senses returned, he heard the angel questioning his existence. "Max Parrish, how and why is it you are alive?"

He licked his lips, wanting to say, "Why not?" He wanted to tell her he had been dead, and alive, then dead again. Now, according to her, he was alive one more time.

"Water," he whispered. This pleased the angel. She smiled, reminding him of—

Damn, his mind was so full of blanks. The angel returned with a glass of water. Before he could ask why he was in the hospital, the netherworld called him back. He took the image of her smile and her dark hair with him as he drifted away, slipping into a world of impossible dreams.

Not quite dreams, they were more like visions fleshed out as memories. Sweeping non-stop through his head, he was dragged heart and soul into another world.

He laughed and cried. He wept and he marveled—and then challenged what he was shown.

"Impossible!" he shouted from the depths of his delirium.

A new and growing awareness absorbed him, an understanding of how he was more than just Max Parrish and why he was alive. He knew all he learned was true ... for he remembered.

One day, she will return to deliver justice upon you.

These words, he understood with clarity, once meant everything to him. And now that he remembered why—they were everything to him again.

The angel returned and he saw with sadness she was not the one of his dreams, but her dark hair was similar enough to make his heart constrict.

She is not Byrgamon.

He struggled to sit up. "What happened?" he asked, feeling disoriented in both space and time.

"You fell off your horse," came a voice from his bedside.

Max turned to see his mother. On his other side, his father hovered close.

Good.

If there was anyone who could help him with an insane search, it was his father. "Dad, help me out of here." Max started peeling off the leads pasted on his body. "There's something I have to do, and I need your help."

Several Months Later

"How do I find her?" Max paced the carpet in his beach-front condo. The sun glittered on the ocean seven floors down, and an endless stream of bikini-clad women paraded the sand. With his thoughts submerged in the past, another perfect day in Palm Beach passed him by untouched.

The only thing important to him was the images and the memories ... and the emotions newly awakened within his heart.

When he walked out of the hospital within hours of waking from his coma, the doctors called his recovery a miracle. "You shouldn't even be alive," they repeated.

"Exactly. How did I get from the back of a polo pony to the most impossible search ever undertaken?" Max pondered. He knew he was alive because he had something extremely important to do—a task he knew was equally impossible. He stared out the window at the horizon. The entire world stretched before him with over six billion people. "Where are you, Gamon? How do I find you?"

What if I fail in this impossible quest?

He stopped and closed his eyes. When the doubts came, he let the memories loose from his heart. Soon, he knew the smell of her skin, felt the silken strands of her hair wrapping around him that night in the pools in Cyrenaica, binding them heart to heart—

"Enough," he demanded. But the visions heeded him not, and soon other dreams came. He wondered what manner of brain tumor brought erotic visions. Without a trace of humor, he said, "Yeah, tell that one to the doctors."

Doubt and rebellion demanded he drink. After three months of this and more insanity, "Gamon," was all he could say. She was all he knew, all he wanted. The women he had known were nameless, the places forgotten, his activities a blur. All that remained in his heart and mind was this woman he had loved and lost in a distant past.

The doorbell rang. Max looked down to see if he was presentable. Grey dress slacks with a button-down shirt and polished leather shoes. Hopefully, he would be able to convince his father the games were over and he was ready to get serious. He opened the door. His father stood with eyebrows drawn and ready for combat.

Max pasted a smile on his face. "Dad, come in."

Derek Parrish, owner of the world's largest software and Internet search-engine, gave Max a quick once-over as he stepped across the threshold. "Son."

Max looked down and squelched a grimace.

Oh boy, this isn't going to be easy.

Max pointed to the deck where lunch and drinks were set up under a striped patio umbrella. "I thought we could have a bite to eat." His father's expression was withering, blasting Max's determination. Feeling overwhelmed, searing defeat pelted him before he could even begin.

In response, a steady gaze of green eyes came to his mind.

Gamon.

Max knew he had no choice. "Please, Dad, hear what I have to say."

Derek humphed in consent, but he was far from forgiving. "When you came out of your coma, Max, you said you had something to do. Sadly, that something turned into an excuse for behavior that was—"

"Disappointing, I know," Max said. "And I'm sorry. I hope you'll let me explain."

Max directed his father to the patio. Derek noted the pitcher of iced tea as he pulled out a chair and sat. His eyebrows lifted and he gave Max a speculative glance.

"I want you to know I'm not drunk—or crazy," Max said. He poured the sweet tea into their glasses. "I told you what happened to me while I was in the coma. My behavior afterward is what I need to explain."

He stared out over the railing to the open ocean, finding it difficult to look his father in the eye. "I was afraid—afraid I wasn't man enough for the job. I tried to erase everything I learned in the coma."

The confession brought relief. He exhaled deep and long. A new strength filled his heart, one that came from finally accepting what he had to do. He looked straight at his father. "I finally understand there is no reprieve for me. What I learned while in the coma only gives me one path. I want you to know my disappointing behavior is over."

"Go on," his father encouraged.

"You told me how impossible this task would be. After I left the hospital, it hit me how right you were."

Derek nodded, eyebrows piqued with interest, opening up ever so slightly.

Max continued, the words coming slowly. "When I first woke in the hospital, I was enthralled by the idea. But soon after, the sheer enormity of the task hit me—hit me hard. Overwhelmed, I tried to deny what I experienced. The drinking and the women were simply an attempt to blur the images ... and the feelings."

His father's eyes softened, and the rigid line of his mouth eased. Max exhaled, not realizing he was holding his breath. In a soft voice, he added, "I know—now—what I must do. I need your help if I'm to succeed." Water filled Max's eyes, but he wasn't ashamed, for it was time to get started.

"I need your help, Dad ... to find a life that was stolen from me."

•

Max watched his father walk out the door and felt a great weight lifted from his shoulders. "Now, how to figure out the rest."

The next day he began searching for colleges, choosing Brown University, and started the long process to get into their archaeology program. He threw his heart and soul into his studies, for his heart and soul drove him. He excelled and graduated with honors.

"What's next, son?" Derek asked.

"Libya," Max answered.

The joy slowly faded from his parents' faces.

"Don't worry," Max rushed to say. "A friend—one of my class-mates—is a Berber from a tribe in Libya. He's invited me to spend some time with his people in the desert."

Max's mother protested. "Will you be safe?"

"I'll be in south eastern Libya, in the God-forsaken desert. No one will know or care I am there," Max replied.

"This sounds dangerous," Derek argued.

"I have to go," Max said. "Dangerous or not." He looked beyond them into the future. Every day that passed in this life brought him closer to what he had lost—a loss he couldn't forget, a betrayal he couldn't forgive, a life he wanted back.

He was packed and gone within the week.

"Welcome, my friend," Amestan said when he picked up Max at the Cairo airport. "You look good." He slapped Max on the back and winked. "Now the desert will make a man of you."

In Libya, Max learned the Berber language while he and Ames-tan combed the desolate mountains that surrounded the 1924 Gebel Oweinat discovery, looking for fresh evidence of an ancient civilization.

"I don't know," Max said. They stood on a rocky landscape as unforgiving as the surface of Mars. He shaded his eyes, looking up at a sheer cliff face. "It's been a while since I was here."

Amestan gave a bark of laughter. "Ha! How funny you are, my friend."

They clambered up a dry streambed to a sheer cliff face shaped like a triangle pointed at the ground. Amestan indicated a jumble of rocks obscuring one side of the cliff face. "Look, do you see?"

"Maybe," Max muttered, not daring to voice any hope. An ex-citement he was afraid to acknowledge made his heart stand at at-tention. "Maybe," he repeated, louder and with more enthusiasm.

They climbed farther up the rugged terrain to get a better glimpse. They reached a perch on a pile of boulders near the top. Amestan held up a lamp and Max looked between the rocks.

"There, now you see, yes?" Amestan insisted.

Max took the lamp. A thin beam of light cut strategically through the darkness—going back, and back, and back.

"We have a cave," Amestan stated with satisfaction.

Max was willing to admit that much, but little else. "Not all caves are tombs," he protested.

They trekked back down the hill when Amestan stopped abruptly in the streambed. He turned to Max with a telltale grin.

"What?" Max challenged.

"This is what inspired me as a child to study archaeology." He pulled an object from his pocket and passed it to Max. "I found this in this very spot the first time I came up here."

Max knew the object immediately. He took it reverently, for here was further proof he was not insane. Grasping the object to his chest, he was consumed by a rush of memory.

The sun glinted off her dark hair as she looked at him with anticipation. Behind his back, he held the silk and ribbon wrapped package.

"What do you have?" she asked, straining to see behind him.

Her expression melted his heart. How could one so bold and powerful be so sweet and childlike? "I have something for you," he teased. She wiggled with excitement and he knew he couldn't keep his gift from her any longer. He passed her the silk package.

"Oh," she exclaimed. She caressed the silk and held it up, admiring the colored ribbons. Her eyes watered and she clasped the package to her heart. "I love you," she whispered as the tears began to fall.

"Why do you cry?" he chided, drawing her into his arms. He held her tight, feeling her quiver.

"Once I gained the power and waged war, I thought I would never know goodness again."

Her simple declaration made his throat tighten. He stroked her back and kissed the top of her head. When he spoke, his words skipped and growled with emotion. "You ... are the greatest good I know. Now, open your gift, so I may see you smile."

She removed the ribbons and set them aside. The silk fell away, exposing a palm-sized puddle of gold. Her mouth opened in silent joy as she shook out the bangle bracelet of gold discs. She peered through the engraved discs, asking him as if she did not know. "What do they say?"

Max felt his vision spiral back to the present, tossing his equilibrium. He exhaled in short bursts to steady his stomach, and gripped the gold disc until the edges cut into his palm. He spoke, answering the past with a whisper. "Gamon and Kedare." With the words, his senses settled back into reality.

He shot a look of speculation and surprise at his friend. "Why didn't you mention this when I first told you about my experience in the coma? You had this all along and didn't feel like telling me until now?"

Amestan shrugged. "At the time of your tale, I didn't have a translation of the engraving." He gave Max a piercing look. "I share this with you now because the timing is appropriate. You, of all people, should know all things come when the time is right."

An awareness evolving from shadowy memory slowly expanded, pressing against Max's heart. These were the words he spoke to Bahk-ir that day in the Temple. But now they meant something else, giving him his first real hope. As though he stood in a tank filling with cold water, the certainty that he was truly on his right path rose through his body. He repeated the words, testing their strength. "All things come when the time is right. Yes."

"I see you are beginning to understand," Amestan said. "The timing of the gods is not on par with human expectation. Look always to your heart. There you will know … when the time is right." He swept his arm up to point to the cave. "Now, do you want to look inside?"

Amestan's simple hand gesture opened the gates within Max. In confirmation that the time was right, he felt a great desire in his heart to see what the cavern held. He nodded yes, even as he looked about, pondering their remote location and lack of equipment. "How do we get in?"

"Berber muscle," Amestan said. "No rock can defeat a Berber."

Max laughed at the tribal humor. "Okay. This I have to see."

They made camp on a flat outcrop of rock downhill from the cliff face and used the streambed for access. The next day, a dozen strong Berber men joined them. For two days they worked to redistribute the rocks so they could reach what they determined to be an entry point to the cave. Another day, and they removed enough rubble to create an opening.

That night Max and Amestan sat by the fire after the rest of the men had retired. Max held the gold disc from Gamon's bracelet, rubbing their ancient engraved names. He sipped his coffee and stared into the seductive flames, hypnotized.

"If we find your queen in the cave—do you think you will find her current incarnation?" Amestan asked.

"Finding this cave—if she's up there—is the easy part." Max shrugged. The gold disc brought him to a place where he could finally be comfortable with the improbability of his task. "I once thought finding any of this was impossible, but I'm a lot closer now than I was eight years ago."

Amestan jumped up to pantomime the search, shading his eyes.

"You're funny," Max said.

"You know, if I had not already possessed the disc when you told me your story, I would have thought you crazy," Amestan replied. He spun one finger near his head, indicating he thought one of them might still be of questionable sanity.

Max threw the remnants of his coffee into the fire. "Eight years ago all I had was a series of visions. Now I have a degree in archaeology and new friends to help me." He held up the disc and watched it glow in the light of the fire. "And I have evidence pointing to a suspected location for her tomb. I call that progress."

"And the man, her murderer—"

"If I am right and she is up there, then Bahk-ir will return. He will have to come here first, you know. You will likely meet him before I do."

Quiet settled between them as the fire crackled. "You have not asked why I help you," Amestan said. He followed his friend's gaze up the hill. "My people have lived in the shadow of these mountains, some say back to the time before the great desert. If your story is as you say, and she is there, then she is my queen, too. Yes?"

"Yes," Max agreed. "If somewhat removed."

"Then let the murderer of my queen come. Perhaps we will have Berber fun with him when he arrives."

"Huh," Max grunted in return. "Careful what you conjure."

•

Dawn came early to Max and Amestan's meager camp, and with it another trek up the hill. A brief flurry of activity ensued before Max heard them call out in their dialect, "'Tis ready."

Rocks were stacked in a staircase to the opening. Max stood at the bottom step, unable to make his legs move. After all this time, would he find her here? Was this crazy quest based on the truth, or was he just plain crazy? In a few steps, he would finally know.

Amestan pointed the way. "My friend, you must be first."

Max slowly climbed the rock steps. He reached the top and without turning on his light, stepped into the cool darkness of the mountain. Amestan came and stood behind him. For several minutes Max couldn't move. On the precipice of discovery, he was paralyzed, his feet anchored to the earth for one last sane moment. While the gold disc was quite encouraging, now he wanted to know if he was actually within reach of his goal.

Dear God, I have worked so hard for this. Please don't let me be here in vain.

The cavern was dark. He couldn't see if she was here, or not. He couldn't see if he recognized anything, or not. Until there was light, he wouldn't know if he was crazy ... or not.

He flicked on his lamp. Amestan turned his on. Two beams shot forward into the darkness.

Max immediately stiffened, impaled by memory ... and sadness.

Palpable grief filled the Temple even though all the mourners had left. As he entered, his footsteps echoed with a whisper, a reflection of the deep sadness that had taken over his heart. The box was tucked under his arm. He looked for a hiding place where no one would notice it until the time was right for the truth to be known.

"Gamon, my love, how I miss you." He knelt, whispering his pain, hoping there was some way she could understand the depth of his loss.

He found a place between two larger chests for his little box and pulled a roll of silk down to provide further cover. Afterward, he sat for some time, unwilling to leave her alone in the dark for the long span until they were united again. His tears splashed to the Temple floor. With her gone, he might as well be dead.

At last he rose, seeing no reprieve from life without her. If he spent the rest of his life waiting for her here, he would never run out of tears. "I will be here," he whispered. "When you return."

"Max? Max?"

Max heard his name being called. He was on tilt, one leg in a dream, his other leg in reality. Someone grabbed his arm.

"Are you all right?"

"Whoa," Max whistled. He set his lamp down and put a hand to his forehead, his other hand pointing to the right. "A room—a side chamber filled with war spoils." He pointed to the left and farther down. "Another room, like the first. More of the same."

Max dared not look at his friend, and took a couple of steps forward. Amestan cast his light to the right, illuminating a chamber filled with a variety of objects. He shone his light to the left, farther down as Max said, and found the second chamber.

Two more steps and Max reached the edge of a massive collection of artifacts. His light showed the corridor was completely blocked. Amestan joined him.

Max smiled, giddy all the way to his bones. Here was confirmation of all he saw while in a coma. Here was confirmation of—

Abruptly, he squatted, knees feeling like water. His heart, while fast and aggressive with excitement earlier, now seemed to stand still. His face muscles went slack and his mouth sagged open. Conversely, his eyebrows met in astonishment.

If this much was real, then the rest—

Past lives, reincarnation ... Magic!

His legs went numb, and he flopped back onto his butt. His breath lagged behind his stalled heart, making sparkles of light dance before his eyes. Astonished and unable to prevent it, he knew he was going to pass out. He put his head between his knees, but the gesture was too little, too late. Blackness swarmed the dancing lights until all went out, and another world welcomed him.

They walked hand-in-hand along a sunny beach, the breeze tossing her shoulder length hair. He raised her left hand where sunlight caught the diamonds of an eternity band, igniting them with fire. Lovingly, he brought her hand to his lips for a kiss. Like the diamonds, their love had survived the test of time, conquering the past so nothing could separate them again.

Consciousness called for Max to return. But the carefree sensation of sand between his toes made him reluctant to leave. The smell of the sea in her hair as the ebony locks drifted on the wind made him smile—

Max's eyes bolted open.

Amestan leaned over him. "Ah, you are back."

Max saw he was propped up against the rock wall by the opening. As his head cleared, he thought about jumping up, but an unpleasant hollow sensation in his stomach dissuaded him from any sudden moves.

"When you are ready," Amestan said. He placed Max's water bottle in his lap and sat opposite him in the shade.

They sat in silence for a long time. Max slowly collected his senses, which had just been blasted into the paranormal stratosphere.

Magic! Reincarnation—

His head started to spin again. He hushed his astonished thoughts.

"So, you believe you have found her?" Amestan asked.

Max felt a chuckle coming on. He worried that this might be the first sign of a rift in his psyche, but the laughter grew, prodded by Amestan's dry sense of humor. The chuckle became deep belly laughter, giving Max incredible relief. He threw his head back as tears ran from his eyes.

"Yes," Max cried. "She is here." He struggled to his feet and wiped his eyes dry as the final ripple of laughter died off. He peered at his friend.

"Excellent," Amestan quipped. He stood and slapped Max on the back, nearly knocking Max back to his knees. "What is next?"

Max shone his light down the sixty feet of corridor to the end. A large object hugged the back wall. "Her sarcophagus. I need to get back there." He gazed over the sea of artifacts, wondering how he was going to reach the back, when Amestan's movements drew his attention.

"What are you doing?" Max cried. He jumped to stop Amestan, who was forging a path down the right wall by pushing material out of the way.

"How else are you going to get back there?" Amestan asked. He continued moving through the artifacts. "Did you lose your common sense when you got your degree?" He gave Max a look of utter amazement.

"Well ... I, uh—" Max stuttered, unable to believe a trained archaeologist would commit such a violation.

"What is the end game here, eh?" Amestan walked over to Max. "What is your priority? Do we care about a few artifacts?" He waved at the objects that stood between them and the sarcophagus. "Or do we save your queen?" He thumped Max soundly on the breastbone.

"Ow," Max yelped, rubbing his chest. "That hurt."

"Are you back on mission?" Amestan replied.

In the face of Amestan's hard knuckle logic, there was little Max could say. He drew up as indignant as possible, but nodded.

"Good. You see the necessity, yes?" Amestan stated.

Max joined Amestan and took what was being pushed back. Some material was destroyed with a touch and Max refused to look. Other items were hauntingly familiar, striking a chord deep within. These he refused to look at also.

For two hours they nudged their way through disintegrated organic material, then pushed through a zoo of mummified animals, and moved furniture until they finally broke into the cleared area surrounding the sarcophagus.

Sweat ran down Max's face. He and Amestan sat with their water bottles. Back-to-back, they gazed at their respective view of the chamber.

"What kind of man do you think he is?" Amestan asked.

"He will be rich probably. Powerful somehow. And evil. I don't look forward to our encounter," Max replied.

"If he wants in here, he'll have to go through me. No one knows these mountains like I do. I'll have your back. We will not let this mongrel get away with killing our queen."

Amestan's words reminded Max of Bahk-ir's speech the day the Amenti brought her here. Bahk-ir, as her murderer and by his own decree, had cast his fate with the dogs. "Think you can get your camp dogs to eat something so nasty?" Max asked.

"Maybe," Amestan grunted. "Might have to throw in a little catsup."

The image from Amestan's words brought Max a chuckle. He stood and offered Amestan his hand. "Up, old man." They stared speculatively at the heavy stone lid of the sarcophagus. "How much Berber muscle will we need to lift that?" Max inquired.

Amestan held out his arm and put up his thumb as they do when measuring an object in the far distance. He groaned and scrunched his face putting on a show as his Berber muscle computed the weight of the stone lid.

Max squashed a burst of laughter. He offered, "You, me, and six strong men?"

"Exactly what I was going to say," Amestan agreed with a show of teeth.

After lunch they returned with a group of young Berbers.

They surrounded the sarcophagus three to a side, with Max and Amestan at each end. Using their shoulders wedged under the lip overhang of the stone lid, Amestan counted and they lifted on three. Slowly, and with a great deal of grunting and shifting of their weight, the lid moved.

Once they had it lifted free of the sarcophagus and stable, Max and Amestan guided the lid clockwise. When they had it angled enough to allow access, Amestan signaled the men to set it down.

The lid landed with a resounding thunk that vibrated down through the stone and up into the soles of their feet. The young men stepped away, rubbing their shoulders and staring at the opened sarcophagus. Gradually, each man's eyes darted about, looking for signs of the newly escaped soul of the one interred.

"Go," Amestan instructed, waving his hand at them.

After the men left, in the quiet as the dust finally settled, Max could almost imagine Byrgamon's soul squeaking out of the sarcophagus once the lid was moved. But he knew her soul was somewhere on earth. All he had to do was find her. Having come this far from zero, the next step seemed daunting—but not impossible.

"It has been a long time. Are you ready?" Amestan asked.

Max took a light and approached the coffin. Deep shadows that had not seen light in ten thousand years shrank back. He peered over the edge and was surprised to feel tears well up. He blinked, making the tears run down his face as he spoke. "I told you I would be here when you returned."

Her remains were scant. The skull, pelvic girdle, and the spinal vertebra were recognizable along with her burial jewelry.

"Gamon," he whispered. The anguish of her loss ripped through him anew as if she had died yesterday. Until he found her current incarnation, seeing these remains made him feel she was completely lost to him. Pain flared in a blaze.

"No," he commanded. "I will not grieve. I will find you." A whisper of ocean breeze and glinting diamonds teased him. "We will have our time together."

He put on latex gloves and carefully scooped up the remains of Queen Byrgamon. She was small, but mighty in life. Hopefully, her remains would offer him a clue as to how she was murdered.

Amestan held open a large evidence bag and Max deposited the bones, setting the jewelry aside. At Amestan's lifted eyebrows, Max said, "She will want these returned one day." He sealed the evidence bag and placed it in a box for protection. The jewelry he bagged and placed in his backpack, unwilling to take the time to inspect anything now.

Max took the lamp to the sarcophagus and shined it thoroughly around the inside. He poked and prodded, searching for secret compartments and found none. When he was sure the journal wasn't to be found here, he signaled Amestan to bring the men back in.

The lid was reset. After the men left, Amestan and Max returned as much as they could of the material they removed earlier, filling in the path.

"Would that convince you?" Max eyed their work critically.

"Take my advice," Amestan offered. He shouldered his backpack with an unconcerned shrug. "Find your queen, take her away and have babies. This place smells of sadness." He marched out without a glance back.

Max would like nothing better than to follow his friend's suggestion. When he exited the chamber carrying Queen Byrgamon's bones, one thought filled his mind.

Where are you, Gamon?

California, The Present

From a small apartment across the alley from Phoenix Donovan, Max watched her with binoculars. Thanks to the discoveries he made in Libya with Amestan, he never once doubted this day would come.

I told Bahk-ir you would return for justice. Now he is here to collect it.

"You bastard. I said your day of reckoning would come," Max growled. Amestan had informed him Bahk-ir was coming to hire Phoenix to excavate her own grave. Seeing Bahk-ir this close to her made Max grind his teeth. He put down the binoculars and turned to his laptop, opening a complex astrology/sky-mapping program, and typed today's time and date into the search window.

A computer-generated scene of constellations appeared, moving in minute increments, causing a long number in a side window to flicker and change.

Next to his laptop was an ancient book on astrology and numerology, *The Numbers of Life and Eternity*, a surprising wealth of arcane knowledge and lore he found via the Internet from a bookseller in eastern Russia. That purchase led to a six-month sojourn in Romania where he learned Tarot from a master of the cards.

He thumbed through the tattered pages, musing. "If not for the computer and this ancient little book, our reunion of old souls would never have happened."

By combining numerology, astrology and advanced sky mapping, he had found her. Amestan's words, "All things come when the time is right," now held more meaning than ever. With the final arrival of Bahk-ir in Phoenix's life, all the players were reassembled.

"Asa Ducaine. At last, the wheel of time serves justice," Max proclaimed softly. "Infinity ends where it begins. In the Temple, my long search to regain all you took from me will end."

The constellations in Max's computer program stopped moving, generating a stable number in the side window. He copied that number, and ran a finger down the fragile page of tiny, handwritten charts of seemingly random numbers.

"Unbelievable," he muttered. His computer program, using a number derived from an equation of both Byrgamon and Kedare's birthdates, gave him a number that appeared in a tiny, ancient chart—corresponding with tomorrow's date. "At last, the time is right."

He gazed out the window at her apartment. They had not met yet, for the numbers weren't right, the dates incorrect. Of all he had endured and achieved since his coma, this waiting with her so close was by far the most difficult. Every time he saw her, he wanted to shout out.

What would he say? How would she react to such insanity? How will she respond when she discovers who she is? He worried about these answers. He worried about how he was supposed to awaken her memories without damaging her psyche. He worried about saving her from a repeat of history.

"My love, I'm coming," he said quietly.

He picked up the binoculars and watched through her kitchen window. She stood by the couch with hands on her hips, consternation lacing her brow. He read her lips as she cried out—

"Who are you people?"

Max closed his eyes and rocked back on his heels. A turbulent mix of trepidation, elation and anxiety ripped through him, curling his toes.

"I did not wait through eternity to lose you again," he vowed. "Tomorrow. At last we meet."

CHAPTER FOUR

Phoenix stared at the closed fortune-teller shop and wanted to weep with frustration. "Come on, it's Monday. You should be open." She banged on the door and sobbed, hearing desperation in her voice as she whispered, "Please, I need to hear what you know."

"Can I help you?" a man said.

Feeling like fool, Phoenix quickly backed up. "No, no. I'm fine, thank you." She gave him a quick look and instantly felt he was … not a threat? She frowned and wondered why a stranger should make her feel safe.

"Perhaps I can be of assistance," he said with a nod to the Tarot sign. "I know a bit about these things."

A casual smile warmed his handsome face, yet Phoenix detected a serious tone in his voice. She also sensed there was more to his ability than he proclaimed.

"I'm Max," he said. "Max Parrish.'

He put his hand out in greeting. Phoenix noted he was tall and muscular with dark blue eyes and light brown hair. His fingers were long and graceful, and his eyes communicated a degree of admiration that made her feel conscious about her appearance. She put her hand out. "I'm Phoenix Donovan. Pleased to meet you."

The handshake was polite, but warm. When Phoenix released his hand, she oddly wished for another reason to touch him. A sudden flash of wildly erotic thoughts raced through her mind, and she felt her face respond with a blush.

What is the matter with me?

His eyes looked right through her. Strangely, she didn't mind. In fact, the thought of opening up to him physically sneaked seductively into her thoughts. Wavering under the onslaught of this sudden, very ripe flush of desire, she feared doing the inappropriate. He smiled again, warm and engaging, and a flutter ignited in the pit of her stomach. She grabbed her purse strap with both hands.

He asked again, "What do you need help with?" He pointed to the sign.

Lost in her thoughts, Phoenix suddenly realized this handsome man had busted her seeking the aid of a fortune-teller. "Oh, no," she shook her head emphatically. "I don't go for this stuff. I was just here to ... to—" Unable to finish her sentence, she felt a slow burn intensify the blush on her face. What an unfortunate time, she thought, to look like an idiot.

His lips thinned with suppressed mirth, and one eyebrow lifted to say, "I'm not convinced."

"All right then." Phoenix laughed. "You got me." She glanced up at the closed fortune-teller and jokingly asked, "Can you remove a curse?"

Oddly, her casual question caused his eyebrows to shoot straight up. After a long speculative look, he probed. "Why? Do you believe yourself to be cursed?"

The tone of his response did not match the tone of her question. She was kidding. He sounded serious. She stepped back and looked him up and down again. "What do you do, Mr. Parrish, that brings you knowledge of curses?"

His eyes connected to hers with an intensity she couldn't identify. Seconds passed before he replied. "I am a keeper of ancient secrets: astrology, past lives, Tarot. These topics intrigue me, and I am blessed with the ability to pursue such interests."

Phoenix felt sure he must have many secrets. "I accompanied a friend here yesterday," she clarified. "I was looking at some Tarot cards, that's all. But Faby—the fortune-teller, made a big deal about the cards I set aside."

"And?" he coaxed.

A young couple passed by, forcing them to move. Phoenix stepped out of the shade into the sun, eliciting a rash of chill bumps across her shoulders. When they were alone once again, she said, "I was told crazy things about two men from my past and the total destruction of my life." She looked up, sheepish to be saying such nonsense.

Instead of a shocked expression, his face creased in concern.

He didn't think her words were nonsense at all. Having shared this much, she felt compelled to continue. With a gulp, and her heart beating a little fast, she rushed on.

"There were the Tower, the Lovers ... uh, and the Empress." She snorted with disdain. "That's me, and I have some ... hidden talent." She waved her hands dismissively. "And supposedly there is power all around me." Running out of words, she shrugged and gave him a glance that said, "I don't see any power, do you?"

A darkening visage was not what she expected. His worried expression sent a shiver from her scalp down to the soles of her feet. Doggedly, she finished. "And there's the Emperor, who's coming for me. Whoever that is," she added lamely.

Her last words turned his face stiff. He suddenly looked so disturbed, she thought she'd said something out of place. In an attempt to make light of the fortune-teller, she wrinkled her nose. "See, it's all a lot of silly—"

Abruptly his attitude turned into good-natured teasing. "Oh, dear," he laughed. "I'm afraid you got the regular," he finished with a sympathetic frown.

He began walking away from the fortune-teller, hands clasped behind him, reminding her of Prof Barnes. "You say you were just accompanying your friend? Ah, so the fortune-teller gives you enough to entice you back the next day. It's an old ploy."

While his logic was plausible, Phoenix still frowned.

I'm here because the fortune-teller's words were prophetic.

She looked back toward the fortune-teller's shop.

"May I?" he asked.

Before she could answer, he took one of her hands, turning her palm up. Gazing intently, he hummed and frowned, finally going, "Ah!"

Phoenix warmed to the sudden game and waited with expectation. A grin twitched at the corners of her mouth.

He hummed for a moment more and said, "You are a deeply intelligent young woman about to make one of the most important decisions of your life."

She couldn't suppress a full smile and laughed out loud.

"You stand at a crossroad, two paths toward your destiny," he added with drama.

"Oh, right," she snickered and rolled her eyes.

His eyebrows came down in a hawkish pose, indicating dire consequences. "You must choose correctly or else all will be doomed."

"Of course! And I must choose the Prince, right?" she added.

Her quick words, meant in jest for the game they played, instantly created a vacuum. All went deadly still. Max's eyes burned with a scary intensity, yet when he spoke, his voice was so soft, the hairs along her arm lifted.

"Yes, you must choose the Prince." He dropped her hand and stepped back.

Phoenix didn't know what to say. They had been walking in the direction of her parked car, and she pulled out her keys as the vehicle came into sight. She didn't want to go, but she couldn't think of a reason to stay and talk to this enigmatic man. "Well, I—"

Max pulled out his keys and pressed a button. The vehicle next to Phoenix's, a Bentley Mulsanne, chirped in response.

Phoenix's face burned with embarrassment. Her little domestic second-hand car looked pitiful next to the elegant Mulsanne. She fumbled for parting words, when she really just wanted to look in his car.

His eyes bright with charm, he asked, "May I take you out for something to eat? I think the time is right."

Phoenix noted he didn't bother to look at his watch, and his words rang rich with a prophetic tone, giving her a splash of goose bumps down her back. Still, she smiled, delighted he asked. She wasn't afraid of this man. In fact, he made her feel ... protected. Was he one of her two men? Counting Mr. Gamon's envelope, there appeared to be three new surprising men in her life.

See, that fortune-teller stuff is bogus.

"I'd love to," she answered. She glanced at the Mulsanne and wondered where people eat when they drive such a car. "I'm dressed pretty casual," she warned. She looked down at her simple summer dress and sandals. She wiggled her bare toes.

"You are a queen wherever you go," he said. His words sent out a wave of good will and made her feel, for the moment, he was right—she was a queen.

He came around to open the passenger door. She peered past him to the incredibly luxurious interior of the Bentley. He was close to her, so close she could smell his evocative scent. Detecting a familiar note, she felt an attraction, as though this particular scent was an old acquaintance. She climbed in, smiling.

The car was large and heavy and incredibly powerful. He drove effortlessly. Phoenix settled into the soft leather seat and relaxed. Oddly, she felt at home in the utterly luxurious vehicle. With genuine appreciation, she said, "How beautiful this is."

They were stopped at a light and Max turned to her. His eyes, at first on her face, lost focus as he shifted to stare right through her for long seconds. His eyes crinkled in sadness even though he smiled. She wondered what she had said to draw such a bittersweet reaction. "Max?"

Behind them a horn blew, but Max was looking at her again with an odd mix of softness and intensity. "Your words," he whispered, "remind me of someone I knew, long ago."

He took her to a Mediterranean restaurant. They feasted on creamy yogurt soup, salad and couscous with roast lamb. Dried apricots and sugared almond pastries left Phoenix licking her fingers.

She felt more relaxed than she had been in a long time. She sat back and eyed this intriguing man who had entered her life. What a shame, she thought, as she was probably going to leave the country in the next week. "Oh, well," she muttered. "Some people just don't deserve life or love."

"What's that?" Max asked. He set his wine glass down next to hers. Their hands were close and he let his fingers drift to caress the length of her little finger.

The meaningless words Phoenix uttered suddenly felt thick in her throat. She struggled to repeat them. "I said ... said, uh, some people just don't deserve life or love." She squirmed under his scrutiny. He studied her for long moments with speculation, again seeming so somber when she jested.

"Why would someone as beautiful and intelligent as you say such a thing?" he asked.

Phoenix's heart began racing at his tone. She fumbled with her words. "Oh, um, that's just something I say at times when the phrase seems appropriate—like now."

He moved closer and took her hand. His fingers, warm and dry, caressed her with reverence, imparting an incredible emotional thrill. He made her feel ... special in ways she had never experienced.

"You are the queen of someone's heart, I'm sure." He brought her hand to his lips for a soft yet smoldering kiss.

A spike of physical delight shot through her body. Languorous, seductive warmth spread outward in waves, encompassing every nerve. Time, she thought, must have stopped, along with her heart and her breath.

Why does this man make me feel so ... different?

Too much was happening, too many questions, too many feelings. She slowly extracted her hand from his grasp and reached for her wine. Her movement broke the spell.

Max leaned back with a look of chagrin. "It's getting late. May I take you home?"

Reality came crashing back to Phoenix. "Oh, my car is—"

"Of course. I will return you to your car and then follow you to your home, to make sure you arrive safely. As a gentleman, I will accept nothing less."

He was true to his word, seeing her to the top of her stairs, impressing Phoenix with his manners. When she opened her door, he peered inside. "May I?" he asked.

Amused at his sense of old fashion protection, she nodded.

He walked quickly through all of her four rooms and returned with an engaging smile. "It's all clear," he said. He stopped at the door to her deck. "What's here?" he asked.

"Just the—" she started, but he was already in motion. He opened the door and stepped out. When he returned, he carried the fat envelope from the Gamon~Search Institute. "You left this outside. It looks important. Maybe you should open it."

He handed her the envelope, suddenly serious again, and she wondered why. He looked past her to the unopened boxes. "Are you going somewhere?"

"Probably," Phoenix said. "I have an offer to head an archaeology expedition—"

"Don't go," he said.

Phoenix stopped, for she wasn't sure she heard him right.

"Don't go," he repeated. He pointed to the Gamon~Search envelope. "At least not until you open the other envelope."

Before she could react, he moved to leave. He stopped in the open doorway. "Call me first," he said. With mischief dancing in his eyes, he gave a deep bow, and was gone.

The door clicked shut and Phoenix looked about, dazed and disoriented, as if she just returned from a vacation she didn't remember. She wanted to ask, "How did I get here?"

She echoed his last words, "Call me first. Now what does that mean?" She sat with a flop on her couch, the Gamon~Search envelope in her hand. Suddenly she jumped up and ran to the door, but he was already gone. "How can I call you," she wailed to the night sky. "You didn't leave me your number."

•

Max left Phoenix's apartment feeling like he was on a rollercoaster. Earlier when he drove to the restaurant, her words had thrown him deep into the past, reminding him of the first moment he saw her.

On that day eons ago, the sun shone like never before. He heard the palace trumpets sound the approach of an arriving caravan, and ran to his balcony overlooking the courtyard.

"She is arrived?" he called out to the servants below.

"Yes, my, Lord. The Amenti are here."

He ran down to the courtyard, straining for a glimpse of her. The Amenti queen was known for her beauty, along with her power as the renowned master of the Magic of War. When word came she would make a diplomatic visit to Cyrenaica, he waited with keen anticipation.

She rode astride a great stallion. As their horses were being held, she dismounted and released her blue head cover, revealing a beauty beyond what he imagined. Her eyes were warm and intelligent, and her long hair flowed loose down her back. She looked about the courtyard, filled with bright flowers, ferns and palm trees, and smiled with delight. "How beautiful this is," she said.

The two worlds—past and present—were pulling Max back and forth, at once terrifying ... and titillating.

"Yes!" he whispered in triumph as he pulled the Bentley into a private garage. He walked the short distance to his small apartment across the alley from her, whistling with every step. In the glow of a streetlight, he checked his phone to make sure it was on.

He entered through the back door and went straight to the binoculars without turning on the lights. "Come on Gamon," he whispered. "Open the envelope."

•

With Max gone, Phoenix felt suddenly alone. She looked at the clock and was surprised to see it was a little past ten.

Where did the time go?

What began as a late lunch extended well past dinner. Too excited to go to bed, she changed into lounging sweats and a T-shirt and poured a glass of wine.

She returned to the couch to view her options on the coffee table: Asa's contract or the fat envelope? She picked up Asa's contract and read it through. Her eyebrows inched up by degrees as she flipped through the pages. "Phew! How could he offer me that much money? That's not only obscene, it's … highly tempting." She put the contract back on the table and picked up the envelope.

"All right Mr. Gamon, let's see if you can top Mr. Ducaine's offer."

She slit open the envelope. Inside she found a thick contract, a letter, and another small envelope. Phoenix sniffed the paper with a deep inhalation.

"That smell again," she mused. "Why is it so familiar?"

The Feather of Maat glyph decorating the return address also graced the top of the opening page. She rubbed the deeply embossed symbol.

"The Gamon~Search Institute," she said.

She started with the letter. As she read, her eyebrows again inched higher and higher. "Oh!" she exclaimed, reading further.

"I wish to buy a spot in this expedition because I believe there is a high possibility the site you are soon to excavate holds the remains of my lover from a past life."

She finished the last page and grunted with disbelief. "Huh. What kind of love could create such a force, such momentum, such desire?" she mused. "Especially over that extended a time frame?" She flipped the last page over, but there was nothing more. "It's impossible, although noble and romantic in theory. But without a doubt, utter nonsense."

The accompanying contract, as with Asa's offer, impressed her for what the Gamon~Search Institute was willing to pay.

"What is going on in Gebel?" she asked.

This location must hold something of great value, she reasoned, for it was generating some rather fantastic monetary offers for her talents. She gazed at the two contracts remembering the fortune-teller's words, that she was surrounded by power. Since money is power, then Faby was correct.

Whatever was at Gebel, Phoenix wanted in on the action. She opened the final, small envelope and found a contact card inside. She flipped the card over and saw the name and number.

"What?" she cried. She called the number.

•

Max put down the binoculars. Knowing he was about to lie to her made his heart accelerate with a combination of excitement and regret. His phone rang and he answered. "Max Parrish."

"Why didn't you tell me earlier?" Phoenix asked.

With a quick prayer Max hoped his words would successfully convince her. "Well, would you have believed me? I mean, my story is a little fantastic, wouldn't you say?"

"As a scientist, or a woman?" she responded.

Max heard the warmth in her voice. He hated to deceive her, even though lying was necessary to bring her gently to the truth.

So she won't crash—like I did.

Changing one's identity, the notion of who and what you think you are is not easily done. He had to bring her along slowly. Were she to ever appear vulnerable to Bahk-ir—

Max hurried to confess. "And so now you know why I am a keeper of secrets. Why I know about Tarot and past lives. I was hesitant to say more when we first met, and afterward, the right time didn't come up. I knew the letter would explain better than I could, once you opened the envelope.

"My contacts in Libya informed me of the discovery of the chamber. I went to Libya and made a quick search to see if this was ... the one I wanted to find. At that time, other arrangements had been made higher up, and I lost my opportunity for excavation rights. I heard Ducaine was going to ask you, so I figured the only way in for me—is with you."

"You were quite charming tonight. Why should I not feel a little used?" she asked.

The slightest quiver in her voice accused him. He silently gave thanks he could tell this lie over the phone. "I hope the generous compensation will ease your ego. As for the pleasure of your company, it was, well ... unexpected."

"I would have to lie to Mr. Ducaine," she said.

"He will not like our arrangement," Max responded. The words echoed back at him from another millennia and he readied himself for the shift. In that single moment, he and Byrgamon were in the tent. The heady smell of the plains in full bloom filled the air. Her skin was satin beneath his fingers. Her cries of ecstasy reverberated deep into the heart of night.

"Max? Are you there?" came her voice.

Max pressed his fingers to the bridge of his nose and scrunched his eyes to loosen the grip of the past. "Your contract with Mr. Ducaine need not be violated. I assume he provides for you to select a team—"

"He says no team. Only me."

A stillness invaded Max's heart as he considered how that would turn out. "You aren't considering—"

"No," she answered. "I'm not so stupid as to go to Libya with only my employer. That would be highly improper and unsafe."

In his most coaxing tone, he added, "Then you should take me along. We needn't tell Ducaine about our arrangement." He held his breath. The last time he made her this offer, she refused him and was murdered.

She didn't answer right away and he could hear her thinking. He closed his eyes and prayed, *Take me, take me, don't go alone, don't go—*

"Do you have any field experience?" she asked.

"Yes. I'm familiar with Gebel Oweinat and, as the letter explained, I've been to this site. I was there last year."

He held his breath.

"I do need an assistant ... but you have to be credible," she said. "Can you do that?"

"I won't let you down," he answered softly.

"Then I'll tell Mr. Ducaine you are a member of my team and part of the package."

"When ... when will you tell him?" Max probed.

Again, the words opened the door to déjà vu, and for the most fleeting moment, he could smell the cloud of Byrgamon's hair against his lips. He closed his eyes and savored the memory until she spoke.

"Come over in the morning and I'll sign your contract. Then I'll call Mr. Ducaine and accept his offer. Max, Asa must never learn you're involved because you think this chamber carries the body of a woman you loved in a past life. However sweet this story of yours sounds—and I say you are allowed to believe what you want, that's your business. But this expedition has to be a purely scientific exploration. I don't want anything found there tainted by this … story. You will keep private your speculations about your relationship with whomever we find. Do we have a deal?"

Tears of relief watered Max's eyes.

Maybe this time will be different. Maybe you won't die.

"We have a deal," he said. "I'll keep my little fantasy to myself, and Mr. Ducaine will never know our secret."

•

Asa Ducaine sat in the living room of his rented suite with a cut crystal tumbler in his hand. Scotch with a name he couldn't pronounce provided a warm glow to his attitude, expanding his already good mood. He turned the glass in the light, admiring the color of the scotch with a smile of infinite satisfaction.

Phoenix Donovan is going to find the Journal of War for me.

Delight and gratification warmed his hardened soul, for he felt the future at last ready to fall into his hands. After countless eons, he was days away from his ultimate desire.

"I found you," he whispered, and swallowed the smooth amber liquid.

There was no doubt Phoenix Donovan was Byrgamon's reincarnation. She looked exactly like her, sounded like her. And she was an expert in pre-dynastic cultures.

Back to the Temple, to the beginning, and to the end.

He chuckled and poured more scotch. "To anger management and shrinks," he toasted. "You showed me who I really am."

Discovery had cost him thousands. But the door to his soul, opened during a past-life regression with a therapist looking to source his uncontrollable anger, led him to this day. From that first session he went on to explore his past lives and memories.

Eventually, he realized how many of his incarnations had been impacted by this rage from an ancient life. The past lives he explored in session after session served only to validate his anger and vindicate his attitude.

"You're damn right I'm pissed," he said to the night. "The potential for vast riches and power was stolen—"

"Stolen—" He held his empty hand up and snapped it closed. "Right out of my hands. Oh, she took everything from me once. Now I will return the favor."

The heat of his long-burning anger nurtured his hatred. At long last, his pent-up rage with interest due and payable, would see vengeance and satisfaction the moment his hands reached the journal.

All was proceeding exceptionally well so far, with her in his grasp and no Kedare in sight. He rubbed his hands together with glee, envisioning the day he would take the journal from her.

"'Only my hands can find the journal now,'" he chirped with a sneer, recalling her last words when he killed her long ago. "This time, your hands will not escape me."

On the day Phoenix found the journal in the Temple, he would take it. On the next day, he would decide what to do with her. A shrug of childish delight lifted his shoulders as he considered keeping her as a toy. Her hands, of course, would have to go—

His phone rang. He looked at the number, expecting to see her calling and scowled briefly when he saw a client's incoming number instead. He answered. "Hey, Dante. What can I sell you today, my man?"

While he listened to Dante's request, Asa held his right hand out, envisioning the power he would wield with the Journal of War's magic.

"Yeah, yeah I can get that. In fact I'm going to be in North Africa in the next few days. I'll contact you tomorrow with quantity and prices," he said. He held the phone to his ear with his shoulder so he could hold both hands up.

When I access the journal, I will once again be the Lord of War and not just a purveyor of weapons.

"Yes, Dante, I can get you more RPGs—as many cases as you want. But the price has gone up since the last time you bought."

Dante's response came across the tiny microphone in rising decibels. "Hey," Asa protested. "Costs go up. That's out of my control. If you don't like the prices, you're more than welcome to buy from someone else. No hard feelings—"

After a brief pause, Asa continued. "Uh huh, that's what I thought. You stand by for my call tomorrow."

He disconnected the call and walked to the windows, staring

out at the lights of Los Angeles and the foggy Pacific beyond. He rocked back on his heels, disbelieving his luck in finding her.

The moment he laid eyes on her, he knew he was destined to succeed. War was his business just as it was in the past. He felt it only fitting and appropriate for him to take possession since he was cheated of the journal long ago.

"Such power should never have been turned over to a woman, regardless of lineage," he complained. "Well, the journal and its Magic of War will be mine now."

He raised his glass to toast her posthumously. "To Byrgamon and finding the Journal of War." He emptied his glass in a single gulp. "This time, my queen, you're going to bring me the journal before I kill you."

CHAPTER FIVE

The next morning, Max walked the short distance to Phoenix's apartment for her signing of his contract. Embracing his coming role as an archaeology assistant, he dressed in faded khaki pants and a Hawaiian shirt from a second-hand store. He rubbed his chin and the beginnings of a goatee, a small step to camouflage his appearance from Bahk-ir.

He stopped to reprimand himself. "Do not call Asa Ducaine Bahk-ir."

In the search for Gamon, Max had acquired an archaeology degree, utilized his father's help as an internet search engine designer, learned Tarot from a Romanian gypsy, explored the desert, robbed a grave and lied to the one soul that was his heart's mate.

Now the hard part begins.

"Fooling Bahk-ir while awakening Byrgamon."

He stood at the top of the stairs to her apartment and knocked. While waiting, he looked down and whispered, "For Gamon," under his breath. The door opened and he looked up.

"Hi," she said.

If it were in his power, Max would stop time in this moment. Her short hair made her green eyes look luminous, and her honey-tanned skin begged for his touch. He had missed her for so long—now she was here, a living, breathing presence—and he could not touch her.

The narrow path he carefully navigated was defined by his strategy to awaken her. Yesterday, he had overstepped the boundaries of sanity when he kissed her hand at dinner. It was imperative he not lose control, lest all his efforts produce a tragic repeat of history.

"Hi," he answered. He pulled his heart back and smiled as if they just met yesterday.

"You look different." She gave him the once over as she stepped back to let him enter.

"I'm an arch assistant," he said, rubbing his chin. "I thought I'd start looking the part. I told you I wouldn't let you down and I meant it. You'll see I can pass credible muster since I have an ancient world archaeology degree from Brown University—"

"You could have mentioned that!"

"Well, I just did," he added with a wink. "As I was trying to say, I did my field work in Georgia. So don't be surprised if you hear me drop into a Southern drawl." He wagged his brows and said, "Mornin' Miss Phoenix. Now, ain't this a purty day?"

A squeak of disbelief came out before she covered her mouth, but her eyes laughed and she motioned him into the kitchen. His contract lay on the kitchen table.

"Come on, you're my witness," she said. She picked up a pen and flipped to the back page of his contract. After signing, she put the pen down and fanned her signature. "There, it is done," she quipped. She looked at him and smiled with mischief, shaking her head slowly. "I cannot believe I let you talk me into this."

Max braced himself, hearing the identical words rush at him out of the past.

Byrgamon unrolled the skin and carefully smoothed it flat on the table. She signed her name in bold letters and blew against the skin to dry the black. When she looked up, she smiled. "There, it is done. I can not believe I let you talk me into this."

The present regained its grip, and Max exhaled deeply. He took the freshly signed contract and placed it in his shirt pocket, over his heart. "What we conspire harms no one," he offered. "You get paid twice, I get to look for evidence of my beliefs, and Mr. Ducaine gets your services. I see that as a win-win situation." He saw she considered a rebuttal, but what she asked surprised him.

"What other secrets do you have, Max? Is there anything else I should know?"

His heart ramped up, eager for this opportunity to tell the truth, even if it was cloaked in disguise. He placed one hand over the contract and looked her square in the eye. "You know everything I know."

"Somehow, I doubt that," she remarked. She put his letter and his card back in her Gamon~Search envelope. "I'll call Asa now."

As she dialed, Max walked off, giving her space to tell her lies. He kept his eyes down and listened.

"Good morning," she said. "I hope I'm not calling too early."

Asa's voice came over the cell phone speaker with a hiss. Max thought of snakes and a flash of chills skipped across his scalp.

"I'd like to accept your proposal, Asa, but I must have a qualified assistant. Surely you don't expect me to handle all the work alone. No ... no, Asa, the local Berbers are not qualified enough to assist in this operation. I'm bringing one assistant who is efficient and easy to work with—"

Phoenix held the phone out from her ear as Ducaine complained, his voice escalating into angry tones. She brought the phone back and interrupted. "Mr. Ducaine, let me be clear. Max comes with me, or you can go to Gebel alone."

An echo of Queen Byrgamon rode in Phoenix's words. Max glanced up and saw a familiar, immovable stance in her posture.

"I look forward to seeing you this afternoon," she said, and snapped the phone closed. "Well, that went down like a snake on a cake." She chuckled.

Max recalled his earlier thought about snakes and joined her laughter. "How did he take it?"

"He didn't like the change and he got a little weird. But in the end, he didn't want to go to Gebel alone." She waved her hands as though the gesture settled the argument.

Max watched her movements and was reminded of the deadly power Gamon commanded. He didn't know if the Journal could be found, or if the power would come to Phoenix. Hell, he didn't know if he could awaken her to who and what she really is—and do it in time to save her life. He just knew he would not let Bahk-ir kill her again. "So when do we leave?" he asked.

"Asa is coming over at 1:00 to discuss the site and leave documents and such. You have to be here. He wants to meet you."

•

In his hotel suite, Asa Ducaine disconnected the call from Phoenix.

"Who the hell is Max?"

Is he Kedare?

And what about Miss high-and-mighty Phoenix? Didn't she sound—

Just like Byrgamon.

His first impulse was to howl and break something. "Relax," he commanded. He drew down his anger using a technique he learned from the therapists. At the time, he was greatly amused that they wanted him to use his hands to calm his anger.

He flexed his hands and stretched his fingers, focusing on the minute detail of the motions. Slowly, his billowing rage contracted. "Ah," he sighed. The relaxation technique drove the urge to kill from his fingers.

But not from his heart.

Soon, my anger will no longer suffer restraint.

This new development would not stop him in any way. "Maybe Max is only ... Max." He cracked his knuckles. "And if he is Kedare—"

Asa made another call, this time to Cairo. "Hassan, my man. I have a slight change of plan. Miss Donovan is bringing an assistant, so tell Amestan we will need another tent in the base camp. Make the necessary changes in supplies. I'm not sure exactly when they'll be arriving in Cairo. I'll call you as soon as I find out the details. I have business in the area pending, so I will see you soon."

He terminated the call. Kedare's appearance could be trouble, but not anything Asa couldn't handle. After all, the Berbers were on his payroll.

"Yes, this could be interesting," he ruminated. He smiled and rubbed his hands together. "If Max is Kedare, I'll just kill him and make her watch!"

He chuckled, a sound humorless and wicked, even to his ears.

•

While waiting for the meeting with Asa, Max passed the time in his apartment preparing. In his bedroom corner was a small round table covered in black velvet with an enameled box containing a deck of Egyptian Tarot cards.

Max drew out his cards, shuffled, and spread them in an arc face down. He took a deep breath, chanting, "For Gamon. Bring me success in this meeting," and drew a card: The Queen of Wands.

"Good, this is Byrgamon." He drew again the Wheel of Fortune, and whistled softly. "An acceleration of events."

Another card, the Knight of Swords. "Power in motion—success." He thanked his cards and returned them to the protective enamel box.

I can do this—

"For Gamon."

Everything from this moment on depended on how he performed when he faced Asa. He must look his enemy in the eye and lie.

"As if her life depended on it."

He remembered the terrible ache that consumed his heart when he learned of Byrgamon's murder. His conviction that Bahk-ir killed the queen sustained Kedare as sure as food and drink through the days leading to their confrontation before the people of Amenti.

When he shouted, "You are the mongrel who killed her," the crowd went silent and still. How those words had brought Bahk-ir's speech to a halt. Even now Max could feel the weight of silence as a thousand grieving Amenti faces turned to question their General. But Bahk-ir was a smooth one.

"You were in command that day, Bahk-ir," Max conceded. "Are you in command now?"

Max sat cross-legged on the floor. He slowed his breath and closed his eyes, reaching deep into his mind for delta level—where miracles begin.

He directed his thoughts to the unseen particles that surround all life and penetrate our being. "When I meet with Asa Ducaine, I will be composed. My heart will remain calm and uninvolved. I command anger to sit silent until needed, while determination is authorized to release the blood debt that exists between my soul and Bahk-ir. I will always call him Mr. Ducaine. He will always see me as Max, the assistant. I command all the particles subservient to my will to see me through to my goal."

In his mind's eye he watched the meeting progress exactly as he desired. He pictured the baffled look on Bahk-ir's face when he could not be certain if Max was Kedare. "Bahk-ir, you will see only Max." He made a series of silent moves with his hands. This was one of the few small spells he learned from Gamon. She had surprised him with her desire to share in her power.

"No, like this," Byrgamon said. She showed him the movement

once more and he saw the subtle difference. He tried again.

"Yes, you have it!" she exclaimed. She crawled into his arms and filled him with her scent, her love, and her power over his heart— which had nothing to do with her magic of war. She shimmied with delight like a small child and made the movement for fire. Flame engulfed the wick of a nearby lamp. "Make the flame expire," she said. "Just do as I described."

He closed his eyes and made the move just learned, but when he peeked, the flame was still alive. He closed his eyes again, gathered his emotional desire for success and released that energy to the unseen forces. He made the move again.

"Oh," she squealed.

He knew he was successful before she cried. When he released his energy and set it in motion, he felt a small window in his mind open briefly, and close.

Max felt the window appear and open again. He released a wave of emotional energy comprised of joy excitement and gratitude to pass through the window. This energy and information was received by the tiny particles Byrgamon described so long ago. He made the hand movement, followed by a flick of his fingers to send the energy and information into the future on the back of tachyons.

The seemingly incongruous nature of Byrgamon's magic made him smile with wonder. "Gamon, my love, you commanded subatomic particles. If I am half as good as you—will it be enough?"

At exactly one o'clock Max watched Bahk-ir arrive at Phoenix's apartment. After five minutes Max walked over. Before he climbed the steps he made the hand gesture again and silently called upon the spell to cloak him with particles to prevent Bahk-ir's mind from fully sensing Max's identity.

Max knew the spell alone wasn't enough. He had to act the part completely. The energy disguising him would dissipate the moment one iota of Kedare's energy appeared. The slightest trigger such as a wrong look or tone of voice, and the game would be up.

"For Gamon," he whispered with each step. At the top he prayed his preparations were enough. He knocked.

•

Asa heard footsteps on the stairs and inhaled deeply. He fully expected Kedare to walk through that door, and he wasn't sure how he would respond.

Don't do anything to jeopardize finding the journal.

To calm his anticipation, he flexed his hands and massaged his fingers. He drew his focus to his breath, keeping it slow and even.

Phoenix opened the door and said, "Hello."

Asa exhaled and relaxed his hands.

A man's figure stood in shadowed relief beyond the screen door, features unrecognizable.

Asa tugged gently on his head, bringing a satisfying pop and release in his neck. He stood.

The man entered. Phoenix said, "Max, this is Mr. Ducaine, our employer for this expedition. Asa, this is Max, my assistant."

Asa took in Max's appearance, head to toe.

"What a pleasure and a great opportunity, Mr. Ducaine. I can't thank you enough for selecting us for your expedition," he said.

The man extended his hand. Asa went still with uncertainty, not perceiving what he expected. This man looked similar to Kedare, but something wasn't right.

He didn't act like Kedare would act.

If he knew.

The possibility that he, Asa, might be the only one present who was cognizant of the past was stunning. He held his hand out in greeting. Max, the assistant, pumped his arm like they were long-lost cousins.

"A pleasure, Mr. Ducaine. I can't wait to see this site. What can you tell us about the discovery?"

A smile was born on Asa's face. When Max said Asa's name, he smoothed the first syllable into Doo-caine, making Asa think of New Orleans and mint juleps on the veranda. And Max said cain't. When had Asa last heard someone say that? His smile froze with speculation too sweet to imagine.

This man knows nothing.

"Hello, Max," Asa said. Max's grip was solid and his shake gregarious, causing Asa's smile to deepen. Everything, he thought, was going even better than he planned. Having what could be an unenlightened Kedare added to the mix was too perfect.

What I earned long ago will finally be mine.

He opened his briefcase and spread out a map. A quick sideways glance at Max showed the man's attention was only for the map. Asa's pleasure increased. He could just feel the journal in his hands.

"Here," he pointed. "Recent earthquake activity has revealed an opening into a mountainside a short distance from the Gebel Oweinat location."

Phoenix joined them. Eagerness spread around the table, taking Asa's expectations for fulfillment even higher. He smiled expansively. His companions were nothing more than lambs dancing to their slaughter.

"This is a satellite photo." He pointed to the right side of a sheer triangle-shaped cliff face. "An opening is here. I've been inside. The interior is like this."

He pulled out a piece of paper and sketched. "There is a main hallway beyond the opening. Two chambers branch off like this, one on each side. From what I saw of the artifacts filling the hallway, this is definitely pre-dynastic." He looked up and saw excitement fill their faces.

Excitement for an archaeological find, nothing more.

"I believe we are going to uncover a pre-dynastic queen existing long before the time of the Pharaohs." He sat back and let them foster the thrill. Such a find was the Holy Grail of Egyptian historians. "They would have existed on the plains west of Egypt during the last glacial melt."

Phoenix picked up the thread. "The plains were lush with life until the last northern glacier died. That caused the Nile to dry up from a vast swampland to what it is today, leaving the plains a desert. The people who lived on the plains are believed to have relocated to the Nile and became Egyptians. Mitochondria studies suggest—"

Max interrupted. "But no evidence supports this theory, for we have yet to find any whole human remains. All we have of these people are the rock carvings at Oweinat. If you are right, Mr. Ducaine, this will be a truly momentous find."

There it was again, that Doo-caine that so reminded Asa of slow paced southerners. He was starting to feel silly for thinking this man was Kedare. "Yes," he said, rubbing his hands together. "I feel this find will serve to be very momentous—for all of us."

"When were you there?" Phoenix asked.

"Last year. I salvaged an artifact remnant that was within reach from the cave opening—a carved wooden ornament showing traces of blue dye and markings in a Proto-Berber script similar to Tamazight. The piece was confirmed at ten thousand years old."

"Are there any human remains?" she asked.

Asa coughed, enjoying the irony. "There is a trove of artifacts visible, and something large at the end of the hall that I am assuming is a sarcophagus. I was unable to get close enough to verify my suspicions. Apparently the opening was blocked many millennia ago and that, combined with eons of dry air, has preserved the find remarkably. These wonders would still be lost to us were it not for an earthquake in just the right spot."

"What are your arrangements with the locals?" Max inquired.

"There is a Berber tribe. I have employed them as our guides, labor and security while we are in Libya."

"What are you after, Asa?" Phoenix asked.

"We'll do a preliminary examination with the usual—"

"No. I mean, what are your goals with this expedition? Fame, riches, artifacts? What drives you to this lonely mountain top in the Libyan desert?" Phoenix asked.

Asa's first thought was to challenge her for asking him such questions, but he tamped his anger. She had to smell this operation moving under the radar. He should expect her, as a professional, to ask these questions.

He gazed at the map and the place where their journey began. Where he intended to end their ties and begin a new journey of his own. "There is much to be learned from the past," he said. "Perhaps knowledge can free us from mistakes once made ... as a species, of course, to create a better life in the future. Isn't that what archaeology is all about?"

"But you are not an archaeologist," she replied.

Asa gazed from her to Max and back. "No, but I am a lover of life. I'll leave the archaeology to you two." He offered her a smart salute.

Phoenix laughed. "Very well, then, Asa. You leave the archaeology to us, and we will leave the loving of life to you."

"I have taken care of everything," Asa responded smoothly.

Phoenix picked up the map. "The terrain is pretty rough. Where do you plan to make base camp?"

He pointed to an outcrop of rock about four hundred, fifty feet down the mountain from the opening. "Here. This is the closest flat area large enough for camp and a heliport."

"When do we go, Mr. Ducaine?" Max asked.

That Doo-caine made Asa smile. "Where are you from, Max?"

"I spent many years in the south," he answered.

"Well, Max, I have business that brings me to Cairo on Tuesday of next week." Asa reached into his briefcase and laid a tightly bundled stack of hundreds on the table. "Here's twenty thousand dollars to cover your expenses from here to Cairo. You only need to bring your clothes and personal items. The base camp is fully stocked with food, water, medicine and equipment. And you needn't bother with receipts for your expenses."

He drew a card from his pocket. The Fairmont Nile City, Cairo, Egypt. "Two rooms in your name Tuesday night, and I will see you at breakfast on Wednesday morning."

He watched them absorb the appearance of cash, a five-star hotel, and the notice of no receipts required. Money, Asa knew, was the universal bait.

Phoenix picked up the bills and fanned the end. "May I ask where the money to fund this trip comes from?"

"I am an industrialist. I'm into international shipping. I own a few cargo planes. Money comes to me in many ways." He shrugged. "Some rich men buy fancy horses and skinny women. I'm interested in the past."

"And the artifacts we find? What happens to them?"

"Artifacts are of no personal interest to me. You may process them in whatever professional manner you require."

"Then what are you looking for, Mr. Ducaine?" Max asked.

Asa wanted to hear Kedare in Max's question, but a long assessing look convinced Asa the man was genuinely disengaged of the past. "The past is a wealth of knowledge, my friend," Asa replied. "And in knowledge, there is power." He flexed his hands and felt a rush of satisfaction.

Come soon, all will be mine.

"Anything else you'd like to know?" Asa added. He rose, signaling an end to their chat, even though the weight of unasked questions filled the small room. Phoenix looked as if she would speak, but the moment passed.

Asa picked up his briefcase and moved to the door. "Then I'll see you next week."

Phoenix followed him to the door and offered her hand. "To Cairo we go," she said.

Asa fixed his gaze on the fingers of her extended hand.

Exactly like Byrgamon's.

When they touched, the feel of her flesh excited him, for they were the hands of power—a great power that would soon be his. He let his excitement show and said, "I can't wait to get you there."

•

After Asa left, Max released a long-needed exhalation of relief.

That went better than I expected.

There were too many unknowns to say if his spell worked. He liked to think of Gamon protecting him from the grave. However, this success with Asa meant they would proceed to the Temple—the most dangerous place in the world for Phoenix. As Gamon's magic reached from the grave to protect him, so he would protect Phoenix. She stared remotely at the bundle of money, prompting Max to speak. "Why didn't you ask?"

Distracted from her deep introspection, she looked up and frowned in puzzlement. "Ask who what?"

"Ask Asa. You know, something like 'how are you able to do this in Libya?' Or 'what is your relationship with Gadhafi?' Aren't you the least bit curious how all this is arranged in Libya?"

She went back to her deep thoughts, long enough to make him suspect he had lost her. Finally she answered him.

"Many strange relationships occur in this world." She stared at her hand, the one Asa had just released. Her face bore an expression Max couldn't decipher.

"I am not qualified to pass judgment on him," she said.

Her words, like a key, opened another door to the past.

Bahk-ir argued to send a message to one of their conquests using the Magic of War. Byrgamon disagreed. Kedare heard the plan as Byrgamon told it to him, and like her, thought Bahk-ir's action unnecessarily cruel. In the end she refused Bahk-ir's request, telling him, "I am not qualified to pass judgment upon these people."

"You are the Queen and you have the power," Bahk-ir argued.

"My magic does not entitle me to make decisions better left to the gods. I cannot condemn these people in peace. The magic of War is for war ... only."

Upon hearing the story, Kedare immediately understood. The

General wanted the power so he could make decisions better left to the gods.

Max shook his shoulders, throwing off the past. A new danger, one he dreaded, was developing right before his eyes. As he watched, a change came over Phoenix.

The light in her eyes hardened, going sharp and feral with desire. Hunger pulled at her mouth, scraping all warmth from her face as she turned to look at him.

"I want to go," she said. "I want to see what's there."

•

After Max left, Phoenix closed the door. "Whew," she whistled. Her mind was in a tumble, but her primary thought was to track down the fortune-teller.

"Two men from my past. Huh," she snorted. "They're both strangers. I've never met them before. How can they be from my past?"

She tried to laugh, to say, "See, Faby, you were wrong—" but she choked, unable to finish her words. To her absolute consternation, all this nonsense from the fortune-teller was turning out to be not so much nonsense after all.

"I think what Faby knows is very important."

When Asa held her hand, adrenaline levels screamed for her to run-or-fight-for-your-life. His words, "I can't wait to get you there" echoed ominously in her head. She tried to chide herself for being petty and argued in his defense. "I'm sure he meant to say, 'I can't wait till you get there.'"

But in her gut, she knew he said exactly what he intended.

What was in Gebel?

She stared at her hand and flexed the fingers. Something about her hands bothered her, but she couldn't exactly say what. Her drifting gaze landed on Asa's contract sitting on the coffee table, unsigned and looking distinctly unimportant.

"I can't wait to get you there," he said.

"That's good, because I really want to go."

She stared at her hands, turning them for her inspection. Not sure why, she said, "I'm coming."

•

In his suite, Asa filled his tumbler, appreciating the extravagant sixteen-thousand-dollar bottle of fifty-year-old scotch. He had always enjoyed cultivating expensive tastes, feeling he was born for wealth and power.

As of today, ultimate wealth and power were one step closer.

Wealth he had attained because he was good at something—selling machines of death. In today's world, there was no shortage of folks looking to kill one another. Asa Ducaine was greatly respected and feared among the mighty of the world. The insane, self-appointed leader, the deranged despot, the raving dictator and the military madman—none messed with Asa Ducaine and lived to tell the story.

"And once I have the journal," Asa projected, "Presidents will bow at my feet." He took a healthy swig, sucking the whiskey through his teeth. His satisfaction over the state of this coming expedition feathered his good will.

"She will be mine, her hands, her journal, her power—all of it. Once I get her there, she will have nowhere to go, no one she can turn to. No longer will time hide her from me."

His phone rang: a client. "Asa."

The caller talked, and Asa drank, silently tallying up his profit on the sale. "Sunday I'll be docking in Eritrea—you know the place. The ship rides low in the water, so tell all your friends. I don't care if they come from Kenya, Ethiopia or whatever they're calling the Sudan these days. Come all ye' merry men and bring your money and a big truck."

"Yes, tell the pirates I have their MP5 stoners." He made a face, hating to deal with the Somalis, for they were nothing more than junkyard dogs. Still, their money spent like anyone else's.

"Sunday at sunrise," he said. His caller droned on and Asa listened, holding his hand out and wiggling his fingers. In his best coaxing tone, he added, "Don't miss out—you never know when I might go out of business."

CHAPTER SIX

The Red Sea, off the coast of Eritrea

Asa Ducaine looked up and down the east African coast through his binoculars. In the vast expanse of nothingness that was northern Eritrea, not a peep of light marred the black of pre-dawn.

"Perfect," he said. "Captain, you know the routine. Beach her right on the sand." He stood in the bow of a fifty-ton LST landing craft, the sort often used for island-to-island ferries. Or for transporting illegal arms to a deserted beach in Africa.

The boat inched toward shore. Water lapped softly at the bow as it eased onto the sand so barely a scrape disturbed the silent morning. By the time the sun appeared over the Red Sea, the cargo bays were emptied and all goods were on shore.

Asa checked his watch and stared at the desolate and unforgiving mountains some thirty-seven miles to the northwest. In the pearly light of pre-dawn, the shadows moved. Asa smiled. Trucks came in from all directions.

"Africa—what a place and time for business," he said. The old black-against-white excuse for war was tired and worn out. New blood for war, the Muslim revolutionary, was filling the frontlines now, ready to kill every infidel on earth—as soon as they wiped out each other. Never was the time better to sell tools of human destruction.

The first truck came to a stop and a lanky black man jumped from the passenger side. He walked with a swagger, carried an MP5 Stoner, and displayed a mouth full of gold teeth.

He walked up to Asa, checking over his shoulder to see if his companions were watching. Assured of an audience, he came to a stop and asked in English thick with a southern Sudan accent. "We are here to buy from you. I am Rabago." He smiled and asked, "Who are you, Mr. Rifleman?"

Asa sucked through his teeth and turned to spit. While soiling his hands with such riffraff was regrettable, as the Lord of War, he had a reputation to maintain and standards to enforce. The first being he was the man with no name.

He brought his right forearm across the man's throat, striking downward to crush his windpipe. The man fell to the dusty ground and spewed blood from his mouth as his shattered cartilage turned into razors.

Those close enough to see froze mid-motion like a cartoon reel stuck on one frame. In that moment of inaction, red laser dots decorated the foreheads of those in the front. Each man turned and saw the red mark of death on his neighbor's forehead.

"No!" was shouted in a variety of dialects by Asa's well-armed group of twenty men.

Asa held up his hand. The final trucks pulled up and he wanted to get on with business. He stepped on top of the dying man, causing blood to gush from his nose and mouth. Ignoring the soon-to-be-dead man's moans, he shouted, "Who wants to buy guns? Who came here to do business?"

He leaped off the body and walked to an open case to pick up a Russian-made AK-47, the darling of assault rifles. "I have rifles and ammunition. I have RPGs, and I have MP5 Stoner mini-handguns." He lifted an RPG into the air with his other arm. "Who wants to buy?"

The murmuring crowd shuffled their feet. After a few taut moments, the dead man's companion suddenly realized his elevated status. "I'll buy," he shouted, coming forward.

From there on, the illegal sale of several tons of arms went smoothly. Prices were set. Haggling was nonexistent. Money changed hands and trucks were loaded. When every RPG, every Stoner, every Kalashnikov, and all their assorted ammunition were paid for, Asa boarded the boat. The Captain gave the order to shove off, and several men shinnied down ropes. The empty boat scraped clear of shore, and the men climbed back aboard.

"Now for the real business," Asa said. Quoting Phoenix Donovan, he instructed the captain. "To Cairo we go."

Asa leaned against the boat railing, eager to see Cairo. Every knot of Red Sea they put behind them brought him closer to his realization of true power. He closed his eyes and saw the Temple where Phoenix would locate the final piece in this ancient chess game.

"Once you find the journal," he whispered to the rising wind, "I'll take it from you as easily as I took that man's life today. Your assistant Max will not stop me."

Cairo, Egypt

Phoenix stood at the Sky Pool on the twenty-fifth floor of their luxury five-star hotel. Far below, the Nile lay at her feet, glittering in all its ancient grandeur. In the vast hazy distance, Gebel was waiting—and an expedition that could make her as famous as Howard Carter. Her shoulders lifted in delight.

No more parking in the last row!

She stared out at the bare landscape until her eyes watered and her focus blurred. While her excitement for this expedition was genuine, something held her back.

Since arriving in Egypt, an odd thought had filled her mind— she dreaded to go out into the desert, sensing somehow her life would never be the same. Just thinking of all the ancient secrets buried in that sea of sand made goose flesh bound across her arms.

The idea was absurd. She shrugged and rubbed her arms.

But the fear was real. Not knowing the origin of this fear bothered her even more. "Stop," she whispered. "Don't fall prey to such silliness."

In spite of this hesitation, something more powerful drew her to Gebel. She had never felt so attracted, so drawn, so compelled—

"Oh, good Lord," she complained. "Ever since I stepped through that fortune-teller's door, nothing's been right in my life."

During the week she and Max prepared for their departure, she'd fret each day over whether or not to go back and see Faby. In the end, Phoenix didn't go because in her heart, she didn't put any stock in such nonsense. This unanswered question in her mind followed her to Egypt as sure as if she'd packed it in her suitcase, leaving her rock solid world wavering.

"That's a pretty serious expression," Max said.

He appeared quietly, pulling her from her thoughts so suddenly, she started. "Oh … Max." She recovered and smiled, asking in jest, "You came out of nowhere. Did you materialize from a spell?"

His face froze as if she said something forbidden. She was prepared to laugh but her smile withered under his serious expression. His knack for wringing the humor out of her jokes was unsettling.

"Magic," she prompted. "You know. We're in Egypt, where you can't walk twenty feet without someone trying to sell you a charm or a spell or some amulet for protection."

He continued to stare at her intently until she cried, "Max, I was just kidding!" At last he snapped out of his reverie. She watched him transition smoothly and pick up the conversation.

"You look lovely tonight." He stepped back and gave her an admiring look. "You travel well."

Phoenix couldn't stop the flush of approval warming her cheeks. Whenever they spent time together, he always made her feel beautiful and special.

Tonight, though she wore a simple blue cotton sundress, his approving eyes were all over her. He took her hand and stroked the silver bracelets stacked on her wrist, spreading them out against the golden brown of her forearm. His touch turned her bones to warm taffy.

Why does everything stand still when he touches me?

She pulled from the spell and asked, "Tell me about Gamon."

"What?" He abruptly let go of her arm and gave her a startled look.

"Tell me about Gamon, the lost lover mentioned in your introductory letter. Tell me about her. Tell me what sort of woman inspires such love."

He turned from her and looked out across the desert, toward Gebel. His words were soft, but his voice cracked.

"She was the queen of my heart, and she was murdered."

"Oh!" Phoenix gasped. When he said murdered the card of death flashed in her mind. She recoiled, backing away. Her hand went numb, dropping the wine glass. It hit the deck and shattered.

Max reached for her but Phoenix backed away. She didn't know why she asked about Gamon, and now she wished she hadn't. If he still loved someone from another life, that was his business. Besides, what kind of man flirted with one woman while looking for a long lost love? She was an archaeologist and he was a client. She needed to remember the rules.

"How ... clumsy," she stammered. She looked at her hand. A houseman came rushing with cleaning equipment. She stepped away, putting more space between her and Max.

His eyes followed her with critical assessment. "Are you all right?" he asked softly.

Phoenix read his lips. His concern was both charming and irritating.

What is the matter with me?

"Ha ... ha." She tried to laugh, but seeing that a failure, she chose to lumber awkwardly through an apology. "I'm ... so ... so sorry. See, you bragged on me too soon."

Great, now I really look stupid.

The houseman left with the shattered wine glass safe in his dustpan. Phoenix felt her face flush with embarrassment. Unable to meet Max's eyes, she looked past him into the desert.

Gebel is waiting.

"I think I'll retreat to my room and eat in," she said. "Obviously, I'm suffering ... some jet lag."

She was suddenly overwhelmed. She wanted to leave, but hated to exit feeling like such a graceless fool. All this sudden confusion over Max and the expedition was affecting her performance. What possible benefit could she be to her clients when she was plagued by her own questions?

This thought reminded her of Asa, her other client. "When we checked in, there was a note from Asa. We are to meet in his room at seven o'clock for breakfast."

"I'll come knock on your door just before seven. If you need anything, I'm right next to you. Get some rest."

"I will," she said, even though knowing he was next door did not give her restive thoughts. She gave him one last glance over her shoulder. He stood with the Egyptian sunset at his back, his face in shadow.

In the safety of her room, Phoenix drew on a light cotton sleep shirt and ordered lobster and a bottle of French wine. "Let Mr. Ducaine enjoy the bill," she muttered.

After her dinner and a goodly portion of the wine, she drew a bath. The extravagant bathroom had a deep tub with a number of jets. She tossed in a healthy dose of Red Sea salts, stripped, and eased into the hot water.

"Oh, yeah," she moaned.

She settled in with her head propped on the special pillow and felt her body respond to the heat. Her pores opened, her muscles relaxed, and her worries released their hold, dissolving away. Thinking of Gebel, she murmured, "What mysteries do you hold?"

In answer, an image sprouted in her mind. She frowned, seeing not Gebel, but Max.

•

When Phoenix walked away, Max had to steel himself against calling out. The pink of sunset turned her blue dress purple, making her all the more regal. He was amazed she had no recognition of this aspect in herself. This lack of awareness, combined with her attitude about the Tarot, led him to believe she was completely blind to magic.

What did Bahk-ir do to you?

The General must have cursed her, for Max could see she had no memories of magic or the love they had. But Gebel was calling her, and Max was willing to bet their love was stronger than anything Bahk-ir could do.

"No matter. The closer we get to Gebel, what was done in the past is unraveling." He headed for the elevators with new determination. "She must regain her memories—of me, of our love and magic."

In his room, he sat on the floor facing her room. After a short time relaxing, he sent his mind to delta, where his actions would manifest at the conscious level of time and space. The techniques he used were ancient, but not forgotten.

His breathing and bodily functions controlled, he sank into a deep state of mind where he could access the special window. He directed his thoughts and emotional energy, moving his fingers as Gamon showed him. The window opened, causing a tiny point of disruption in the time/space continuum, allowing him to see into the next room.

Her blue dress was tossed across a chair. The silver bracelets rested on the vanity. A room service tray that had seen better days sat nearby with an empty bottle of wine. Through the bathroom door he saw the back of her head. She reclined in the tub.

Having seen all he needed, Max called his essence to return. She had a bottle of wine, a hot soak, and was exhausted from travel. This would all work to make her receptive to his suggestion.

Time and her magic were weaving the past and the present closer together. Her earlier remark about him materializing through a spell had instantly transported him.

"Did you arrive on a spell, my love?" Byrgamon purred. *"Shall I teach you another move of magic from the journal—the one to make you appear at my side with a snap of your fingers? Then we can be together whenever we desire."*

She lounged in the steaming hot water of Cyrenaica's royal baths. Around her face, errant curls popped up in the moisture, giving her a childish appearance. But the sultry message in her eyes came from a passionate woman. He watched through the crystal clear water as she brought her hands along her ribcage to cup her breasts in offering.

Enough games, he decided. With a snap of his fingers he released the clasp that held his robe together. The soft woven linen fell without a sound.

"My Lord, is that for me?" She rose in the water, exposing the top half of her breasts to the cool night air and the heat of his gaze. He entered the water, his rigid manhood waving at her. "My Queen, let nothing separate us, not even the snap of a finger."

Max pulled from his reverie with a smile. This was one of the memories he must return to her mind. While he wished he could physically go to her room and join with her as they did that night in Cyrenaica, he knew this was impossible. He felt the corners of his smile twist with irony. "So close, and yet so far."

To initiate physical contact was likely dangerous for her psyche. He must bring her to full awakening slowly, giving her subconscious levels of mind time to process.

"First, she must remember our love."

He climbed out of his sitting position on the floor and walked across the room to check his watch. He would need at least two hours for her to get to deep sleep. There, in the safety of her dreams, he would awaken her heart.

"Sweet dreams, my love. We'll be together soon."

•

Phoenix crawled under the covers, pushing her exhausted and

relaxed body deep into the cool cotton sheets. She sighed and stretched from fingertip to toe. "Don't anyone wake me before tomorrow," she whispered.

In the span of several breaths, she fell deeply asleep.

She entered a rare state of mind, producing that feel-good dream you always search for in sleep. She sighed, content and warm, drifting deeper and deeper.

Exotic scenes swirled through her head. She rode a horse across a green land with blue sky, felt the sun on her face and ... tears.

Why do I cry?

This was not a part of her feel-good dream. She turned to evade the pain, but her agony only increased. She silently cried out, *Why must I turn my back on love? Why must I always sacrifice?*

A breeze, salty and reminiscent of desire and freedom fanned her face, drying the tracks of sadness on her cheeks. A power bright as lightning pierced her emotions, illuminating the sadness. "Kedare ... I can not—will not live without you."

She turned her horse around and gave him her heels. On the wind, they raced back to the palace of Cyrenaica. Entering the gate, she dismounted her horse and fell into his arms, crying, "Kedare!"

Phoenix rolled over in the luxurious hotel bed and pulled the covers over her head. But her subconscious mind burned with a new inquiry—

Who is Kedare?

•

While Phoenix dreamed, Max lay in his bed fully conscious of the past and the present. Even though he worked from delta level to seed the memory into her dreams, the effects of his immersion in that memory left him swamped with the emotions of that day long ago.

He watched her leave the palace and ride away until the vast plain swallowed her tiny form, unaware of the tears on his face. He had never felt so alone, so lost and untethered. She had become the most important aspect of every day, no matter what that day held. With her gone, crushing emptiness blew cold through his chest.

She was long out of sight before he turned, but found himself unable to make a step in any direction. He stood in a stupor, his mind rushing through a wealth of memories of her.

Shouts interrupted his reverie. Daring to hope, he cast an ear.

The pounding hoof beats of a rider sent a bolt of joy blasting the cold from his chest. "Gamon," *he shouted.*

He ran to meet her, catching her as she threw herself from the horse. Their tears of happiness mingled as she kissed and held him tight—as though she would never let him go.

"Kedare!"

"You came back, you came back—," *he whispered, burying his face in her hair.*

"I love you," *she muttered hoarsely into his neck.* "Of course I came back."

Max let the tears run past his temples and into his hair. He had been working on an impossible mission for years, but this explosion of memory opened the gates of his heart, allowing a great catharsis. Gone were the doubts about success.

"She will come back to me again."

•

Asa Ducaine lounged comfortably at the dining table in his suite at the Fairmont. The window provided a panorama view of the desert all the way to the horizon. "Gebel, at last," he hummed. He poured coffee from the silver pot and checked his watch. "Okay, everyone should be here—"

A knock at the door and a voice called out, "Room service."

"About now," Asa finished. He opened the suite door and stepped back as an attendant wheeled in a cart and began setting a service for three at the table. As the attendant exited the door with his cart, Phoenix and Max arrived.

"Good morning," Asa called, motioning them in.

Max entered with a Doo-caine/southern greeting, pumping Asa's arm like it would produce oil. "Mr. Ducaine, good to see you again."

Phoenix followed, looking refreshed. "Morning, Asa."

Asa brought them to the table where a multitude of silver covered platters awaited. Phoenix took her seat and the two men sat after her. Asa asked, "I hope your accommodations were sufficient."

"I slept like a log," Phoenix replied. "Feed me, and I'm ready to go."

"Here are all the usual offerings," Asa said. "Look until you find what you want."

"Just like love, life and archaeology," Max said. He lifted one dish cover and sniffed.

Phoenix laughed and added, "Unless you don't deserve love or life." She speared a pair of pancakes and added them to her plate.

"What did you say?" Asa asked. He stopped to see her answer. She looked up and gave a stunning smile, and for a quick moment, he thought she was Queen Byrgamon again. Her face was so beautiful, so perfect, so desirable—as he remembered.

"Oh, pay me no mind, Asa," she answered. "That's an old saying of mine." She reached for the syrup.

Asa realized he was holding a silver cover in the air like a shield. He set it down, no longer interested in poached eggs. Straining to appear nonchalant, he moved his focus to a bowl of fruit and picked. "The words are unique. Where did you first hear it?"

"I have no idea," she shrugged. "The phrase has been with me forever."

Asa looked down, trembling with sudden fear.

My exact words cursing Byrgamon—

Did she know? Was the queen awakening by being close to Gebel and the Temple? Or was the journal's energy stirring her memories? "The words are quite dismal," he said. "Almost a curse, don't you think?"

She looked up from her plate, unconcerned. "Apropos to the land of curses."

"Exactly," Asa said carefully as a pit of alarm opened in his belly. The queen must not overcome his curse and recover her memories. Were that to happen, she would be extremely formidable. He glanced at Max and saw the assistant with a mouthful, fully dedicated to his plate.

No Kedare there. Asa silently chided himself for any suspicions Max was Kedare. He also made a mental note to watch Phoenix more carefully.

With a nod of appreciation at their healthy appetites he said, "If you two are recovered enough from your flight to proceed, we'll leave right after breakfast. We're going in a helicopter. With fueling stops, I'd say we're about five hours from base camp. We'll have dinner at the site."

"Excellent," Phoenix commented. "A sarcophagus. How exciting to be the first. I really must thank you for selecting me for this expedition."

Asa adeptly speared the last pancake. "You were my only choice. I wouldn't think of anyone else."

After breakfast, they moved to a large table where maps and documents lay scattered. Asa directed their attention. "This is what I have. Here are photographs of the approach to the opening. As you can see it is quite rough." He passed the photos around.

Max peered at the sheer cliff face in one photo. "Are you the first to breach the area?"

"Yes," Asa answered. "I made a preliminary expedition last year after an earthquake exposed the opening." He passed the first interior photo of the Temple corridor to Phoenix. "Here is the interior of the chamber."

Phoenix examined the photo.

Asa handed her a magnifying glass. While she bent over the photo, he fixated on her hands in his excitement. "Do you—" He choked off his sentence, almost asking if she recognized her Temple.

Without taking her attention from the photo, she asked, "Do I what, Asa?"

"Do you see the abundance of artifacts? Even in shadow, you can see the richness of the find."

"How can you be sure the site is secure since you were last there?" Max asked.

"I have exclusive rights from the government for the archaeological examination, and I have hired the local Berber people to guard the area. I feel confident we will be walking into a virgin setting." Asa passed around more photos.

Even in the poor light and shadowy pictures, the abundance of artifacts was apparent. "If only a fraction of this is salvageable," Phoenix mused, "there is still significant potential."

She looked up, the fevered glow of pure excitement in her eyes. "I can't wait to get there," she said. "Let's get going."

CHAPTER SEVEN

Phoenix sat strapped into a bench seat on Asa's helicopter. After three stops for fuel, they were now on the last leg of their flight—the ascent from the desert floor up to the base campsite at four thousand feet.

She looked out the window with a curious mix of excitement and anxiety. The excitement she expected because that's part of a new expedition. The anxiety she gave up to flying into Libya.

Beyond this, greater turmoil churned.

Faby's words continued to spook Phoenix, with the death card blasting into her mind at times without warning. This sense of the mysterious and unknown contributed to her fear of setting foot on the shifting sand.

In defiance of this fear, she couldn't wait to get to the site. The latest information indicated a great discovery awaited their arrival. Since this project held the potential to make her famous, she wished she were a little more clear-headed. Were she not so distracted by the events that lead to this moment—

I should have gone back to the fortune-teller.

"Too late now," she said.

"Too late for what?" Max inquired.

Phoenix thought the wind would cover her words. She felt a slow burn invade her cheeks, and she stammered. "I mean, er, rather ... what I meant to say was—"

Max laughed with teasing eyes, putting her instantly at ease. He glanced forward to where Asa sat next to the pilot before taking her hand. He mouthed, "I understand," and gave her a supportive squeeze.

She sat back, even more puzzled. What exactly does he understand? His actions sometimes were such a mystery to her, she wanted to poke him in the ribs and shout. "Hello' Where are you?"

The helicopter was slowly climbing over the most desolate and bare expanse of rock she had ever seen. From the window, nothing seemed to be alive down below, certainly nothing bigger than a mouse or insect.

What did it look like ten thousand years ago when the Sahara was a lush endless plain? How did a people live here and prosper? At least some of these answers, she knew, would be found inside Asa's discovery. If the artifacts were indeed preserved, they will provide a vision of life in a time pre-historic.

She heard a change in the engine sounds and knew they were ready to land. Twisting in her seat, she saw the tents of their base camp. The helicopter landed, and she and Max unstrapped their seatbelts. Phoenix stood at the door while Asa jumped out and came around to her side. He opened the door and offered her one hand while the other spread expansively toward the camp. "Your kingdom awaits you."

Phoenix couldn't help but smile. Asa looked like a kid on Christmas morning about to open the gift of his dreams.

A gift he was willing to share with her.

She took his hand and jumped down, grateful to put her feet on mountain rock instead of desert sand. "Where?" she asked.

Asa pointed upslope. "See the triangle cliff face?"

She shaded her eyes. Max came to stand behind her.

"Look about fifteen elevation feet down from the top right corner. You'll see the opening—a three-foot crawl hole."

Phoenix saw the opening. She frowned, thinking of the difficulty of getting there and removing artifacts when she realized her heart was pounding and her ears ringing.

She slowed her breath and closed her eyes, alarmed at this reaction. Their altitude was not enough to produce such a physical response. She panted, struggling to breath. She felt like she teetered on a precipice, about to fall because she missed something critically important.

What? What?

She brought her attention to Asa, who peered a little too close. "Are you all right?" he asked. "Is there a problem?"

She laughed, unwilling to share her inner conflicts with a client, and waved off his piercing look. Pointing to the cliff face, she asked, "How the heck do we get up there?"

Asa didn't respond right away. He seemed reluctant to let go of his concern. Finally he shrugged and said, "We take the stream bed about a quarter mile up to the cliff face. There's a small plateau just outside the cave opening. Tomorrow, Amestan's people will erect a large tent for storage and examination of what you retrieve."

Phoenix looked over her shoulder to the setting sun. "It's too late to try an entry today. Show me the camp. I'd like to turn in right after dinner and get an early start tomorrow."

Their accommodations were strictly first class. They took a tour, and Asa showed them the galley and each of their tents.

After Asa left, Phoenix whistled with appreciation for her tent. "Oh, my," she exclaimed. "This is nicer than my apartment." Her tent had three rooms. In the front was a sitting room complete with couch, worktable and stool. Beyond the first zippered opening was a sleeping area with a standing clothes closet and a queen-size air mattress made up with bed linens. The rear compartment was a vanity, private shower and commode.

She gazed in wonder at the luxurious field conditions, thanking her lucky stars for this rich client. She sat on the bed and bounced. "Yes," she squealed.

"Knock, knock," Max called. "I hear you in there."

"Come in," Phoenix answered. Max entered and she rolled across the bed, flinging out her arms. "Oh, I feel like such a princess." She rolled over and looked at him with her head hanging upside down. "Have you ever seen a camp this nice?"

He smiled even though his eyes crinkled with pain, making her wonder what he was thinking. Before she could ask, a sudden thought chased through her mind, too fleeting to catch, distracting her. She felt her smile fade and a frown begin to crease her forehead.

Something there I'm supposed to remember—

"Phoenix?" Max asked.

He stood over her as she lay on her back overhanging the side of the bed. She giggled, suddenly wanting to pull him down on top of her. The images flowing from those thoughts prompted her to cover her mouth and lurch to a sitting position.

As gravity drained the blood from her upright face, she focused on Max, once again seeing his expression serious. "Stop doing that," she said.

"Doing what?"

"You're always serious when I'm kidding, or kidding when I'm serious. You make me not know how to act."

He looked down, she suspected, to hide his smile. When he looked up, he made that transition again, sliding into the conversation as though he just stepped through time from somewhere else. "Are you an extraterrestrial?" she blurted.

He laughed, the sound a static bark of surprised humor. He seemed to think about her question again and threw his head back to laugh more heartily. He kept on, and when the tears rolled from his eyes, she started laughing too.

"No," he replied at last, wiping at his eyes. "I'm not an extraterrestrial."

Phoenix opened her mouth to ask what was so funny about her question, when the dinner bell rang.

He held his hand out. "Come on, let's see what Asa has in the galley."

Dinner was as much a surprise as their tents. A wiry little man claiming the dubious title of Chef Andre humbled Phoenix. While her mind kept thinking "not possible," he surprised her to the end, producing a crème brûlée for desert.

"That was incredible." She wiped her mouth.

Asa was lounged back in his chair like the lord of the land. "I refuse to eat … grub," he commented. "Andre is renting a cow and several chickens from the Berbers, hence the brûlée. The rest is the miracle of a gas-powered generator for refrigeration. I see no reason to suffer just because … we are on the frontier."

He emptied the second bottle of wine into Phoenix's glass. "Please, enjoy while you can. For tomorrow, I expect you to earn your keep."

Phoenix accepted the wine, murmuring, "Thank you." She sipped, enjoying this special rush of excitement that comes the day before a dig begins. She mused aloud. "This is the moment when we don't know what's going to happen. Tomorrow and the following days will show us reality, but for now, we are allowed to exist within the realm of potential—envisioning what we desire to find."

She pointed to Max. "As you said at breakfast, we look until we find what we want. That's possible for us at this moment." She raised her glass for a toast. "To our desires, gentlemen. May we find them tomorrow."

•

Max zipped up the front exterior panel of his tent and pulled down the flaps, knowing the temperature would drop significantly in the night. The curtain panels over the two large windows in his bedroom came down next, providing a place of privacy.

Alone at last, he collapsed onto his bed. "Oh, my God," he moaned into his hands to muffle the words. "What have I done?"

If only he could go back to the insane moment when he thought up this hare-brained plan. "I must have been drunk," he protested. "How in the hell did I think I was going to pull this off?" He rose and went back to the rear sink. Cool water hit his face. When he looked up into the mirror, he saw a ghost.

"I am not Kedare," he whispered. He looked haggard, worn with the strain of pretending he was just Max the assistant, pretending he didn't know Asa was Bahk-ir, that they were on a regular expedition and he didn't know Asa was going to kill him and Phoenix when this was all over—whether she produced the journal for him or not.

He dried his face on a towel and looked in the mirror again. The biggest lie … pretending he didn't love her, was the most difficult to maintain. He pressed the towel into his eyes.

When he felt like it was too much, when he was swamped by these moments of weakness, when he was sure he couldn't take any more, the most criminal lie of all rose to frighten him most—this entire pretense was a gamble with her life.

"I should kidnap her and take her away," he muttered. While brushing his teeth he pondered how that would help, and by the time he spit out the toothpaste, that idea was discarded.

He leaned on the sink counter and spoke to his reflection. "I guess we'll just have to play this one out."

Finally able to relax, he returned to the bed. The closer they were to the journal and the Temple, the stronger the past came to merge with the present. "Whew," he breathed, recalling his reaction earlier when Phoenix was rolling around on the bed in her tent. Her actions and words swept him through another door to the past.

Byrgamon walked into his tent and squealed. "Oh, look what you have done." She jumped onto the bed he had fashioned in the middle of his tent.

Four posts hip high were sunk into the ground with ropes pulled tight to make a sling. On top of that were the finest bedding and silks he could find in the royal stores.

"Oh, I cannot believe this bed. I have never seen such a campsite." She rolled onto her back and threw out her arms like a child. "You make me feel like a princess," she exclaimed.

He came to stand over her. "Gamon—you are a queen."

Her eyes turned sultry and she lifted her arms to reach for him. "No, with you I am a princess, having no duty except to live my life in your arms."

Max accepted the piercing sadness that always accompanied these bittersweet memories. He looked around his tent, not so different from the one they shared on the plain ten thousand years ago, and knew the separation between the past and the present was little more than a slip in space and time.

The light went out in Phoenix's tent. He closed the window flap and returned to the bed, sitting upright with his back to the headboard. He would wait for her to reach sleep.

With his eyes closed, Max saw Byrgamon of the Amenti dressed for royal court. He saw Byrgamon the Queen riding break-neck across the plains on her stallion, her long hair streaming behind her, the thrill of daring death lighting her eyes. Then there was Gamon the woman, waiting for him in the baths of Cyrenaica the night their passion rocked his soul.

And hers, as I recall.

"Let her remember that passion," he said.

After a few breaths, he took a heart filled with love and desire and descended to his delta level. The window in his mind opened and his essence slipped through to rise above the camp. He saw the galley, cold and deserted. Asa's tent had one light on, which expired as Max watched.

Max stayed above camp, seeing out to the desert where the fires of the Berber camp dotted the hillside. With no threat to be discerned, his invisible essence came to hover over Phoenix's tent. He heard her sigh deeply in her sleep. He sank down through the tent to linger over her. She slept like a child, on her back with her arms tossed above her head.

Within her heart lies a woman's passion.

His essence slipped into her dreams.

•

Snuggled down in her bed, Phoenix's excitement and exhaustion from the long day combined with the wine and the meal to take her deep into sleep. Slumbering emotions from her heart, along with images in her mind, roamed free of her constrictive consciousness, seeking a place of expression in her alternate levels of mind.

"Max," she mumbled, as his image materialized in her thoughts.

"Here," he whispered in return.

"Is it really you?" The warmth and comfort of his presence gave her so much joy. "I'm so glad you're here." She reached for him and felt the wonder of his hands on her shoulders. "But how?" she thought.

"Shh," he whispered.

She felt his warm breath on her neck and his lips kissed lightly. Chills flashed down her legs each time his breath fanned the junction of her neck and shoulder. She allowed him to reach more of her sensitive flesh. Her body moved slowly, feeling as though she pushed through some unseen resistance, leaving her limbs feeling heavy, swollen. A sense of need built to an ache in her core.

"Oh," she moaned, wanting to feel him, feel more of him, closer. She couldn't stop this rising need to join with him. His touch was relaxing, yet exciting. He caressed her hips and her thighs, making her legs stretch and then relax, opening naturally for his attention.

Her ribs were stroked, her breasts palmed and the nipples loved lightly with his tongue. The wetness against her flesh sent shivers down her spine. Her toes curled with delight.

She reached for him, wanting to feel the heat of his rigid flesh in her hands, against her thighs, pushing into her. Dampness warmed her woman's core. Her hips rocked with need.

She licked her lips, intending to ask for more, but he was already there.

His mouth, hot and seeking engulfed her breast, sucking and pulling, taking her internal heat higher. Lips and tongue, seeking her heart and soul stole the breath from her lungs. She gasped, but he claimed even more, as she desired. "Take all," she muttered in her fever. "Take me."

He stroked her belly and legs as he kissed her. He teased her breasts and rubbed her inner thighs, coming ever closer to the part of her that wanted him most. She moaned deep in her throat, letting her legs ease open.

His wandering hands roamed closer and closer. She felt her breath stutter in her chest, waiting for the release of anticipation at his first touch. She willed him to reach lower.

Up and down along her thighs, his fingers caressed, fanning the growing heat inside her, reaching between her legs, stroking, coaxing her flesh, coming closer until his fingers probed her moist opening.

"Ah," she cried softly. Tears of joy watered her tightly clenched eyes as his fingers delved deep.

A wet finger slipped out and worked a slow circle around her engorged nub. He circled and rubbed against her, slow and tantalizing. His ministrations captured her breath, her heart and her body as she felt the stirrings of her release. She surged against him to increase the pressure, signaling her need for more.

Breath was forgotten as he took her mouth with his. She wanted to pant, for the fire was starting. She pushed harder, clenching her belly. A flash of heat washed up from her feet, bringing sweat to the backs of her legs.

She mumbled encouragement. Her hips picked up the pace in perfect timing with his fingers. Around and around he stroked, bringing the waves of climax exploding out through her belly. She moaned with ecstasy as her body went slack. Aftershocks of pleasure twitched through her unconscious body.

•

With the completion of Phoenix's orgasm, Max withdrew his essence from her tent and dipped back into his. While his mind joined with hers to create the scenario that gave her pleasure, his body, in concert with his mind, reacted fully.

He eased back into his body just as his own orgasm began. He grabbed his hard-on as the first tremors of release sent exquisite spasms through his body. He grunted into his pillow as he went rigid and collapsed.

•

Phoenix woke before dawn, eager for the day, stretching with an ease that only comes from a good night's rest. She thrust her arms above her head, pulling taut her abdomen and breasts.

Feeling good, she brought her hands to her ribs and lifted her breasts, smiling when her nipples hardened with a flash of goose bumps. A sense of fullness throbbed in her core, as though she had just had an orgasm. She felt swollen, and semi-excited enough to want more.

She slipped a finger into her mouth and reached down to stroke herself. She lay back, suddenly in terrible need, and rocked her hips, rubbing her finger over her already excited sex. She was shocked to feel an approaching orgasm. She threw her head back and clamped her lips tight as a vision of Max splashed through her mind just as the orgasm began. She jerked her hips and felt her belly tighten as she soared with the ecstasy. Waves of hot pleasure poured through her limbs, leaving her inert on her bed, panting and twitching as the last vestiges of her orgasm passed.

She sat up and looked around, feeling slightly disoriented. "Whoa ... What the hell?" she muttered. She looked down and saw her swollen breasts with the nipples still hard. She pressed her breasts with her hands as if to wring this sudden wantonness out of her body. Wondering what made her so—

"Horny. I feel like ... like I'm in heat."

What the hell was in that wine last night?

A need coursed through her body, one that went beyond one orgasm. She felt ready for sex again and froze, panting with desire. She rose up on all fours, and before she could wonder why, heat and desire pulsed through her, eclipsing all logical thought. Even though she just had an orgasm, she wanted another.

"Oh," she moaned and rose up on her knees. Her breasts were throbbing and alive in a way she couldn't explain. She palmed them and felt her knees wobble. The heat expanded and she slowly began rotating her hips. "Yes," she whispered before clamping her hand over her mouth.

The rising desire was overwhelming and she couldn't stop. Never in her life had she felt this ... this unbearable need, as though she had never really tasted true satisfaction.

She closed her eyes and dropped one hand between her legs where she was still wet. Back and forth she rocked her hips against her hand while her other hand squeezed one breast.

The flash of ecstasy was so close to the surface it didn't take long to complete. In a matter of seconds, another orgasm emerged to scream through her body. She jerked and twitched in spasms, using the hand from her breast to muffle her cries, before collapsing to the bed. Her body was swollen and used, but at least her desire was quieted.

"Phoenix Donovan, that is not normal." She recalled last night's dinner. Was there something in the wine or in the food, an aphrodisiac?

She struggled out of bed on rubbery legs. After a brief shower, she dressed in khaki shorts and shirt, ready for a day of archaeology.

Outside, she glanced at Max's tent and saw his light on, as was Asa's. She entered the galley tent, and headed straight for the coffee urn.

Remembering her concerns over being drugged, she bypassed the coffee and opted for tea instead. She selected a cup from the back of the pile and rinsed it well with hot water before proceeding with her drink.

"Good morning."

The voice came while she was intent upon preparing her tea. Startled, she turned and jumped, tossing her carefully prepared cup of tea across the carpet.

Asa stood behind her with a dry smile of amusement. "Should I wear a bell?" he inquired.

"Oh," Phoenix cried. She looked with dismay at the tea stain on the carpet at her feet. "I'm so sorry, you really sneaked up on me," she protested poorly. She reached for a towel and bent to clean her mess.

"Not to worry," Asa said. He took her elbow and lifted her up. "Please, Phoenix, you are not paid for this."

Asa had hold of her arm when Max walked in. Phoenix saw Max tense with alarm, stricken terror filling his face. The reaction passed in an instant before he sauntered over to the coffee urn. "Mornin' ya'll," he called out over his shoulder.

"Max," Asa greeted. He looked at Max, releasing Phoenix's arm.

Phoenix prepared a new cup of tea. While she stirred, she shot a glance at the two men, sensing an undercurrent. Something was wrong here and she couldn't place how or what. She just knew that at the oddest moments, she felt like she was out of step with what was going on around her. She chided softly.

New day, got things to do—keep moving.

One of Chef Andre's assistants began placing food platters on the white cloth-covered table, and Phoenix brought her focus to bear on the feast at hand. She sniffed with appreciation and took a place at the table between Max and Asa.

"Max, good morning," she said, sitting down. "Are you ready to work?"

He gave her a cool glance over his coffee cup. "I am at your command," he said.

"Did you sleep well?" Asa asked.

"Out like a light," Max quipped.

Phoenix wanted to give Max a long look, but with Asa watching, she resisted. She joined in, answering, "Me, too. My bed and tent are superb. Thank you again for the first class appointments." She lifted a cover revealing eggs Benedict. "Oh," she mumbled in approval.

Asa nodded absently, his eyes drifting to stare at Phoenix's hands. "You have delicate hands for archaeology," he commented.

Phoenix had noticed his apparent fixation with her hands. She flexed her fingers. "They may be small, but they're powerful."

On the tail of her words, an unexpected silence bloomed, pressing all the air out of the tent. She frowned, again feeling like she was missing something important.

Their meal passed without any more oddities. Phoenix made a note to keep her eye on Asa, if for no other reason than to understand why he seemed so interested in her hands.

"Getting to the cave is not easy," Asa said. "We'll work until noon, come down for the meal and take a brief siesta before going back to work until dark. If you need anything from your tent or to freshen up, we meet back here in fifteen minutes."

Phoenix returned to her tent to brush her teeth and collect her backpack and hat. She always took a few of her own supplies and water to a remote site, even one within view of camp. Outside, she waited for Max. When he appeared, she chuckled.

"What?" he asked. He turned around in a circle, looking. "Do I have toilet paper stuck to my shoe?"

"No. We look like twins," she said. Because they shopped together, they had matching pants, shirts, boots and backpacks.

"Let's hope he knows which is which," he added drily.

They met Asa at the galley tent. He gave their identical attire a fast glance, but he declined to comment. "Amestan and his people have been running supplies up to the site. They are erecting the examination tent as we speak. Just follow me."

The rock plateau they were camped on sloped away at the edges. Where it dropped off too far to go on foot, a rope ladder was pegged into the rock face.

They crawled down fifteen feet to the next level where another ladder took them about ten feet down to a dry streambed.

Phoenix glanced at the incline. "How long does it take to get up there?"

"It goes quicker than you think," Asa replied. "From camp to site is about thirty minutes."

They climbed and stumbled over the round boulders in the streambed. The sun had already removed the chill from the air and Phoenix swabbed the sweat at her neck with a cloth.

After fifteen minutes, the streambed dead-ended square into the bottom point of the triangle cliff face.

They stopped and collected their breath. Phoenix stepped into the shade and looked up the angle they had to climb to reach the cave.

"Just go slow and take your time," Asa directed. "The terrain is steep."

She saw what he spoke of and winced. This was mountain goat country. She shifted her backpack and started climbing. The sun was low and the hillside opposite the cliff provided shade, but once Phoenix climbed high enough, the sun hit her full in the face. She pulled her hat down and put her eyes on the ground, slogging up the last twenty feet.

The plateau opened up. A massive tent, open on the bottom half like a circus tent, filled the level space. She turned and scanned the cliff face for the cave opening about three feet above their heads.

Max crested the plateau and came to stand beside her. "That was fun," he volunteered, breathing heavily. He saw the tent and followed her gaze to the elevated opening. "Wow," he said. "Good thing I brought frozen Snickers."

"Why are frozen candy bars so important?" she asked.

"So you don't turn into Betty White," he replied.

He answered so smoothly, so deadpan, she burst into laughter. "Betty White?"

"You know, the commercial—" he protested, joining in her laughter.

They squelched their humor as Asa walked up. He nodded to the massive examination tent the Berber's had erected. "You will find all you need there." He pointed to tables lined end-to-end.

With Max and Asa following, Phoenix admired an impressive display of the latest electronic GPS recording and measuring devices, camera, flags, and boxes in the tent.

She turned back to examine the cliff face. Two Berbers were installing a rope ladder from the opening. One man stood on another's shoulders and pounded spikes into the rock face.

"More permanent fixtures will be added," Asa said. "We wanted the cave to be as undisturbed as possible for your first inspection."

The rope ladder was fixed to the metal spikes and the two men stepped away.

"Who wants to go first?" Asa asked. He looked at Phoenix.

Phoenix shrugged off her backpack and walked to the edge of the tent. All she could see of the opening was a black hole in the cliff face.

What mysteries are you holding?

Chill bumps rushed over her arms. This was the thrill of archaeology—this moment when the door to another civilization was breached.

She looked down at her hands. In a few short hours these hands would touch the goods of someone who lived before recorded history in a life Phoenix couldn't even imagine.

Who are you? Who loved you? Who attended your funeral? How did you die?

She took a step, wanting to know these answers. While she would never know the "who" questions, she just might, depending on whether there was a sarcophagus with remains, be able to determine the quality of life and the cause of death.

The card of Death sprang up in Phoenix's mind, but she pushed it away. This was where she excelled. Here, she was the trained expert. Here, she was supreme. Here, she didn't need Faby's answers.

She would find her own.

"Let me take a look."

CHAPTER EIGHT

Phoenix tugged on the rope ladder leading up to the cave opening. Like the other ladders closer to camp, this one was store-bought, made of rope and sturdy wood slats.

She climbed the first two steps and paused to let the ladder take her weight. All was secure. She looked over her shoulder at Max and Asa. Each watched her with a level of concern.

"I'm just going to take a quick look," she said. "Hand me a light."

Max passed her a halogen lamp. She looped the handle over her wrist and climbed farther up the ladder. When her head cleared the top of the ladder, she clutched the rope and shined the light into the chamber. As Asa described, there was a center corridor extending about twenty yards. Panning the flashlight around, she saw the openings to the two side chambers.

She set the light inside the chamber and climbed waist high in the opening. "Oh my," she exclaimed softly. The corridor was at least hip-deep, and in many places the artifacts were even higher, all of which she judged to be excellent quality grave goods. She resisted the urge to whoop with delight.

The light exposed a hauntingly surreal scene of wild animals side-by-side with carved furniture. Here and there an occasional reflection brightened the darkness, indicating the presence of precious metals. As she panned with the lamp, particles of dust drifted through the light, giving the illusion of movement.

Once inside the chamber, she stood in the semi-darkness, feeling the cool, dry air perfect for preserving artifacts. Sniffing lightly, she detected none of the musty reek from insect or rodent infestation. More odors were roused from deep in the chamber and they brought a familiar note that teased her memory.

What is that smell? Something so familiar—

At the end of the corridor the supposed sarcophagus was barely visible in her light. Between her and that object, the corridor was packed from wall to wall. From what she could see, the volume was immense, and that wasn't counting the side chambers.

"This," she said, casting the light around, "will at the very least equal Tut's tomb."

Suddenly her heart was pounding and her ears ringing, as when she first looked up here yesterday. A sense of spatial disorientation swept over her, like waking up in a strange bed and not knowing where you were. She closed her eyes to control her breathing, but that served to aggravate a fast-rising sense of vertigo. She reached out for the rock wall as a change in pressure squeezed her eardrums.

Utterly perplexed to know why, she felt different somehow, not at all like herself. Yet she had no sense of fear. She pressed her ears with both hands and the ringing faded. New sounds reached her— a feminine voice, too faint for Phoenix to make out the words. A masculine voice joined in, drawing feminine laughter.

They sound happy.

She cocked her head to hear more. The joy she detected from their voices was alluring, like a glimpse of something ethereal that leaves you begging for more. She strained, wanting a clearer picture of—

A sudden shiver cut Phoenix to the bone. She blinked. The voices and the laughter, the sensation of feeling she was not in her own skin, all evaporated.

"Are you all right?" Max asked softly.

"Oh!" She jumped and pressed back against the rock wall, clutching her throat. Max looked up at her from the rope ladder, his head just above the opening at her feet.

"For heaven's sake," she hissed. "You scared the ever-living crap out of me!" Feeling like her heart was trapped in the wrong place, she glared at him. "I swear if you ever do that again—"

He gave her a thin smile. "I was worried. We hadn't heard from you in so long—"

She waved her hand at him in dismissal. "What's the hurry? I've been here all of five minutes," she protested.

"No," he said slowly. "You haven't."

That serious look she had come to dislike filled his face. She sighed with frustration. "Okay, then I've been here ... ten minutes. Whatever. I just crawled in here."

His expression deepened with nuances she liked even less. She shook her head in denial as he spoke.

"No," he said. "You crawled in here over an hour ago."

"That's not—" With her lips pursed to say "possible" she stopped and looked at her watch.

He was right.

The end of her sentence faded, leaving Phoenix to come up with an explanation he would accept, and one she could understand. Recalling her recent claim to discover her own answers, she looked over her shoulder at the ancient chamber.

Obviously something beyond her training as an archaeologist had just occurred. The conditions creating the anomaly, she reasoned, resided in this chamber, hence the answers to the mystery were here.

As for her anomalous perception of time, she could only say, "Something strange—" and roll her eyes to the heavens. Her more pressing interest was the job she came here to do. She pointed to the chamber. "We have a lot of work ahead of us." She gave him a wink. "And I think I'm ready for one of those Snickers."

•

Asa kept his eye on Phoenix as she sat under the examination tent. She watched the workers as they came forward with a wooden stairway to the cave opening. The rig was freshly made out of cut timber, and the Berbers attached it to the rock wall using more of the steel pegs that anchored the other rope ladders. Now they could walk up stairs to a landing and step through the opening.

He continued to watch her closely for signs the queen was stirring. When he asked what happened to her in the chamber, her response, that she simply lost track of time, told him nothing.

What happened to you in there?

Asa wanted to know if her experience duplicated his. When he entered the chamber last year he never reached his goal, the sarcophagus, for the passage was clogged with Byrgamon's grave goods.

When he stood in the opening, exactly where she stood today with the ancient still air surrounding him, he recalled feeling as though no time had passed since that ancient lifetime. There were no past lives of accumulating anger. He was simply Bahk-ir, filled with fresh hatred for her and all the dreams she had ruined for him.

Is that what happened to her this morning? Did the past envelope her?

Did she find the journal and hide it again?

"No." He shook his head. She could not have managed this, for the entire passage was impassable. There was nowhere to go in the chamber—except back in time.

If she went back in time, did the queen return?

He walked across the tent and sat next to her, peering at her. She had a crumpled Snickers wrapper in one hand and a steel water bottle in the other. He searched for any appearance of Byrgamon and saw none. Testing her, he asked, "Do you want to take lunch early. We can get a fresh start this afternoon—"

"Why would we do that?" she asked. She pointed to the Berbers who were disappearing now that their work was complete. "The staircase greatly facilitates our access. After we take some measurements and get a better look at the structure on the inside, we'll see about enlarging the opening. When we have a workable entrance, we must put up plastic containment strips."

Assured Phoenix harbored none of Byrgamon, Asa was collectively relieved and annoyed. He nodded as she gave instructions and made a mental note to pass her orders on to Amestan.

At the equipment table she picked up a laser gun used for measuring. Asa noted how deftly she handled it, her movements conveying assurance and strength.

There is more than a touch of the queen in this one.

She collected her equipment and approached him with steely determination in every nuance—her stride, her posture, even the glint in her eye. Just to think of her awakening as the queen sent a flash of fear through him.

She handed him a pair of high output lanterns and said, "Let's go."

•

Max sat at one of the other tables, keeping Phoenix and Asa in his peripheral sight. He was torn between needing to keep an eye on both of them while desperately wanting to keep them separated. He sipped his water and munched on his Snickers, wondering how to get rid of Asa. When they walked up, he acted surprised.

"Oh, ready to go?" he said. He tossed his candy wrapper in a trash can, put his refilled water bottle in his backpack, and took one of the lanterns from Asa.

They walked to the stairs with Max bringing up the rear. Earlier, when he entered the galley tent and saw Asa's hand on Phoenix, he almost reacted. He silently scolded himself.

Remember the game—keep her alive.

Phoenix bounded up the stairs to the opening. She stomped around on the landing and announced, "Nice. Good and stable. Now we can get some work done."

Max climbed the stairs with Asa and joined her on the landing. They turned the lanterns on and placed them through the opening, one on each side. She passed the camera to Max. "I took a picture of the opening before the stairs were added, so the GPS coordinates are locked in. You're responsible for all the photos."

She turned to Asa. "Until we clear the interior, you and the workmen are not allowed inside this opening."

Asa opened his mouth, eyebrows drawn in combative furrows.

Phoenix cut him off before he could start. "I am in charge because you pay me to do my job. I will follow protocol to preserve the validity and value of what we find. These are my rules. If you don't want to do things like this, we can terminate my contract and call it a day."

Asa shrugged, twisting his lips in a silent "no problem."

"You and any qualified workmen," Phoenix continued, "will assist in transporting items from the chamber to the examination tent. This gives you hands-on access. Does this satisfy you?"

"You're the expert," Asa said, stepping aside to give her the lead.

Max gave a mental grunt.

Oh, he's smooth all right, just like the old days.

Max joined Phoenix as she continued.

"Max and I will take measurements and photos and set up the grid. After we return this afternoon, we'll see about enlarging the opening."

Asa's eyes bulged when he realized he was dismissed. But he recovered and gave Phoenix a salute like he did that day in her apartment. He went down the stairs and called out over his shoulder. "I'm satisfied to watch from the tent until I am needed." He walked into the artifact tent without a backward glance.

Alone with her on the landing, Max's heartbeat rose in anticipation. At last, the queen was returning to the seat of her power— to right the events that went so horribly awry in the past.

Earlier when he climbed the rope ladder and found her, she was staring into space, as though hypnotized. He had no idea what she experienced. Had she heard the same—

"Max?"

He shook himself. "Sorry, lost in thought," he muttered.

"It's all right," she said in a whisper. She looked around to make sure no one could see or hear, and put her hand on his arm. "You don't have to worry. I think your Gamon is here."

Uncertain what she meant, he went still. He was afraid to ask, but he had to know. "What makes you say that?"

"Just a feeling." She shrugged as if unsure how to speak.

"Go on," he encouraged. "You can tell me."

"I can't explain, but, when I was here earlier, I heard—"

She stopped, looking embarrassed and hopeful at the same time. "I know it sounds ridiculous, but I heard ... I heard your voice—from out of the past." She squeezed his arm for emphasis. "She's here, Max—you found her. I think your Gamon is here." She turned and stepped through the opening. "Come on," she called out.

When she turned and entered the chamber, Max deflated with a silent whistle. Having no time to consider the impact or meaning of her revelation, he stepped through behind her. Their lanterns cast spotlights on a wealth of material, amazing to him, again, by the sheer volume.

They gave from their hearts, so she would remember them on this day.

He took photos of every vertical inch in front of them. Grave goods filled the corridor to a depth of three to five feet.

Phoenix took measurements with ease using the electronic laser gun. "Twenty yards exactly to the back wall," she said. "And five yards across the corridor at this point." She followed the beam of light and admired all the wonders barely revealed. "Wow, if this is your Gamon, she was apparently well thought of by her people."

She gave him a teasing look, eyes sparkling with mischief. "That must make you important as well. Who were you?"

Within her words he heard her begging him to elaborate. But he knew she was not ready for the truth. "It doesn't matter who I was," he said, hearing the sadness in his voice. "I was unable to save her."

I will not fail you this time.

He returned to taking photos.

She took one light and examined the rock surrounding the opening. "This all looks like debris separate from the bedrock of the chamber. Possibly it was deposited here in an effort to hide access to the site. I think much of this can be removed to give us a bigger opening."

They went out onto the landing. The cool dark of the chamber was instantly replaced with heat and bright sunlight. Phoenix shaded her eyes and put two fingers in her mouth for a piercing whistle.

Asa stepped into view from the artifact tent.

She gestured a triumphant two thumbs-up.

•

Back at camp, lunch consisted of cold sandwiches, chips and iced tea before everyone retreated to their respective tents.

Phoenix pressed her tea glass to her forehead, appreciating the chill lingering from the melted ice cubes. Her mind was filled with images of the vast find in the chamber. She gave a short whistle of appreciation and drew her shoulders to her ears pure delight. "I'm going to be famous," she whispered.

There was no doubt the find was spectacular. She felt her smile broaden and thought about jumping up to do the happy dance across the carpet of her tent.

On the sober side of reality, she expected the Libyan government would confiscate everything, in spite of Asa's claims she would be allowed to choose the artifact dispersal. Still, she would oversee the excavation, retrieval, and cataloging of the entire work, cementing her name to the find.

She put the tea glass on the bedside table and stretched between the cool sheets. Even though she was full of nervous energy and doubted she would fall asleep, it felt good to shower off and take a few minutes to cool down with a short nap. She rolled over and tucked her hands beneath her pillow and closed her eyes. While her mind ran in busy circles, her body slipped away, eager for oblivion and the sights and sounds of another life.

The palace halls rang with excitement. Everyone was so elated and filled with triumph—yet she could not join in the celebration.

How I wish to escape, to be free, she thought, knowing her voice could never utter the words. Her impossible yearnings opened the gates to loneliness and despair. She was always going to war, could not remember when she was not on campaign or preparing for a new one. Images of death and destruction joined her loneliness and despair. Tremors of sadness rocked her body.

I do not remember any of the sweetness of life. I am so tired. I want love, she cried silently. I want love—

"Wake up," he said.

Phoenix felt a hand shaking her shoulder but she resisted. There was something in her dreams she needed to see. She rolled away from him.

"Come on, wake up," he coaxed.

"No" was on the tip of her tongue as she drew her lips into a teasing pout. But she could never deny his requests for she loved the sound of his voice. Her pout slipped away as she thought, why will he not lie next to me and we will make love again?

Phoenix's eyes bolted open as she shot out of her drifting slumber. "Max," she said through dry lips.

He was sitting on her bed, but when she spoke his name, he stood and backed away. "We're getting ready to go back. When you didn't answer, I came in and—"

Phoenix couldn't think. She felt like she was part here and part in her dream world. Her brain was sluggish, but her body was quickly warming with desire. She felt her nipples harden and dampness invaded her core.

I am so ready. We could do this in about thirty seconds.

Startled at her thoughts, she felt her face turn red. She reached for the tea glass and gulped what remained. Waving him out the door, she mumbled, "I'll be right out."

He gave her a curious look before he ducked out the front of her tent. When he was gone, she sat up and shook her head.

She dressed and checked her watch. "Impossible," she muttered, seeing two hours had passed. She tossed a little water on her face and quickly dried off with a towel. A quick glance in the mirror proved she was Phoenix, but she paused to wonder aloud. "Where did that little explosion of passion come from?"

Max and Asa waited for her in the galley tent, Max more patiently than Asa. Even though she felt Asa's eyes crawling all over her, she didn't bother to speak up in her defense. She filled her water bottle and stuffed it in her backpack. "I'm ready."

The second trip up the hill was slightly easier than the first. Phoenix felt her leg muscles pumping up as they climbed the streambed, and knew she would be sore tomorrow. The sun was on the other side now, casting shade over the artifact tent and the opening to the chamber. While she slept, the Berbers had been busy. The opening was enlarged and covered with a row of vertical plastic strips.

"Excellent," she commented to Asa, nodding to the expanded opening. "Max, we can start bringing out the forward most layer of material. Let's get boxes and tags up to the landing," she directed.

"Asa, I'll place artifacts in the boxes up there and Max will photograph and catalogue everything here in the tent. You and the workmen will transport the boxes from here to Max in the big tent."

While they brought containers in an assortment of sizes to the landing, Phoenix walked through the opening, dodging the vertical strips. Once inside, she paused, letting her eyes adjust as she pulled on latex gloves.

The first materials she faced were the last items placed in the chamber. She guessed this layer to be mostly organic items such as animal skins and fabrics, for it was all badly deteriorated.

She was ready to begin against the right wall when she noticed a disturbance in the material. She scanned the area with her light. "If I didn't know better, I'd say someone isn't telling the truth." Her sharp eye spotted where a path was recently cleared and then filled back in.

"Asa," she said.

She carefully scooped up the organic material and placed it in boxes she had already marked. Over fifty boxes were carried to the tent before she came to the next layer. Here she faced items made of sturdier materials like hardwoods, metal, plaster and pottery. As she cleared away more debris, a fantastic zoo slowly emerged. The animals were exquisite. Phoenix wanted to clap her hands.

The first piece to come out was a plaster giraffe over three feet tall. Most of the color had faded and two of the hoofs were crumbled, but the eyes were smoky topazes the size of small plums. Next, a troupe of monkeys had lost their hair, but still held their stuffing. Their eyes were made of rubies. Phoenix placed the animals carefully in boxes marked *precious* for the stones.

A carved pair of wooden cheetahs was adorned with gold collars embedded with emeralds. The cheetahs carried in their mouths the remnants of what appeared to be a stuffed hare, representing the cheetahs' captured prey. In total, an interesting array of animals was set to accompany the deceased in the sarcophagus.

Three times she ran out of boxes, and when the next round didn't appear in time, she burst through the vertical strips, ready to holler at someone. She was stunned to see the sun almost set.

"But we just started," she complained.

Asa came up the stairs. While he seemed pleased, she could tell he held no special thrill for anything found so far. She remembered him saying he looked for knowledge, but even with such lofty claims she expected a little more excitement over rubies the size of almonds and a pair of pure gold and emerald collars weighing at least eight ounces each.

What, she wondered, would spur his excitement?

"We should let them close up now," he said. "The walk back is difficult enough in daylight. I wouldn't want my high paid archaeologist breaking her leg on the way back to camp."

"The artifacts we removed—" she asked.

"Have been tagged and photographed," Max said. He joined them as he slung his backpack over his shoulders. "I have everything prepared to begin cataloging tomorrow. For now they are all boxed up, resting in transportation containers until we return tomorrow."

Phoenix saw her day's work was done and stepped aside.

Berber workmen brought out a pair of wood panels bearing hinges. Electric drills, fed by extension cords that snaked up from the camp, whined as they drove screws into the rock, anchoring the hinges. The two panels went up to hang across the opening—a heavy clasp and a substantial lock was added. The men came down from the landing, and one offered the pair of new keys to Asa.

He took them and immediately passed them to Phoenix. "I think it's appropriate you keep these."

Phoenix took the ring with both keys and put it in a zippered pocket of her shorts. The Berbers were packed up and ready to descend back to camp, standing with the lights on the path. She fell in behind them, hearing Max and Asa crunching down the rocky path behind her.

She fingered the key ring in her pants pocket, knowing it represented a show of professional courtesy. Asa wasn't worried about someone getting in, for they could see the locked chamber from camp. A shiver rippled across her shoulders, and she resisted the urge to look back at the locked opening.

He's not keeping someone out. He's keeping something in.

•

Asa paced his tent, his anger liberated by alcohol.

"Only my hands can find the journal now, she said. What the hell does that mean?" he hissed with a sneer. He stood and shrugged his shoulders like he didn't care, drawing a long pull on his drink. Squinting through a substantial haze of whiskey, he peered at the shallow remnants in his glass. "Tell me, please," he begged with a slur. "What do you think that means?"

He tipped the glass back and emptied it before placing the empty vessel to his ear. In spite of his deep desire to hear what the glass had to say, not a whisper of solace came forth.

Who the hell knows what she meant?

He threw the glass at the table, aiming for the now empty sixteen-thousand-dollar bottle of whiskey. His shot missed and the glass thudded into the side of his tent before falling to the carpet.

"The journal is there," he whined. "It has to be." In an abrupt move, he slid to the carpet-covered ground, laughing and hiccupping. "She thought she was so—so smart—" He snarled and sobbed until he choked.

She was smart all right, for the journal was never seen again. In the two days between her murder and her state funeral, he spent every minute searching for the journal. He went through her apartments and found nothing. He thoroughly inspected both side chambers in the Temple and found nothing. He crawled every inch of the stone floor of the Temple looking for a hidden chamber, and still nothing. The only place he wasn't able to search was the sarcophagus.

"Sshhh," he sputtered, holding his finger to his pursed lips. He whispered softly, adding a myopic wink. "She hid—hid the journal using magic." He nodded with drunken assurance. "She'll need ma—magic to find it."

That sobering statement made the whiskey in his belly turn sour. "No," he quickly protested, immediately refuting his own logic. He waved his hands in a mad course correction. "She will not—not remember magic because I—" He tapped his chest with attitude. "I took that away—way from her."

He chuckled as he labored to pull his shoes off. Succeeding at last, he kicked the stubborn and offensive objects across the tent. With his shoes out of the way, he stripped and staggered to his shower, whistling a nameless tune in between fits of chuckling and bouts of chest rattling hiccups.

"She's no threat to me," he muttered with a snort. Inside the shower, he let the water run freely over his face. He grabbed the soap and lathered, humming, remembering how easy it was to kill her once before. "After killing you—" He stabbed the water. "At the peak of your power—killing you now will be easy."

He stepped out of the shower and dried off, forcibly pushing away the alcohol's effects. He shaved and combed his hair, feeling refreshed with the beginnings of sobriety. His sojourns into alcohol and the temporary reprieve they brought came periodically, but the internal argument never stopped. He peered into the mirror, squinting to settle the issue once and for all.

"Fool with me—and I'll cut your arms off and find the journal without you."

CHAPTER NINE

That night, dinner was everything Phoenix didn't expect.

First, Asa was absent. Second, Max was so distracted he might as well have been somewhere else. That left Phoenix the only one thrilled about the day's accomplishments.

She tried to capture the proper level of elation, but a damper seemed to have taken over the camp. "Do you notice anything strange?" she asked.

Max stared into his wineglass, lost.

"Well, I guess that in itself is an answer," she muttered.

He looked up, stirred from his reverie. "I'm sorry—what did you say?"

Phoenix abandoned her original inquiry, switching to ask, "How will you know your Gamon? How will you know if you've found her? What is your confirmation?" The look he gave her came from another place and time, and apparently so did his words. She was astonished to see him search for a response, prompting her to wonder what was so difficult about answering that question?

At last he said, "If I can find something with her name, I'll accept that as ... confirmation."

"Provided there is some written record, which is possible, are you able to read it?" she probed.

"I have her name written in the ancient symbols likely used." He looked down and played with his wine glass, giving her nothing more.

She felt cheated by his answer, prodding her to challenge him. "You still love her, don't you?"

He froze so briefly she almost missed it, but he shifted gears and smoothly managed to look surprised. With a snort of denial, he protested. "That would be absurd, don't you think?"

"Really?" she blew back with disbelief. "I would call you absurd to do all this if you didn't still love her." His response mystified her, for she thought he would admit his love freely. Now, she didn't know what to believe. She pushed her chair back. "I think I'll re-tire."

She rose slowly, hoping he would make one of those abrupt changes and ask her to stay. But he looked less chatty than a stone. "I'll see you in the morning, then," she said. She walked out without a glance back, leaving him with his thoughts.

After Phoenix left, Max sat quietly in the semi-dark with one lone candle flickering on the table. Her questions were too close to the heart of the matter, creating the necessity for him to lie—when all he wanted was to tell her the truth. A truth she desperately needed to save her life.

"But until she's ready, what would the truth do to her?" he asked softly. When she asked if he still loved his Gamon, he nearly laughed out loud. "Of course I still love you," he wanted to shout. "Why else would I be here?"

Instead, he had to deny it and in the process—made himself look like a fool.

He picked up his glass and twirled the remaining drink, staring into the softly moving fluid. When she asked how would he know if his Gamon was in the chamber, again he was forced to lie about the message in his own hand, left for them eons ago. That day was seared into his memories.

"Losing her is unbearable," Kedare said.

The metal smith responded with a simple grunt, managing to offer neither consolation nor argument.

"By all the gods," Kedare swore. "We will return to this place and the scene will play out again, and differently next time. On that day, my friend, let this be a declaration of the truth."

The smith poured gold into a flat mold, making a sheet as thin as animal skin. When the gold was at the right temperature, he nodded. Kedare pressed his clay tablet into the gold sheet. As the gold set, the writing on the clay tablet was passed into the precious metal, telling the truth of Byrgamon's demise in Kedare's own hand-writing.

Max sighed deeply and swallowed the bottom of his glass of

wine. He knew Kedare's declaration of the truth was waiting for them in the chamber. Since he was the original author of the ancient message, no language experts would be necessary.

Again, he was forced to tell a lie in the interests of easing her toward the truth.

Max closed his eyes, seeing Phoenix that first time in the chamber, lost in a trance, mesmerized by something. If she heard voices, she was awakening. The chamber, she would learn, was filled not only with the past, but also the emotions of that fateful day. All the grief, lies and anger remained bottled up in the Temple, just as these emotions remained with each of our souls.

Events were moving quickly—proving the power of the words "when the time is right." His intuition told him soon she would face the truth beyond denial. The seeds he planted of Kedare and their love were growing, aided by the Temple, the past, and her magic. Soon, he would complete her awakening by consummating their passion.

Which brought him to his next problem: Asa. What kept him from dinner? "I'd be happy if he never left his tent," Max mumbled.

Even better, what if Asa left camp?

Max had pondered how to make this happen all through dinner. Abruptly he stood and checked his watch. "Only 8:30. Still early." He tapped his finger on his chin. "Hmm ... what to do, what to do."

Peeking out the galley, Max saw Asa's tent filled with light and movement. He went the long way back to his own tent, going around the other side of the galley so as not to cast a shadow across Asa's tent.

Once inside, Max stripped down, crawled into his bed and set his internal alarm for three o'clock AM. He thought of Phoenix and hoped her dreams were lonely tonight, for he would not be in them.

Other business demanded his attention.

•

Phoenix left Max in the galley, baffled by the lot of them.

One day, I'd like to know what's going on around here.

Asa's lack of appreciation was off-putting to say the least. "Knowledge," she spit. "Yeah, that and my hind end."

After a quick shower, she changed into a nightshirt. Later, the night would grow cool, but for now it was still warm. She opened the flap on her small window and saw Max's tent go dark.

"I guess that shuts down a fireside interlude before bed."

She opened the other window and saw lights blazing in Asa's tent. Intuition clearly shouted, "Do not go there."

"Fine with me," she said.

She turned her light off to discourage any visitors and paced across the carpets. The find was priceless, and that made their situation dangerous. Even though they were in the middle of nowhere, she worried how long before reports about the treasure they were finding in Gebel leaked out.

Seeing no answers to lessen her anxiety, she gave up and crawled into bed. "Don't borrow trouble. Camp's weird enough as it is," she muttered. She rolled over and snuggled down, knowing tomorrow would be filled with more hard work and mystery.

What will we find tomorrow?

That query bobbed in her mind as she slipped into a dream state. The need for answers mixed with anxiety to drag her dreams again into unknown territory.

She sensed danger, for the darkness was suffocating. Being constantly on guard against those who wanted what she knew, how she wished for a safe haven, a place where she could be herself. She twisted, kicking the covers from the bed, just as she wished to kick him from her life. There was no escape. He was always watching her. Even now she could feel his eyes—

Phoenix woke with a start and sat up in bed. "Ugh, what a horrible dream." She got up for a drink and to straighten the bedcovers. In the night chill, she noticed one window open and stopped to secure the flap.

Seeing movement outside, she watched as a shadow slipped from Max's tent and disappeared into the darkness. When she could see nothing else, she checked the time. Her next thought was for the keys to the chamber, but they were on the table by her bed.

"I wonder," she said, frowning. "Where does Max go in the middle of the night in the middle of nowhere?"

•

Max traveled like a night shadow, moving silently across the rocky ground. He eased down the rope ladder at the edge of the camp plateau and turned away on the path to the Berber camp, heading for his friend's tent.

"Amestan," Max called softly.

The tent door hanging was pulled aside and Amestan peeked out. "Max, come in. You should not be here," Amestan said softly.

"I need to get him out of camp for a couple days," Max said.

"I am surprised he has not been called away already," Amestan replied.

Max heard the alarm in Amestan's voice. "Why, what's going on?"

"War is brewing on the sand."

This was the last thing Max expected. His eyebrows shot up.

"Religious extremists are making their move, using public unrest as cover," Amestan said. "A wave of social revolution is sweeping Africa, and the Colonel is high on the list for removal. A civil war is sure to come—soon."

A mix of relief and disbelief flooded Max. His relief over having an excuse that would draw Asa away was quickly overshadowed by the ugly prospects of war. "Are we safe?"

"Rebel forces are forming in the East, but they are vastly under-equipped. I don't give them a snowball's chance in the Sahara." He gave a toothy smile of pleasure at his play on words. "But I don't see you under any threat out here. We are too remote, and the expedition is not publicized. I expect Ducaine will get a call from the Colonel soon."

Max paused to consider the duplicate chronological order being rolled out by the Universe. In the past, Bahk-ir had been drawn away to the frontier by a rebellion ... allowing Kedare and Byrgamon the opportunity to consummate—

"Got to go," Max said. "Keep me posted—"

"Your safety is always a priority."

Max gave his friend the shake of comrades and ducked out into the night. He smiled all the way back to camp.

•

Asa woke early and looked out his tent window to see a full moon setting on the cusp of dawn. A new day was born, and he felt lucky. Today, he mused, she will find the journal for me.

He didn't know where the journal was or how she would retrieve the book, but he was certain she would find it. Even more certain, he would be here, watching her and everything that came out of the chamber. Nothing would keep him from the journal and her magic this time.

Anticipation that everything he deserved would be justly delivered to him rendered a heady rush. "Once I have the journal, the world will experience a new weapon of mass destruction—me."

While the rest of camp woke up, he waited patiently, feeling the minutes pass as seconds. When he smelled coffee, he walked out of his tent and saw Phoenix disappear into the galley.

"Just the person I wanted to see," he said. He set off after her, whistling.

•

In the galley tent, Phoenix stepped lightly, filled with fresh excitement for the new day in spite of last night's dismal atmosphere. The smell of breakfast drew a rumbling response from her stomach. "I'm famished," she said.

"Good. My bones proclaim today we will be especially fortunate," Asa said behind her.

Phoenix jumped. The only reason she didn't pitch her tea onto the carpet this time was because he caught her before she prepared it. "Asa," she cried. "I hope to hell I find a bell to put around your neck."

His smile oozed charm. "Cats and cows wear a bell. I assure you, I am neither," he said. He hurried to the table in front of her and pulled out a chair. "What happens next?"

With a slanted look, Phoenix took in Asa's charm and his obvious effort. She decided to avoid his question with a question of her own. "What happened to you last night?"

Caught off guard, he hesitated before responding with an obliging tone. "I had to let an old friend out of a bottle."

His smile made Phoenix wish she hadn't asked. She glanced down and stirred her cup of tea, disturbed by the way he sometimes looked at her.

What the hell—nothing about this expedition is textbook.

He offered her a bowl of fruit, but she declined. After looking at her so strangely, she didn't want to eat anything he touched. She opted instead for an almond pastry the service staff had just placed on the table.

"Oh," she moaned, sniffing the hot breakfast treat. Before she took a bite, she shot him a sideways glance and said, "Domestic goods and furniture. I'll need some muscle for a few of the pieces."

Slowly he realized she had answered his first question. His whole countenance gradually morphed from creepy and disturbing to that of an eager little boy. "May I come up to watch?" he asked politely.

Phoenix nibbled on her pastry. The chameleon-like changes Asa produced made him the last choice for joining her in the chamber. She much preferred having the chamber to herself, but she couldn't think of a valid reason to deny him—creepiness or not. "Sure," she agreed. "As long as you don't get in the way."

Max entered the galley. Phoenix noted he looked a little rough from his night out.

"Mornin' ya'll. Sorry I'm running a little late," Max tossed over his shoulder. He collected a well-filled plate and joined them. Realizing he had no time for chitchat, he dug intently into his breakfast.

"Max, we have some larger pieces to move today," Phoenix announced. "Asa is coming up to the chamber to observe." She shot a look at Asa. He responded with a nod, deferring to her authority. When she looked back at Max, she caught a fleeting look of panic in his face before he went on with the business of his meal.

That man. What makes him tick? For that matter, they are both—

She stood, suddenly sorry she had to put up with either of them. She would go to the chamber where she knew what was going on. "Call me when you're ready," she said.

In her tent, Phoenix washed her face and brushed her teeth. She stopped to look in the mirror over her sink, peering deep into her eyes. She saw the same green eyes she had always known. There were no monsters, no ghosts, no surprises.

"Just as I thought. Everyone here is nuts. I'm the only sane person in camp."

"Ready," Max called from outside.

Phoenix took one last searching look at her face. When she saw nothing unexpected, she nodded. "Good. Now, let's get busy."

The climb up the hill to the chamber was becoming familiar. Phoenix's legs ached, but in a good way. At the top, she went immediately to the tent where yesterday's material was stored. She breathed a sigh of relief when she spotted the two cheetah collars exactly where they should be.

"Is there a problem?" Max stood beside her.

She wanted to ask where he went last night, but there was no time. Asa waited for her at the foot of the stairs. "No, no problem," she said. She walked down the row and scanned the artifacts he had tagged, photographed and stored the day before. The work was clean and orderly. She couldn't ask for better. Still, seeing him slink about in the middle of the night made her wonder what he was doing. She hated to suspect him of anything nefarious.

"I get to spend the day in there with him," Phoenix mentioned. They walked over to the water table where she handed Max her steel water bottle. He filled both their bottles from the same pitcher put out by the kitchen.

"Drink only from your bottle," he said casually as he handed hers back.

Phoenix looked at Asa. He stood with his hands on his hips, one foot tapping. She waved to say she was coming. She took her bottle from Max and wiped it dry. His quiet instructions made the hairs lift on the back on her neck.

Was it the nature of the comment or the tone of his voice?

Without looking at him she replied, keeping her face smiling. "Are you trying to tell me something?" She stuffed the bottle into her pack.

Asa was walking their way, putting an end to their conversation. She met up with Asa and climbed the stairs to the landing. It was becoming increasingly difficult to walk the tightrope between these two men. With Max's words still ringing in her ears and Asa looming over her shoulder, the early morning shadows crowded. Standing at the chamber doors, pressure expanded all around. She felt like she was being pushed into the rock. She stopped, hands trembling.

"Are you all right?" Asa asked.

His voice made her want to scream. Instead, she blew him off with, "Yeah, I'm fine. Just a morning sugar rush." She inserted her key. The lock clicked and popped open. She left the lock hanging on the hasp and swung the doors back. Dry air tainted with the odors of the chamber wafted out through the vertical plastic strips. Phoenix recognized the smell that had plagued her since ... since she opened the Gamon~Search envelope.

"What is that smell?" she said, sniffing.

He sniffed as she did and smiled. "Yes, I know that smell," he replied. "I know exactly what it is. You smell the past." He pulled the vertical strips apart, opening the way.

Phoenix stepped into the chamber and turned on the lanterns. As with any ancient place, there was a preternatural stillness borne of isolation and long-term abandonment. The expectant archaeologist, projecting what he hoped to find, sends his anticipation into this stillness. The result was a feeling the artifacts wanted to be found.

Artifacts do not have desires. And yet, a ... sense of pregnant discovery, of secrets ready for revelation, speaks loudly here.

"Do you feel that?" she asked.

Asa stood next to her, so close his sleeve touched her arm. Their breath mingled in the stillness, stirring particles to rush through the light. He was so long to respond, she looked up at him. His face was relaxed and happy. He seemed to have come home.

"Asa?"

He finally answered, speaking remotely and without looking at her. His tone gave her chills.

"Yes," he said. "I understand what you feel." He looked straight at the end of the hall, to what they hoped was a sarcophagus. His voice dropped to a whisper. "It's waiting—"

Phoenix didn't like the sound of "it's waiting." She recalled her thought last night about his lock on the chamber door keeping something in rather than out. A rash of chill bumps flashed down her arms. "It?" she probed.

Her voice broke the spell and Asa looked at her with a vacant, hollow smile. "You know, all of it." He spread his arm out, indicating the entire mass of artifacts.

Phoenix thought *yeah, right* and stepped away. With a long day ahead, she wanted to get started. She adjusted her lamps on the next layer they would extract. When she told Asa they would need some muscle, she wasn't kidding. Before them, the next layer went from wall to wall and extended over ten feet back. "Since Max is busy in the artifact tent, I'll have to take these photographs. Can you bring me the camera? Max has it in the tent."

He went quickly and returned. For the next hour she intricately photographed the front face of the layer before they could remove anything. Another two hours was spent brushing residual debris from the previous layer into containment boxes to clear the way.

At last, her lights panned back to the starting point. She whistled. "Look."

The chamber looked like an ancient yard sale with enough furniture to fill a queen's apartment. "Much of the furniture survived—looks to be hardwood," she said.

In the center of the corridor was a great banquet table topped with black and white tiles in a checkerboard pattern. A smaller eating table was at the end, with the rest of the items cascading out from the banquet table.

There were numerous long couches and several shorter ones, small end tables, a throne, what appeared to be the headboard of a large bed, and a dressing table covered with personal items like brushes and a hand mirror. More beyond that she couldn't identify.

Phoenix shot a quick glance at Asa. He stared at a cushioned couch with its matching table nearby. His expression was hard like she had never seen before. She reflexively stepped back, not wanting to be within reach of that face. "Asa?"

"She was well loved," he said,

His tone grated with familiarity and ... hatred. Phoenix put more space between them. "I see cosmetics on the table. Perhaps we have found, as you believed, a pre-dynastic queen."

The plastic strips moved, and Phoenix looked up—Max waved for her attention. "Let me see what he wants," she said. She stepped out onto the landing and breathed deeply of the fresh air. Asa's presence made the chamber feel claustrophobic ... and threatening.

Max gave her a sympathetic look and jutted his chin toward the chamber. "How are you doing?"

"I think you should both be pleased," she said. "It's possible this pre-dynastic queen could very well be your—"

Max looked over her shoulder, and she stopped. She turned as the plastic strips moved and Asa stepped though. She said, "It's close to lunch. How about we break here and come back fresh?"

Asa's nostrils flared and his lips tightened. Just as he began to object, her stomach rumbled, cutting him off. With a half-hearted salute he said, "As you wish."

They left their lamps inside the chamber, but locked the great doors. Phoenix secured the keys in her pocket.

Camp was subdued. Over vichyssoise and poached halibut, conversation was sparse. As soon as lunch was over, Max promptly made an excuse and left.

After Max's departure, Phoenix rose. "We did good this morning. I expect this afternoon to be quite exciting. If you'll excuse me, I'd like to lie down."

Asa stood while she exited. She felt his eyes on her back, and forced herself to walk an even pace. Once she zippered her tent secure, she gave in to a shimmy of revulsion. "God, there is something so strange about that man," she mumbled. She rubbed her arms, scraping the feel of his eyes from her flesh.

She brushed her teeth and stepped into the shower, grateful to rinse away the dust and cool off. She dried, remembering Asa's words.

"As you wish," she said. Why was that familiar? Where had she heard that recently?

She climbed into her bed, giving up on mysteries for the moment. "Oh, that feels so good," she said, looking forward to resting before tackling what they would retrieve later today. She closed her eyes and remembered Asa's comment about the smell in the chamber. "He says I smell the past."

As she lost consciousness, her mind asked, *Why does the past make me so sad?*

After a brief nap, she woke feeling cheated of any real rest. She saw her watch and said, "Oops, time to go." She dressed and joined the men in the galley. Max was stuffing two frozen Snickers from the small freezer into his backpack, bringing a smile to her face. She handed him her water bottle to fill.

The climb up the hill was getting easier. At the site, Phoenix opened the chamber doors. Seeing no Berber workers about, she asked, "Where's the muscle?"

"Asa and I thought we were better equipped for moving ancient artifacts," Max offered. He tipped his hat to her and drawled, "Where would ye' like the sofa, Miz' Phoenix?"

"All right then," Phoenix said, laughing. She pulled the vertical strips aside. "This way, gentlemen."

They entered and stood side-by-side, still and silent in the cloying darkness of the chamber.

Phoenix blotted out the two men beside her. Entering another culture always captured her, and opening a door into another person's life was deeply moving. While she had long ago gotten over the feeling of being a voyeur, something about this site felt more personal for her—perhaps because they explored a woman's grave.

Would this prove to be Max's Gamon, fulfilling a search for him that had obviously consumed much of his life? Where does a man go after finding the lost love of a past life?

And Asa. What was he after?

What about her? What did she want?

Memory chose that moment to deliver the answer cloaked in Faby's words, *as you wish*—the same words recently echoed by Asa.

Since I first heard about this place, I wanted to come.

She was drawn here, and not entirely for archaeology reasons. Like the two men beside her, something other than science brought her here. Since she possessed a scientific mind, this small pocket of mystery irritated her greatly. Yet she could not discount her experiences in this chamber. Regardless of how strongly she felt about magic and such, she knew in her bones there were mysteries waiting for her in here.

Mystery, she realized, had dogged her all the way here, beginning with Faby's words.

There's only one way to find out.

She snapped on a pair of gloves and passed the box down the line. "Ready, gentlemen?"

The three of them gently moved piece after piece, sweating, groaning, and cursing. Once they discovered a working rhythm, the furniture flowed quickly out of the chamber.

Phoenix paused on the landing, wiping sweat from her face. She fanned her neck, watching as Max and Asa carried the last piece into the artifact tent. When they started back for another run, she stopped them.

"Break," she called, putting her hands in a T.

In the artifact tent she drank from her water bottle as she strolled down the row of furniture. Most was hardwood, likely from the sub-Sahara jungles she thought, and was surprisingly well preserved. She stopped to survey the lot, seeing Max had everything tagged and was ready to begin photographing each piece. She said, "Something is missing."

Max came to stand beside her. "This is everything. How can something be missing?"

"What I mean is, the mate to this table is missing." She stood by a zebrawood table and pointed down the line. "See, just like Noah's Ark, everything is in pairs—except for this table."

Every couch had a mate. Chairs and tables all came in pairs. Only the bed, throne and dressing table stood alone. She walked to the dressing table with Max. "That would make sense," she said, pointing to the three stand-alone pieces. "One bed, one throne, one dressing table."

She walked to the dressing table and picked up a silver hand mirror. The face was dark grey with tarnish, around the border was a delicate trail of roses. "How beautiful," she said, and held the mirror out to Max. When he didn't respond, she looked up. He stood with his eyes closed.

"Max?"

He opened his eyes, coming from that faraway place he went to periodically. She wanted to ask where were you? She wanted to touch him. She wanted to feel that thread of attraction that existed between them in California.

He watched her now with eyes gone dark and suddenly intent with passion, clearly wanting her. His desire for sex reached out to surround her, bringing her a vision of heat and passion and sweat. With this erotic vision rose a need to feel him within her. Realizing a bit more than the thread of attraction she hoped for, she gasped and stepped back.

At her movement, Max coughed and cleared his throat, but Phoenix refused to look at him. She replaced the mirror and turned as though nothing had occurred. "Keep working. I want this all photographed before we go down the hill."

On shaky legs—proof something had happened—she walked away. She exited the tent and saw Asa standing at the base of the stairs, watching. She hoped what happened between her and Max escaped Asa's notice.

When she reached the stairs, she told Asa, "This find is turning out to be well beyond my greatest expectations." She looked around their isolated and obviously inaccessible location, feeling somehow a sense of vulnerability. Seeing no way for a thief to approach the artifact tent without being noticed, she labeled the thought absurd—and yet she worried.

"Is there a problem?" Asa asked.

He peered too close. She wanted to tell him to back off. Instead, she smiled. "Oh, no problem. Unless finding treasure in the desert is a problem. I'm going to help Max so we can finish procedure at his end before we start on the next layer of material. We're done in here for today."

She closed the chamber door and snapped the lock tight, leaving him no opportunity for rebuttal. Thankfully, he turned away without so much as a shrug.

Phoenix joined Max in the artifact tent and silently began assisting. Still reeling from their wild, erotic moment, she managed to be of help without talking to him—or him talking to her. They closed the last box as the sun touched the rim of the mountain above them.

After an afternoon of Asa watching her every move and Max alternately desiring and ignoring her, Phoenix hoisted her backpack and announced, "I'm done for today." She took the descent to camp alone, got to her tent, and dropped her backpack by the bed. She stripped and went straight into the shower, letting the water wash over her head and shoulders.

"Oh," she moaned. "Thank heaven for the miracle called a shower." She exited and toweled off, feeling fatigued but satisfied with the day's efforts. She reached in her backpack for her list of the day's find and discovered why her pack seemed heavy.

"What are you doing here?" she asked. Tucked into her field notebook was the silver hand mirror.

She put on gloves from her backpack and examined the mirror. To see the rose-and-vine detail along the edge, she held the mirror in a thin beam of sunlight cutting through her tent window. As she turned the mirror in the light, the tarnish slowly disappeared.

"What?" she whispered.

The grey faded away and the silver turned bright. With every exposure to the sunlight, the silver lightened even more. Another turn and the silver turned completely shiny.

"Holy crap!" she exclaimed and dropped the mirror on her bed. A wave of panic and fear of the unknown suddenly washed over her. She jumped off the bed, fully frantic, and stripped the gloves from her hands, throwing them to the floor, staring at the gloves as if they were the problem.

What happened to the mirror?

The artifact was brand-new shiny.

"What—?" she muttered as she leaned closer to peer into the ancient artifact's now highly reflective face. Her eyes reached the mirror's face, seeing—

Instantly she recoiled away from the bed, tripping over her backpack, falling on her rump. "Oh, oh—" she sputtered.

Footsteps sounded outside her tent. Shoes grated loudly on the rock. "Are you all right in there?" Max called.

Phoenix blurted out, "Oh, yeah," managing to sound strangled. She knew he stood just inches away on the other side of the tent wall. His feet shifted on the rock.

"I'll see you at dinner," she said.

"Are you—?"

The concern in his voice made her cringe. "Yeah, I'm fine. A little tired. I'm going to lay down before dinner."

He fell quiet. She held her breath.

"Okay," he said. "I'll see you in the galley."

Phoenix listened to Max's footsteps fade away. When she knew he was gone, she sat on the carpet with her back against the tent. She recalled this morning when she entered the chamber, how strongly she felt this site wanted to be found.

"Inanimate objects do not have desires, they do not have emotion," she argued. She glared at the hand mirror.

Her protest fell of deaf ears, for without any doubt, she felt her assessment this morning was correct—that this site and these artifacts wanted to be found. Again, she was troubled that she knew this with such certainty, when she couldn't explain why or how. Was this connected to Asa's disturbing "it's waiting" remark?

Having so many questions with questionable answers gave her no relief. She rubbed her face and groaned, "Damn. I hate when things don't add up!"

The mirror frightened her so much she was afraid to touch it. How did the artifact come to be in her backpack? Max?

"What are you?" she asked the mirror. "Are you friend or foe?" As soon as she said the words, she frowned.

Now, why would I ask that?

CHAPTER TEN

Phoenix threw a pillow over the mirror. Not only did the artifact provide no answers, it created questions she couldn't even
voice. She backed up, making the sign of crossed fingers until she
bumped into the tent wall. Chagrined, she realized how supersti-
tious she was behaving.

Seeking distance and a distraction, she retreated to the front
room of her tent and sat on the couch with her field book. The
missing zebrawood table bothered her. She scanned her notes to
confirm the inventory. "Yes, everything came out in pairs."

Could there be a hidden chamber?

"Maybe the matching table will turn up in one of the side chambers." She wrote *missing zebrawood table* and circled the notation.
"Something to look for," she mused as she returned the book to her
backpack.

She dressed and walked to the galley tent. Dinner was a quiet
affair in spite of the extent of the day's discoveries. Asa had little to
say, thankfully, for Phoenix had heard enough out of him today. His
phrase "it's waiting" still echoed in her head and generated chills
down her spine.

After dinner, he rose to leave. "I look forward to tomorrow," he
said, and left.

Whatever, Phoenix thought as she made a mental note to keep
him out of the chamber tomorrow. She pushed her plate away and
glanced at Max. He was examining his partially filled wine glass.
After ten minutes of strained silence, he stood. Phoenix raised her
eyes to his face, wanting to see something she could understand,
but his expression was a mix of pain and joy that completely baffled
her.

Did he regret this search for Gamon? Or did he wonder, like she did, where he goes from here? What future exists for him, or for her growing feelings?

"Tomorrow," he said bluntly. He offered to fill her wine glass and she declined, sensing his greater need for it. "No, you take it."

He collected his glass and left with the bottle.

Alone in the galley, Phoenix sighed deeply. Even though the day was long, she wasn't in a hurry to return to her tent, knowing the mirror was still parked on her bed.

"Maybe now that it's dark, the phenomenon witnessed earlier in the sunlight—" she mused. "Yeah. Maybe this is all just a simple … freak case of, ah—photo-chemical reaction."

The statement, while sounding scientific, was ridiculous. "Well, there's only one way to find out," she offered.

Back in her tent, she closed the flap separating the bedroom from the front room. She put a light in the vanity area and closed that flap, leaving the bedroom area lit indirectly.

"Okay," she whispered. "No sunlight and no opportunity for a photosynthesis driven chemical reaction of any kind."

She pulled the pillow across the bed, exposing the mirror. The artifact was shiny, looking more reflective than she expected at this level of light.

The mirror waits to show me the truth.

Phoenix gasped. What an absurd yet titillating thought. She slipped on a fresh pair of gloves, curious now, for if there was ever a time in her life when a dose of the truth was needed—

She picked up the mirror and eased her eyes up the handle. When nothing looked ready to bite, she continued on until her eyes reached the face of the mirror.

A quick glance showed her the same strange anomaly that startled her earlier. She flipped the mirror over and stared at the back before setting it down on the table by her bed.

"Huh," she snorted, feeling silly. "No truth in there."

Needing a decent night's rest, she prepared for bed and settled in. Tomorrow would be another long day. She closed her eyes and felt the swift pull of exhaustion, taking her not to rest, but to a well of memories deep in her subconscious.

A salty breeze from the ocean gently lifted her long hair, making her feel like she was flying on the air currents. "I want never to go home," she cried. "I am free ... so free."

His warm breath blew against her neck, bringing hot, passionate chill bumps across her shoulders.

"Stay, never leave," he whispered.

She knew his words came from his heart and she wanted nothing more than to grant his desire. She let her head fall to the side so he could kiss her neck, praying to feel more of him soon. The gods answered quickly as his warm breath became a kiss, so gentle, so reverent. Tears filled her eyes. "How can you love me?" she asked. She reached for his hand, needing to hear the truth, to feel the truth in his touch.

"Because you are beautiful," he teased.

"No," she protested, even though his words made her feel beautiful. She turned to see his face, to see the truth in his eyes. "Give me the truth," she commanded in her most queenly tone.

He winked and removed an object from his robes.

"Now what do you have?" she cried.

"For you, something special, made by a friend."

He held up a silver hand mirror with roses along the border. The silver face gave an astonishingly clear reflection, like pure water.

"How does this give me the truth?" she asked, taking the mirror.

"By the magic of love," he said. "To protect you with the truth wherever you are."

She had never experienced such a reflection. While her eyes received an image, her heart also felt ... his love for her. "How beautiful." She reached for him, needing to show him the truth residing in her heart.

They kissed, long and slow and sweet, gradually stoking the fires. Only her desire for life was greater than her desire for him. Were he taken from her, that life would be worthless. "I need you," she whispered, wanting to feel them united as one.

He caught her urgency, understanding she wanted to waste no time. With a growl, he lifted her up. She pulled their robes aside, freeing them to come together. She was wet and ready and he entered her with one long stoke.

"Yes," she panted, fanning the flames. He kissed her deeply, plundering her mouth as he filled her below. She wrapped her legs around him and strained for that point of contact that always brought her heaven.

"*There,*" she gasped. *The heat was rising. She felt her inside become slick with anticipation. Her hips moved faster, feeling the tingle flare across her breasts and down through her belly. He abandoned her mouth and descended to her sensitive neck, kissing and sucking lightly.*

The stimulus was all she needed.

Her flame ignited into a blaze. The pulse began deep within as he drove against her, going faster, deeper, consuming her completely. Ribbons of intense pleasure exploded through her body and she stiffened. Her scream of ecstasy was captured by his kiss as he, too, found his release.

She sagged against him. He staggered and they fell together, gasping. His manhood filled her still, his spasms pulsing against her swollen insides, bathing her with his seed. She prayed she was fertile and ready to receive his child.

Slowly their breath returned to normal. When he slipped from her flesh, she pouted and grabbed to hold him tight. "Never leave me," she begged. *"Love me always, do you promise?"*

More than words could say, his eyes were dark and intent with passion—and love. She saw the commitment there she demanded.

"Always," he said, *his voice husky and ragged. "I will love you through all eternity, always and forever, I promise."*

Phoenix woke the next morning, feeling … physical, feeling sore and swollen inside, as though she had sex last night.

She lay back in bed and pulled the covers up. The desire for sex rumbled just below the surface of her mind making her want an orgasm … badly. She licked one finger and her hand slipped beneath the covers. The heat rose. "Oh," she moaned as she circled her fingers.

"Yes," she grunted when the flame quickly caught. Rubbing faster, she pulled the heat to a rapid peak. Her hips thrust and she arched her back as an exquisite sensation washed up though her feet into her clenched center. The orgasm flashed like napalm. She pulled the pillow into her face to smother her cry.

Panting, with orgasmic tremors still twitching down her legs, she pushed the pillow from her face and rolled over on her side. There on her table was the mirror. She frowned, suddenly thinking she knew something important about this artifact.

But the details would not coalesce.

She pushed the covers aside and put her feet on the carpet. Without gloves, she picked up the mirror. The handle fit her hand perfectly, as if it were made for her. The silver felt cool, even after she held it for some time. Too late, she realized her hand was contaminated with her sexual fluids and saliva. She didn't care.

She held the mirror up to look.

Oddly, there was nothing there. While the silver was highly reflective, she was astonished to see nothing of the inside of her tent. Instead, the mirror cast a blank shiny image that reflected nothing.

"Why is there no reflection?" she asked. This was the anomaly that caused her to recoil yesterday. She set the mirror down gently and looked at her bare hand, wondering if she had contaminated the artifact.

Or ... had the artifact contaminated her?

She wrapped a small towel around the mirror and stuffed it beneath the covers and pillows on her bed. She stood back to evaluate her work and cursed. "Dammit," she said, shaking her head. "What is the matter with me?"

Huffing and puffing with righteous indignation, she jumped on the bed and dragged out the mirror. "There," she said. She stuffed the mirror securely inside her backpack. "You're going back where you belong."

After a quick shower, she dressed. A tentative look in her vanity mirror proved she appeared just as sane as she did yesterday at this time. But a fast glance at her backpack proved her sanity might not be so rock-solid as it was yesterday.

Outside her tent, Phoenix breathed in the fresh, cool odors of the early morning. She closed her eyes and drew another deep breath, filling her nostrils with the rich moist scent of the vast fertile plain stretching as far as she could see—

"Whoa," she gasped.

Her eyes flew open and she lurched, as though she stepped off an unexpected drop. She stumbled and went to her knees. A flash of vertigo washed through her ears, tilting her world on its side. She struggled back to her feet and put her hands to her ears, tucking her chin.

The vertigo and the olfactory phenomenon stopped.

What the hell was that—the prelude to a seizure?

The dry scent of desert air once again filled her nose and the world was stable beneath her feet. "What the—" She peered hard at her surroundings to make sure she was where she was supposed to be. But the camp looked perfectly normal. The smell of coffee and the delicious scent of something baked stirred her stomach to growl. Another rumble came and she shrugged, setting off for the galley.

She went straight for the coffee urn, needing to blast away the morning's disorientation. She filled her own steel coffee mug and took a sip of the steaming, black African coffee. Appreciatively, she said, "Oh, yeah, that works." She put together a substantial plateful: pancakes, scrambled eggs, and sweet watermelon.

Max was the first to step into the shade of the galley tent, temporarily blinded. As he stood to let his eyes adjust, Phoenix admired him, noting the strong, tanned legs in his khaki shorts. His goatee had filled out to a small beard, making him look like a pirate.

"Mornin," he called, seeing her at last. He ambled over to the coffee table for a cup before coming to sit with her.

Phoenix couldn't forget his reaction yesterday when she showed him the mirror, remembering acutely how the heat in his eyes sent a wave of passion to wash over her.

I could have used a little of that action this morning—

Feeling her cheeks turn pink, she dared not look at him and busied herself with her pancakes. He sat across from her as though nothing happened between them yesterday.

Asa arrived, smiling with enough excitement for all of them. He whistled a little tune and fixed his coffee with a spring in his step before coming to sit with them.

Irrationally, Phoenix wanted to wipe the joyous look from Asa's face. Ignoring her out-of-control urges, she said, "We have another big day ahead."

"What do you have in mind?" Asa asked. He sat next to her.

Phoenix took a quick look at Max. While he appeared not to notice Asa's move, Phoenix saw Max's fingers tighten on his coffee mug. She announced, "We have a choice coming today," and gained their full attention.

"The next layer is a row of chests from wall to wall. I have looked into the first chest and it appears to be decomposed organic material. I'm thinking food and clothing. Once we clear the row of chests, we'll have access to the first side chamber flanking the main corridor. Do you want to enter the side chamber, or go straight to the end of the corridor?"

Max puttered with his plate, leaving the decision to her and Asa. "Asa? What would you like to do?" she asked. He answered so fast she knew he had already considered this option.

"I say we go straight to the end."

She looked at Max and lifted her brows.

He waved his hand as if he didn't care. "Whatever you two decide."

"Straight to the end it is," she said. Seeing Max was still eating and Asa was just starting, she rose. "Come for me when you're ready."

She returned to her tent and brushed her teeth, unable to keep her eyes off her backpack, knowing the hand mirror was there. "What?" she mumbled with a mouth full of toothpaste foam. "You think it's gonna get up and walk out?"

"Ready," Max called from outside.

Phoenix wiped her mouth and reached for her backpack. She got two steps when she stopped and said, "I'm coming." She pulled the mirror out of her backpack and returned it to the hiding place under her pillows. A quick look to see the mirror wasn't visible and she bounded out the front of her tent.

With a pounding heart and sounding a little breathless, she said, "You were fast. Where's Asa?" She looked past Max and saw Asa entering his tent in a hurry.

Max ignored her question and stared at her. "Have everything?" he asked.

Phoenix felt his question was a little too pointed in tone. She managed to ignore his tone and deeply probing gaze as she zipped her tent closed. The unspoken question laced within his words couldn't be missed. She hoisted her backpack into position and returned smartly, "Yep. All is right where it belongs."

With her backpack in place and her heartbeat under control, she dared to look at him. His dark blue eyes probed longer than was necessary, she thought. But she refused to squirm and stared back like nothing at all was amiss.

His gaze softened and he smiled, surprising her.

"Shall we?" she asked, thinking to end this strange moment.

Now his smile went ear-to-ear, as if she offered something more. His response came in cryptic tones. "Yes ... I think we should."

Phoenix laughed, enjoying the double play. He spoke slowly, his words heavy and pregnant with multiple meaning, turning their simple conversation into an event smacking of secrets and seduction. While she wasn't sure what just occurred under the radar of this conversation, she felt like they made a date for something sensual, something strictly between the two of them.

"Yes," she purred. "I'd like that." She liked having secrets with him, and wanted him to know she was eager for more.

"I will hold you to that commitment," he said.

The words fired shivers of premonition to dance across her shoulders. The dark blue of his eyes was suddenly like yesterday, when she had to step away from the heat. But today she wasn't sure if she would turn away from him. At their next encounter—perhaps today, she might, instead, encourage him to take her in his arms, to open her shirt and bare her breasts to his gaze so he would want to place his wet mouth over her budding nipples—

"Phoenix?"

She lurched back from the carnal world that had been expanding since her arrival in Egypt. Afraid she might have just embarrassed herself, she longed for the solitude of the chamber. His eyes were no longer stormy with passion. Instead, his look was soft, making her feel she could melt into his arms—if only he would make the offer.

What the hell is the matter with me today? I'm acting like a twit—a horny, schoolgirl twit.

"Forget it," she said sharply. "Let's go." She shifted her backpack and started off toward the trail, taking the lead to avoid looking at him. He followed her up the hill, the disturbed rocks from their passage making the only sound.

Her normal procedure was to check first on the previous day's material, but she didn't want to bring any notice to the missing mirror. Instead, she went up the stairs to open the chamber while Max went on to the tent.

She opened the lock. Just before she swung the doors open, she remembered Asa's remark. A chill skittered down the back of her legs. She paused and placed her forehead on the door panel, straining to hear movement on the other side. Asa's remark had tainted her view of the chamber. He brought fear to the chamber. She wished she hadn't let him in yesterday. With a deep breath of resolve, she carefully drew the doors open.

The plastic strips were as they should be. She pulled one aside and peeked into the chamber. Again, all was just as she expected. Silent, dark—

Waiting.

"Stop it," she snarled. She stomped her foot for emphasis. The impact shock ran up her leg and helped disperse the insanity of her thoughts. She would not fall prey to the countless oddities running free in this expedition. She was a scientist who dealt with reality—

In spite of her resolve, a knot of dread seized her lower back, preventing her from stepping over the threshold. Her palms went sweaty and she wiped them on her shorts. She didn't want to face the chamber alone today. She looked over her shoulder for Max and saw the camera flash go off in the artifact tent.

"I am not afraid," she declared. She took a deep inhalation of fresh air and plunged through the plastic strips. To further prove she was fearless, she stood in the dark before turning on a light. At the far end of the corridor, the darkness was absolute. She closed her eyes, saying, "There is nothing to be afraid of—relax."

The now familiar odor invaded her nose and brought that perpetual sadness to tug at her heart. Beyond the sadness, another sensation slowly emerged as she was swept away to another world.

She strode boldly down the center of the Temple, feeling her power expand and envelop her as she walked through the side chambers. Here were the spoils of war, evidence of her proficient use of the invisible forces she called the Magic of War. Here she was invincible, here she was one of the gods. She motioned with her hand and flame jumped forth to ignite a lamp wick.

A shocked gasp tore though Phoenix. She opened her eyes. The dark chamber offered no source for the strange manifestation she had just experienced. Intrigued, she quickly duplicated the hand move, but the vision had been too quick. "Darn," she mumbled. She was oddly disappointed she didn't produce the flame.

"Okay, now you've gone over the edge," she mumbled. "This is how you get light." She turned on the battery-operated lamp.

Instant light flooded the chamber.

With all they had removed, she was able to step past the organic rubble in the main corridor and enter one of the side chambers. She flashed her light in the first chamber: weapons and loot.

"She was a woman of war," Phoenix said.

Behind her, the plastic strips opened, letting in a beam of lamplight. Max came in and stood beside her, so close their clothing brushed. His presence gave her comfort. "Where's Asa?" she asked.

"He is being detained by a series of rather important phone calls. He said he would come up later."

"Hmmm," she mused. "I wonder what a satellite phone costs these days." She glanced up at him with humor. "It must be satisfying to be so important."

"I wouldn't know," he said, rocking back on his heels. He stared at the end of the corridor and what they hoped was the sarcophagus of his Gamon.

She followed his gaze. "You were important to her."

"And why do you say that?" He took his eyes from the darkness of the corridor and gave her a skeptical look.

She lifted one shoulder. "Call it woman's intuition."

He took one of her hands, gently tugging on her fingertips. "I thought you didn't believe in that stuff."

"I didn't ... I mean I don't," she protested. Her unintended words said more than she was willing to admit. She frowned at the disconnect evolving between what she experienced and what she believed. The glaring disparity left her baffled.

"Will you stay with me? I could use a little help in here today." She grabbed his other hand. His fingers were warm, and she fought the urge to hold his hand to her face, wanting to feel his strength supporting her.

"Of course," he answered slowly. "Whatever you need, I am here for you."

His words answered her immediate request—and a great deal more. Again, his tone was serious and she knew he spoke of more than helping her here in the chamber. She shook her head.

Will I ever know what this man is talking about?

She released his hands reluctantly and pulled on a pair of gloves. "Let's get busy. After all, 'it's waiting' you know." She laughed and tossed him the box. Having Max with her took the fright from Asa's words.

"It's waiting? What does that mean?" Max asked. He pulled on a pair of gloves.

"Asa's words yesterday," she said. "You know what? That man is creepy in the dark." She passed Max the camera and pointed to the right side. "Start photographing there. When you're finished, we'll extract all these chests."

Max hadn't moved. "What else did he say?"

"That's just what he said, 'it's waiting' and then he acted like he referred to the entire site. He spooked me, making me feel like the Mummy was in here."

"Did he say anything else ... odd?"

His voice was calm, too calm. Phoenix glanced at his pinched, hawk-like expression and knew he was not as casual as he pretended. She didn't want to think about what drove this man. With all these oddities surrounding her, a shift in awareness was slowly building, trending a certain direction—one that was vastly beyond her understanding. It seemed what was unbelievable today became possible the next.

I don't want to know!

She stood with her hands on her hips. "Stop that," she demanded. "You scare me sometimes. I get enough of that from Asa. I don't need it from you, too." She motioned him to get started, waving both hands and shooing him into action. "Go, take pictures so we can move the chests."

One by one the chests came out of the chamber to a new home under the tent. Some chests were wooden and solid enough to move whole. Others were woven and had deteriorated to the point where they were swept into boxes and removed. In all, fifteen chests of various sizes were taken from the chamber.

When all the chests were removed, Phoenix walked out to the tent for a break. Amazingly, the hardwood chests had survived, with still functional hinges of solid gold. The interior goods, likely fabrics and foods, were unrecognizable. "After we photograph each chest, I'm ready for lunch."

Gazing down the line, she said, "It's Noah's Ark again. Everything is in matching pairs." She strode down the row until she came to a small hardwood box. "Except this one. Is this an oddity, like the table? Where was this box in the photographs?"

Max pulled up his recent photos and handed her the camera.

She took the camera and peered at his face, wondering at his silence this morning after their earlier discussion when they held hands. Without a reasonable explanation for his behavior, she excused his actions as more of the strangeness afflicting camp.

Examining the photos, she said, "Ah, the placement here looks haphazard. Maybe this box is not one of a pair." She nudged it. "Little guy's heavy. Have you opened it?"

After a long moment, he said, "No, I haven't."

Phoenix drew back and looked at him, completely baffled. She expected a quick yes or no.

Why would he take so long to answer? And what's with that sad look on his face ... why does he do that? What am I missing here?

She sighed and shook her head, feeling her world overrun by all these mysteries. With a gloved hand, she lifted the lid from the lone box.

"My guess this is silk," she said, using a probe to gently push the decayed remnants aside. The probe tapped something solid. "Ah, we have a package, I believe." She pushed more of the silk aside and a sheen of gold broke through. Delicately, she lifted the gold free of the box.

A solid gold sheet about nine by five inches was filled with writing. Phoenix bit her lip and gave Max the "oh boy" look, her shoulders lifting with anticipation. "Perhaps this is an identification of who is interred here." She used a fine brush to sweep away the debris, exposing letters in an ancient script pressed into the gold.

"This script looks familiar," she said, frowning. "But something isn't right. You said you have her name as it should be written?" When he didn't answer right away, she looked at him—

He wasn't even looking at her or the gold sheet. His eyes were vacant, gone to that far away place. From the crinkle of grief in his forehead and the grim tightness to his lips, to the watery shine pooling in the corner of his eyes, his expressions were so personal and intimate she had to look away, feeling an intruder. If this was what he looked for, if this was his Gamon, Phoenix was viewing a very private moment.

The gold sheet was obviously made with great care. She looked close and saw the same rose detail as the mirror. She ran her gloved fingers over the writing. "Not written by her," she mused. "Looks more like a man's writing. I would need a computer to search out this writing. It looks like an ancient Libyco-Berber script." She looked at Max, but his eyes were now closed.

"Yes, it is," he said. "My language samples are down the hill. I'd like to take the sheet back with me when we break for lunch, if you don't mind?"

"Of course," she replied. She trusted Max without a doubt and hoped this was his much sought after identification of Gamon. But something bothered her about what he just said. A curious chill shot down her backside, making her want to dash out into the hot sun.

Max wrapped the gold in a sheet of packing paper and gently slipped it into his backpack. "As soon as I can work up a translation, I'll return it. If you're ready for lunch—"

"Sure," she said. "If you'll secure this end, I'll get my backpack from the chamber and lock up."

Phoenix walked up the stairs, allowing her mind to worry over Max's words. She eagerly plunged through the vertical strips and stepped into the cool, dark relief of the chamber. Pausing to catch her breath with eyes closed, she listened to the echoes stirred to life by her sudden appearance ... and was once again in another body, another life, another time.

The Temple was filled with a palpable grief. She was alone and wanted to cry, but there were no tears. Only a deep, penetrating sadness she knew would follow her into the next life.

She knew when he entered. His footsteps echoed the same deep sadness she felt. He carried a box and looked furtively about, searching. She felt his grief, and her heart, like his, was crushed. At last, her tears were falling—like great stones.

He stopped and knelt down, whispering. She could not make out his words, but his pain reached her. She wanted to cry out to him, but she had no voice ... only tears of stone and this great aching sadness.

His whispering stopped and the box was tucked in between two larger chests. A roll of silk came in front of the box, hiding it. For a long time he sat there. Each of his tears striking the cold floor reverberated through her heart. He rose at last, even though his shoulders still rocked with grief. He was leaving, but she knew he would be back.

Always and forever he promised, and she believed him.

Come back, my love, I am here.

Phoenix staggered. "Oh," she sobbed. The vision stopped, but the emotion lingered on. One of her knees buckled. The other sagged, and she dropped to her haunches.

"No," she sobbed, meaning to deny such deep pain, but her heart was crushed with intensity. Sweat sprouted at her hairline. Her stomach, while empty, threatened to hurl, making her tear up with angst. She bent over and dry heaved. More tears came, for she was lost ... so lost without him.

"No!" This time she cried for all they had lost and could never reclaim. Liquid grief poured down her face, dripping to the ground.

On hands and knees, Phoenix stared at the puddle of her tears. A last retch rose from her stomach and she spit. She closed her eyes, gasping.

What just happened to me?

She sat back on the chill floor and pressed her palms to her eyes. She took a slow, deep breath.

The chamber was still and silent again. All was normal, as if the vision ... the burst of emotion ... never happened.

She rose slowly and leaned against the rock wall, one hand pressed to her stomach. Her legs were wobbly, but the event was gone. She spit the sour remnants of her retching and wiped her mouth on her sleeve.

Her backpack was on, and she was ready to flee when she noticed the puddle of her tears. The moisture glistened with silent reproach of her refusal to accept the evidence.

"I said no!" she exclaimed, and ran her boot through the puddle when she went by.

Once outside, she closed the doors and fixed the lock with trembling hands. She exhaled, resting her forehead against the locked portal. Before she could catch her breath, her mind chose that moment to challenge Max's story about the gold sheet.

"He knew the language before he saw it."

CHAPTER ELEVEN

With her forehead resting on the chamber doors, Phoenix waited until her breath calmed. She wanted to tell Max what just happened, but she was afraid—

Am I losing my mind? Or is the woman buried in the chamber possessing me?

Burning tears flooded her eyes at the thought. She scrunched her eyes, shutting off the flow. "Stop crying," she hissed under her breath. She snatched at the tears with her fingertips and flung them aside. A quick swipe with her dirty hand across her face was all the clean up she could manage.

"Everything all right up there?" Max asked. His voice came from the foot of the stairs.

Phoenix sniffed and coughed before turning away from the chamber doors. She crossed the landing and walked down the stairs, refusing to look at him.

"You look like you've been crying," he said.

He blocked her passage at the foot of the stairs. She wanted desperately to fall into his arms sobbing, but for that to happen she would have to admit the impossible. She brought her gaze slowly up to his face, hardening her resolve with each precious second. When her eyes met his, she clamped her lips tight.

"What happened in there?" he asked. "Are you feeling okay?" He reached for her chin.

She jerked her face free from his hand. "Nothing happened. I'm fine." She spoke harshly, daring him to contradict her. Without looking at him, she challenged, "What reason would I have to cry?"

When he didn't answer, she couldn't bear not to look at him. She glanced up, her eyes begging him to speak, to explain what was going on. But he offered no answer. Seeing he chose to be silent, she stomped past him and headed down the hill.

As soon as they reached camp, she said, "I'm going to lie down." She turned and strode off before he could respond.

She reached the sanctuary of her tent and dropped the backpack, an instant relief as it felt like it was loaded with stones. She stripped her soiled clothes off, grateful to be free of the chamber's grit and walked straight into the shower.

Blessed cool water rained down. She tilted her face up and let the water take the residue of her tears. The grief that consumed her in the chamber had marked her heart, for she could never forget such pain.

Whose pain? From when? And how? Dear God, am I being possessed?

"No," she hissed. "Do not think about it." In spite of her commands, a trickle of tears began.

Oh God, I'm afraid, so afraid!

Phoenix hunched her back against the stream of water, feeling her face crumple as she let the tears come.

She held her hands out and whispered, "Why does the mirror feel so right when I hold it? And why is my mind suddenly so filled with erotic images and thoughts?" she begged as she hugged her chest, shielding her breasts.

"Max, why is he so terribly important to me?" Feeling completely lost, she covered her face and sobbed into her hands. Abruptly she thrust her hands out.

"Fire—I can make fire. How in hell is that possible?" she gasped. "Oh God, I am losing it," she groaned. Sobs of disbelief hitched through her chest as her tears continued to pour unabated.

"Stop," she whispered. "Please, stop." She pressed a fist to her forehead, fighting for control. "I must keep my cool," she chanted. "I must keep my cool ... I must keep cool." A forced calm settled in her breath and mind. The tears stopped.

Needing to feel normal, she lathered and rinsed, washing her hair with robotic movements. The tension in her scalp at last gave way under her massaging fingers, spreading down through her body. A sense of relief moved into her tight chest and she blinked, feeling her usual, academic and well-controlled persona returning. A brisk rub down with a thick towel brought a flush of circulation to her skin. She applied lotion, massaging her aching shoulders and legs, her mind tuned only to the simple task at hand.

"There, I am who I am," she announced. She put on a pair of silk lounging shorts and a soft T-shirt and crawled onto her bed. As she slid down into the cool sheets, she stretched long through her aching legs. One hand slid under her pillow—and wrapped around the handle of the mirror.

"Oh no," she whimpered. "Not you."

She sat up and looked at the mirror. The handle fit perfectly, molding to her hand, making her feel as if it were made just for her—

"Please, no more," she said, shaking her head in warning. "No more mysteries, no more paranormal events, no more making me think I'm losing my mind ... or being possessed ... or gaining access to someone else's body."

In spite of her admonitions, when she looked, the mirror face remained unchanged since the last time she saw it—the surface cast no reflection. The anomaly paralyzed her mind because she could see no reason why this should happen.

"Huh," she grunted. "Key word, *reason*." She set the mirror on the bedside table, resisting the urge to wipe her hand free of the mirror's touch. She rolled onto her back and stared at the top of her tent.

She held her hands up and examined them front and back, unable to grasp how so much could be beyond her understanding. The sex, the vision of making fire, the dreams, and the perceptions in the chamber were all creating a dynamic force strong enough to flatten her reality.

"I can't allow that to happen. I have to take control," she stated. "It's that simple. I will accept no more mysteries."

The hand mirror was a perfect example. She spoke to the artifact. "I refuse to be drawn into the mystery of your missing reflection. Obviously, there is a simple scientific explanation."

She rolled over and closed her eyes. Soon her consciousness retreated, leaving her alone with a subconscious filled with memories.

He was tickling her. She squealed and laughed, turning in his arms to evade his onslaught, but he seemed to know every sensitive place on her body. Madly, his fingers danced across her ribs, bring-

ing more gales of laughter.

"Stop!" she commanded, breathless. She had nowhere else to squirm as she lay on her back, half off the bed.

He heeded her order and ceased, hauling her back up to the bed. They lay side by side in the silence, slowing their breath as they listened to the tent move with the constant wind.

Soon, his hands roamed to other sensitive parts of her body. He brushed his palms across her nipples, and they hardened in response. His lips followed, descending to caress each bud. She moaned and arched her back, throwing her arms over her head, giving him her body.

A trail of kisses marched up her neck, bringing shivers along her spine. "Love me," she panted. "Only in your arms am I free from war. Love me, bring me peace."

He massaged her legs and stroked the insides of her thighs. His kisses on her fevered flesh brought the heat to rage all though her body. "Please," she begged.

Her hips, moving slowly at first, gained momentum. The flames were ready and she reached for him to come up and enter her. He rose over her. His hard member slid in easily.

His chest rubbed against her breasts and his kisses left the salty taste of her sex on her lips. As he drove deeply within, the fire of ecstasy caught and exploded, making her gasp. She clenched and squeezed tight, her hips bucking wildly with each sweet, expanding spasm. He answered her demanding hips with his own drive for release. She screamed her climax as he plunged deeply.

Aftershocks of pleasure rumbled down through her limbs, leaving her body thoroughly consumed by their passion. Consciousness wavered and she closed her eyes as the last spasm trickled across her body. Energy flowed out her fingertips, leaving her filled with utter contentment. She sighed and reached for his hand, whispering, "Only with you do I find this absolute peace."

Phoenix tossed and turned in her bed. When she woke after a brief nap, she was instantly aware of her need. She moaned and rolled over. "No, not again," she mumbled.

Why is this happening, what's causing this?

She couldn't wait. She wet a finger and opened her legs to touch her already swollen sex. She was so close, only three strokes and she felt the waves of pleasure begin. She grunted with amazement and collapsed. Peace of mind and body spread through her like a soothing balm.

The serenity was short lived, for the unforgiving turmoil in her mind waited. With stiff movements, she got up to shower, turning on the water carefully as she fought once again to establish control over one small aspect of her life.

The water trickled down through her hair. When it hit her shoulders, her pretense of control melted and ran. She held her face as more tears poured painfully from her eyes.

"What's happening to me?" she whispered.

She stepped out of the shower emotionally drained and feeling disconnected from her reality. She put on a summer dress and walked to the galley for dinner. The shade was immediately inviting. Max sat at the table with an opened bottled of wine. She took a seat and looked around, still feeling a little disoriented. "Where's Asa?"

Max filled a wine glass and placed it in front of her. "I haven't seen him," he said. "But there is a good deal of movement and agitated conversation coming from his tent."

"I wonder what's going on." She took a sip. "Nice," she said, noting the French label. She took another sip, eager for the dimming effect of the alcohol.

The kitchen staff came out and placed covered plates on the table. Before Phoenix could comment, Asa stalked into the tent. He looked like he hadn't slept or bathed since Phoenix last saw him. Without a word he stomped into the kitchen and exited quickly with a plate. He paused, seeming to consider sitting with them, but the satellite phone in his pocket began ringing.

"Yes," he barked into the phone. Immediately he veered out of the tent with the phone in one hand and his covered plate in the other.

Phoenix looked at Max and raised her brows. He shrugged, but again, she thought he knew more than he was letting on. She wanted to ask, "Is there something I should know?" But she had asked him this before, and was still in the dark about so many things.

She reached for her wine glass and tossed a worried look to where Asa just stood. "What's going on? He has the look of trouble on his face. Do you think we're in danger?"

"Maybe, but you don't have to worry—I'll look after you." He lightly caressed the back of her hand.

She blurted out, "Maybe?"

"You're never in danger while I'm around," he countered.

Phoenix frowned. He certainly didn't look alarmed. In fact, his soothing touch was so effective, she forget why she was worried.

"Huh," she grunted and reclaimed her hand. Uninterested in another emotional challenge, she gave him a slanted appraisal and let the topic go. Picking at her salad, she asked, "Did you have a chance to work on translating the gold sheet?"

"I found her name," he said quietly.

Phoenix put down her fork, ready to jump up like they had won the lottery, but his somber expression was an instant killjoy. Instead of being elated, as she expected, the corners of his eyes crinkled with a deep sadness. When he said "found" his voice cracked.

She stabbed at her salad and probed further. "And the rest of the message? What does it say?"

"That's all I have so far," he said. He reached for his wine and swallowed the last in his glass.

This reaction wasn't what she expected. The mysteries around him disturbed her more than anything, for she knew deep down there was something he wasn't telling her. This lack of full disclosure on his part left her clutching her own secrets close.

She stood and covered her plate. "I think I'll eat in my tent. I'm exhausted."

He grabbed her fingers. "Are you feeling okay?"

"Didn't you ask me that once already today?" she accused.

"Yes, and I am as worried about you now as I was then," he said. His brows drew together and his lips pursed with worry.

Seeing his sincerity, she was tempted even more to drop into his arms and tell him about her experiences—if Asa weren't so close by.

Instead, she picked up her plate in one hand and reached for her glass with the other. "I'm fine. I just miss the beach. I could use a little humidity."

One of his eyebrows shot straight up. She opened her mouth to elaborate when her mind was filled with a scene of them locked in embrace, arms tightly clasped, legs entwined ... sweat trickling down between her breasts—

She clamped her lips together, fearing she would act on this desire running so close to the surface. She backed out of his reach. "Really, I'm fine, don't worry," she protested, taking another step.

His mouth turned down in disbelief.

She spun on her heel and walked off before he could speak.

In the quiet of her tent, she nibbled half-heartedly at her dinner. Unanswered questions and abnormal events had taken over her usually predictable and orderly life. Since she first heard of Gebel, her life dipped and soared like a roller coaster with a madman at the controls.

Artifacts displaying unnatural properties—paranormal events, erotic images—no wonder she constantly felt out of step. Her failure to understand these events made her doubt her senses. That alone frightened her more than she dared express.

"This chaos has to stop," she said. 'Either I'm losing my grip on reality—or reality is losing its grip on me. I think it's time I got some answers."

She remembered thinking the silver hand mirror was here to show her the truth. She sat on the bed by the table and peered into the blank face. "What is happening?" she queried.

The mirror remained unchanged.

Phoenix sighed with disappointment. While she didn't really expect anything to happen when she spoke to the mirror, within her existed a tiny dash of hope burning for the truth. She set the mirror down, a rush of frustration welling up, tightening her throat and watering her eyes.

She snatched up a package of tissues and went to the front room. Sitting on the couch with her feet tucked under her, she gazed through the open tent flap.

In the desert night sky, the deepest, absolute darkness was obliterated by the brilliance of a million galaxies. She wondered, were the ancients correct when they said, "As above, so below. As within, so without?" If this was accurate, would the truth likewise illuminate and dispel the darkness in her life?

"I want to know what's happening to me," she announced to the universe. She waited with her head cocked, hoping for some sort of instant enlightenment, but all she heard was the tent rustling in the light breeze. She nursed the last of her wine and sat staring out at the night sky.

Somehow the answers are right in front of me.

The view was hypnotic and her head fell back to the couch. Her eyelids closed, and the door to memory opened.

Her hands would not perform and she was frustrated. She flexed her fingers and tried the move again without success.

"No," her father said. "You have to consciously control the power, with your mind and your hands. See here—move these fingers before the flick." He did it again, quickly, expertly, and the flame erupted.

"Oh," she quipped. "Father, you should have shown me that sooner." Again she imitated the move and the flame came at her command. "Yes," she cried, jumping up and down. "Yes, I have the move—"

Phoenix's eyes snapped open and she sat up, groaning. Her neck was stiff from the awkward position on the couch, and the wineglass had slipped from her fingers to spill its contents on the carpet.

"Damn," she cursed. She stumbled to the bed, stripped, and crawled in, falling quickly back to sleep. More deep memories breached the subconscious barrier, invading her mind in a rush.

It seemed preparations for this day had been underway forever. While she only took up the studies of strategy and the Magic of War in the last year, the process had consumed her old existence. So complete had the Magic of War transformed her life, she could not remember one day as a carefree princess.

"Good," she murmured. Never would she return to her old life, or her old dreams.

"Are you ready?" her father asked.

Hot tears came quickly. She knew he loved her and had not wanted this. But he was dying and she was the only one to take the responsibility. Father and daughter must remember they are king and princess.

She wiped her eyes and stood, showing him she would make him proud if he would only live long enough. "Yes, I am ready."

She walked slowly, keeping with him all the way to the Temple. The Amenti were waiting, ready to see the power and crown passed to their favorite royal daughter.

"Praise be, let the power always know a home," they sang. "Praise for the power."

Yes, she agreed. Praise for the power.

Her throne, newly constructed of hardwood from the southern jungles, had been placed next to her father's. She stared straight ahead, looking neither at her father nor at the General, unable to bear witness to the one's pain, or the other's desire.

She closed her eyes. Her ears shut out her father's words. But despite her denial, the weight of the gold crown came down upon her head. Next, the weight of the journal as the Magic of War was pressed into her hands. A tear escaped her closed eyelids and slid down her cheek.

"Rise," her father called out to the people. "Rise before the new ruler of the Amenti."

"Long live the Queen! Queen Byrgamon! Long live Queen Byrgamon!"

Phoenix woke with a heavy sadness coiled in her chest. She sat on the edge of the bed and rubbed her eyes, feeling them swollen.

"Ugh," she grunted as the shadow of some unpleasant dream flitted through her mind. Her mouth was dry from the wine, and a headache lingered at the base of her skull.

"No more wine for me," she pledged, rubbing her forehead. A long look in the mirror showed deep shadows beneath her eyes, a sure sign she had not slept well.

She showered and pulled on her khaki shorts and a short-sleeved shirt. Before leaving for the galley, she pushed the hand mirror under her pillows. "Don't get into any trouble," she admonished on her way out.

"Oh, yeah, talking to inanimate objects, that's a sure sign," she grumbled as she walked to the galley.

"A sure sign of what?" Max asked.

Phoenix lurched in recoil and grabbed her chest. "Max!"

"Sorry," he said. "I wanted to check on you after last night. I was a little distracted, and you seemed—'

She walked in step with him. "I've had a lot on my mind lately, too." She looked for Asa before she spoke. "There's a lot of strangeness going on around here. Have you noticed—?"

He pulled her aside so they were sheltered from view. He grabbed her hands and gave a squeeze. "Don't worry, everything's going to turn out different this time, I promise."

His confidence in future events only served to increase her worry. "What are you talking about?" She looked about to make sure no one could hear. "Please, tell me what's going on around here?" He gave her a long look. She could feel his wanting and expectation ... for what?

"I can't say any more, but don't worry," he said. "You'll see everything will be fine." He released her hands and nodded to the galley, smiling. "Come on, we have a fresh day and plenty to do."

Phoenix followed him in spite of what he said. His comments had actually sent a curl of dread down her back. But his smile and self-assurance was a beacon that drew her along.

They entered the galley and filled their breakfast plates. Sitting with Max in the silence, Phoenix let go of her questions. Being with him made her feel everything would be all right. The questions and the visions only de-railed her when she was alone. "Have you seen Asa this morning?" she asked.

"No. If he doesn't show—"

The helicopter fired up, cutting off Max's words. Asa strode into the galley looking clean, refreshed and ... busy. He grabbed a cup of coffee and picked up a pastry before stopping in front of them. He gave Phoenix a long look before speaking. "How did it go yesterday?"

"Nothing spectacular. There are several chests we still have to open, but I don't hold hope for anything other than a lot of degraded organic material. The next layer looks interesting. Toys or pets maybe?"

She shrugged. Asa was staring at her with an unsettling intensity. He made her feel like a bug on a slide, helpless and exposed.

"Are you going somewhere?" she asked. He looked down, but not fast enough to prevent her from seeing the compressed line of his mouth, the flaring nostrils.

"I'm afraid business and events are interfering," he said. "I'll be gone a couple of days."

Phoenix's first thought was they were here by the grace of his helicopter. "What if we have a problem?"

Asa motioned and a Berber young man stepped into the tent. "This is Izri. If you need anything in my absence, he's here for you. He'll stay with the galley staff."

Phoenix thought Izri looked like a nice enough young man, but he was, in her mind, unqualified as her only link to civilization— and that being a Berber tribe. She opened her mouth to protest, but Max spoke.

"We're fine. We have an abundance of work and plenty of food and water." He shrugged and looked at Phoenix with a subtle glint in his expression. "We still have the two side chambers to open up—I think we have enough to keep us busy for a couple days. Don't you?"

Phoenix suddenly comprehended the appeal of working without Asa looking over her shoulder. "When are you coming back?"

"Two days, maybe less," he said. "I can't say exactly how long. Unexpected affairs are . . ."

"Unpredictable?" she offered.

"Very," he added. "But you are not abandoned. I assure you, I go reluctantly. I'll return as soon as business allows."

When he said "I go reluctantly," Phoenix saw a flash of agitation in his eyes. More than ever, she was glad to see him go. "We'll be here working when you return," she promised.

Asa glanced from her to Max. "I look forward to seeing what else you find."

His tone was harsh. Phoenix detected anger and frustration. Not knowing how to respond, she just nodded.

"Izri will take care of you," Asa said. "Well, I have to go. I'll see you in a few days." He turned and marched out, leaving Phoenix with the strangest feeling she had lived through this scene before. After the helicopter took off, silence returned. But the sense of déjà vu was so strong, so compelling, a knot formed in her stomach.

Why is his abrupt departure so familiar?

"He's not telling us something," she said. She glanced at Max. His faint smile mystified her as much as Asa's unexplained exit, fostering her underlying sense of disconnect. Again, she was out of step somehow.

Phoenix stood. Max rose with her and gave a quick glance at Irzi, reminding her of the open ears in camp. "Call me when you're ready," she said.

In her tent, Phoenix brushed her teeth and collected her backpack. She hoped Asa's departure would lighten the mood in camp, but now she felt a sense of menace she couldn't place. Why did she suddenly feel something was at great risk?

What's in danger? The artifacts? My sanity? My life?

"Ready," Max called.

Phoenix saw the silver hand mirror and suddenly wanted to

take it back to the artifact tent where it belonged—in a box with a tag. Instead, she sighed and pushed the mirror under her pillow.

"I can't figure out anything anymore," she complained. She stomped through the tent muttering, "I give up—I don't care what happens."

Max waited outside. She glanced at his face and asked, "What has you so pleased?"

He just smiled and took the lead with a jaunty step. They climbed down the rope ladders at the edge of camp and started up the trail. He took her hand and pulled her along. "Come on, it's waiting, you know," he teased.

His delight had expanded into pure infectious exuberance. Forgetting her earlier confusion and dread, she climbed, huffing and puffing to keep up with him. Playfully, she added, "Yeah, and it's going to get you if you don't watch out—"

They reached the top of the climb, and she followed him to the artifact tent. Leaving camp had lifted her somber mood. Being here alone with Max made her feel invincible. "Do you want me to help you with the chests, or do you want come up and help me with the next layer?"

He stopped to look at her. "Wouldn't that be a breach of procedure?"

"The next layer is all that keeps us from the sarcophagus. We could push ahead to the sarcophagus and come back here to inventory the chests later." She waved her eyebrows, suggesting he join her in this wild abandon of protocol.

"You're the boss."

They bounded up the stairs. She removed the lock and pulled the doors open. They stepped together through the vertical strips.

The scent came first, bringing a twinge of sadness, but not so much with Max beside her. She turned on the lights to reveal the next layer. "Wow, more animals. I wonder why these are separated from the others?"

Suddenly Max grabbed her hand, pulling her to him. "Does anything look—?"

His eyes were bright with expectation. Not understanding the half sentence, she didn't respond. He dropped her hand and turned away.

She thought to stop him, to ask, "Does anything look—what?"

But he was already busy, cutting off her opportunity.

"We should get busy," he said, his voice full of gravel. He reached for the box of gloves.

Phoenix was content to let the incident and his actions fall into her file marked *mystery*, a file that was becoming harder to ignore. For now, she preferred to delve into the task at hand. Archaeology was her sanctuary, and this site would likely be the highlight of her life's work.

The next layer was primarily stuffed animals, degraded but some pieces remained recognizable. Most notable was a full-sized cheetah and a monkey. The single most spectacular piece was a saddle and bridle with its leather desiccated into a hard mass, leaving only the metal buckles and bit recognizable.

Phoenix wiped her forehead and sat back in the cool of the chamber. She looked at her watch and was dismayed to see they had worked through lunch.

"Max," she called.

He stood just feet from the sarcophagus. With everything removed, it was possible to walk right up to the enormous stone coffin.

She went to stand next to him. They stared at the sarcophagus. "Brought in," she said. "Not carved here—a different stone." The lid looked to weigh more than they could handle. "We'll need help to move that lid."

He grunted in agreement without looking at her.

"Tomorrow," she said. He didn't move and she saw he was in his other world. She wanted to bring him back and took his hand. The warmth of his fingers moved into hers. After several breaths, his fingers twitched before he squeezed her hand.

Knowing he had returned, she asked, "Ready?"

He gave her a long speculative look. Instead of answering her question, his expression slowly burned with enough smoldering suggestion to draw a gasp from her. This time, she couldn't back up, for he held her hand tightly.

The unspoken suggestion in his eyes drew her in, bringing to mind their "Shall we? I think we should" conversation this morning. From the beginning, this man had ignited within her a sensual fire she couldn't explain. He was the one mystery she wanted to explore.

At last he responded. "Yes," he said. "I think the time is right."

His tone made the simple words sound like a riddle, inspiring goose flesh that went well beyond her desire. Suddenly it was no longer a game. Phoenix knew she was making a commitment. An erotic vision of them wrapped in embrace filled her mind.

"Are you ready?" he asked.

Her nipples instantly hardened and her knees weakened.

I thought you'd never ask.

"I'm ready," she whispered.

He stepped in. She held her breath as he placed one hand at the base of her neck and gently guided her closer. She turned her lips to him.

His breath fanned her face and she closed her eyes. She felt his lips lightly brush hers, his beard tickling her face. She parted her lips, encouraging him. His breath became hers. Their gentle lip-to-lip contact mutually grew more possessive, more demanding, more consuming.

Phoenix absorbed his smell, feeling the happy flutters deep in her psyche. She wanted to share her body, her heart, her life with him. Within her heart an emotional vacuum was exposed—and just as quickly filled with a long desired need.

She moaned and wrapped her arms around his neck. She pressed against his chest and slowly moved her hips. The wanting had been with her for so long—

"Phoenix," he whispered.

She realized he called her name, and opened her eyes, not knowing when the kiss ended. She saw him through a glaze of desire and burning need. "What?" she croaked.

"Not here," he said.

She stepped back and blinked. Her lips were tender. Her core ached with desire. Slow comprehension of what she was doing made her cheeks burn. She stammered. "I'm … sorry. I don't know … don't know what happened—"

He drew her back and crushed her against him, surprising her with his ferocity. "What happened needs to be—but not here. I want to see you with all the luxury you deserve."

His obvious desire warmed her heart. She stuck out her lower lip, knowing the display was childish. He responded with a blistering look that promised they would have it all.

"No one will love you as I do," he said.

Phoenix saw the sarcophagus and felt shame for lusting after a man in the presence of ... what? The past? She nodded to the stone coffin. "What about Gamon?"

The heat of desire filled his look and his stance. His voice was ragged, but the truth of his words was undeniable.

"Gamon is dead."

Phoenix nodded, silently praying he was right about Gamon. She grabbed her backpack. "I think we've done enough today, don't you?"

He stood behind her and helped position the weight of her backpack, stroking her arms. She felt him bend toward her and arched into him. He nuzzled her neck, whispering. "We haven't even started."

"Are you here?" called a voice.

Max instantly drew away. Phoenix looked to the chamber opening. Izri peeked though the vertical strips.

"Yeah," Phoenix answered. "We're here. We're just leaving for the day."

Izri held the strips aside for her and Max. "We were worried when you didn't show for lunch. I came to see that you are all right." He smiled, eager for their approval.

"We'd prefer to skip lunch and have an early dinner," Max said. "Will you inform Chef Andre for us?"

Izri bounded down the stairs ahead of them. "I will tell them," he shouted as he sped away.

Phoenix laughed. "He certainly tries hard."

Max took her hand. "Come."

They did not hurry, instead taking their time as though returning from a picnic. Knowing a sensual encounter was most likely near at hand, Phoenix's heart pounded with anticipation. Having to wait till they reached camp was torture.

They stopped at her tent. Her heart beat with a mix of excitement and ... completion. She sensed her desire for Max had always been a part of her, that his declaration of love and their coming together was somehow an act of destiny. Intuitively she knew the mystery that overtook her life was rooted in this physical act they were speeding toward.

"Now what?" she asked.

"I would like to shower and eat first."

Phoenix nodded, appreciating his gallant rules. "I'll see you at dinner, then."

"An early dinner," he reminded.

"A brief dinner?" she offered, teasing, yet sincere.

"Perhaps," he answered, smiling.

His tone warmed her heart as much as his eyes warmed her insides. "I'll shower and see you in the galley," she said. She stepped through her tent flap and turned back to him. "I'm famished, you know."

His eyes sparkled with understanding. "I know. Me too."

After he left, Phoenix squealed and danced from the front room of her tent into the bedroom. She stripped off her clothes and ducked into the shower.

As she lathered her torso she thought about what lay ahead. Her breasts were already sensitive and her nipples hard. A heat warmed her core with eagerness.

She dried and sat on the bed to apply lotion. Thinking of the hand mirror, she pulled it from under her pillow. The handle that had always felt cool was oddly warm. She closed her eyes. Her hand holding the mirror felt tingly. With the sensation coursing up her arm, she opened her eyes and peered into the mirror. "Show me the future."

What she saw came from the past.

Her fingers smoothed across the warm skin and hard muscles of his chest, bringing a sigh of contentment. His magic of love had brought life back to her tired world, and she was suddenly free ... free from battle and death, free of the loneliness of a queen at constant war.

"What you propose, my love, has never been done before," she said. "We will turn the world upside down. Finally, I can bury my Journal of War."

Phoenix opened her eyes and blinked, feeling lost. She didn't remember closing her eyes. She was on her bed, but she didn't remember why she sat here. The mirror was in her hand. She frowned, having no memory of picking it up or why she held it.

"Now what was I doing?" she said slowly, her brain churning for answers. "I must have, must have ... intended to ... to put it somewhere else ... it seems."

She stashed the artifact in a drawer in her garment closet, beneath her underwear. "There, stay safe," she whispered. She drew on a summer dress and added a touch of bronzer to her cheeks. A little lip-gloss and she was ready. "Oh." She dug in her toiletries bag for a tiny, expensive bottle of scent she picked up in the hotel gift shop. A couple of quick dabs warmed her throat.

In the vanity mirror, her reflection stopped her. She was truly beautiful. "Huh," she grunted in amazement. "When did that happen?" For the first time she saw what Lacey tried to tell her—that she was exotic and sensual and beautiful.

Phoenix knew exactly where the change came from and looked out her window at Max's tent. "What other changes do you bring?" she whispered.

Nothing in her life was the same since she received the Gamon~Search envelope. She was on a different continent in a different land and culture. Sometimes, she admitted wildly, she thought she was in a different time and space. Other times, she felt she occupied someone else's body.

Am I possessed ... or am I her?

She looked at her image in the vanity mirror. "Please," she begged. "Let me be me ... in this body ... tonight."

CHAPTER TWELVE

Phoenix exited her tent and stopped. "Oh, my God," she whispered.

A peculiar sensation filled her body, like heat and ice simultaneously firing through her nerves. The effect was surreal and she wobbled, feeling disconnected again, as though she was not in her own skin. She felt separate from her surroundings, but—

I am part of something else.

She looked over her shoulder. The tent was just inches behind her, but the level of her disorientation made her feel she had actually passed through an opening of another kind—a portal to something beyond her ken.

Above, the sunset generated ribbons of pearlescent pink so stunning she gasped, knowing she had never seen a sky so breathtaking. She closed her eyes and inhaled. A floral scent wafted on the breeze, coming from flowers she couldn't see.

Pleasure and pain, relief and confusion joined and rippled through her body. She reeled as all her senses reinforced the surrealistic perception she moved in another world.

I no longer know where—or who—I am.

Her senses—that bastion of solidity she depended on—were delivering input she couldn't qualify. Like the scent of flowers she couldn't see, she could no longer argue her point. She was forced to accept what she couldn't believe.

At the galley tent she paused, eyeing the door opening. She peeked through without entering.

Candles filled the tent with an ethereal light. Next to the table, a silver bucket, misted with condensation, reflected the room in foggy reverse, creating a rabbit-hole realty.

Phoenix sighed.

There is no escaping these altered worlds.

She smiled with acceptance and stepped in.

Max rose. His excitement was palpable. Her ears hummed from his joy. His eyes raked over her, his look calming her nerves and increasing her excitement at the same time.

"You are lovely," he whispered.

He pulled out her chair. Phoenix spied Izri in the shadows as she sat. She gave him a polite nod.

"Thank you," she said to Max. When he pushed her chair in, his fingers caressed her back.

"I'm ready," she said.

"I see that," Max replied. He signaled Izri, who darted back to the kitchen.

Phoenix watched Max pour the wine. She admired the strength in his fingers as he handled the wet wine bottle, marveling at the grace of those same fingers when he lifted his glass.

"To today's discovery," she said, raising her glass.

His eyes danced with understanding and he tipped his glass to the heavens. He opened his mouth to speak when Izri suddenly appeared with salads and placed them on the table.

"Thank you, Izri," Max said with a nod. He leaned forward to speak, elbows on the table, but stopped, seeing the boy had not left. "Yes?"

"If I can be of help with anything, you'll let me know?" Izri offered.

Phoenix tucked her head and made busy with her napkin.

"Of course," Max said. "That's all for now."

"I'll be back for the plates soon," Izri elaborated. "I can stay. I wouldn't want you to miss me if you needed something."

Phoenix picked up her wine and sipped, striving not to laugh.

"You'd have to go first for us to miss you," Max clarified.

Izri took his time to ponder this. At last he gave Max a conspiratorial look. "Exactly," he said. A quick salute and he retreated to the kitchen.

"What's so funny," Max protested. He wagged a finger at her.

"You," Phoenix said. "Trying to make your move."

"I was not making a move," Max bristled. "I'm a gentleman."

"Gentlemen don't make history," Phoenix quoted from a popular T-shirt.

"Ha!" he burst in laughter.

Phoenix nibbled at her salad before pushing the plate aside. Max followed her lead. Within seconds, Izri arrived, scooped them up and disappeared.

"He tries—" Phoenix defended.

"I just want a little time alone with you—"

Phoenix dipped a finger into her wine and ran that finger across her lower lip before sucking the finger into her mouth.

Max's words evaporated, yet his mouth remained open.

Phoenix heard Irzi walking up behind her and dabbed daintily at her mouth with her napkin just as he came tableside. He brought them a bucket with metal utensils and left immediately.

Max watched the boy's retreat. When they were alone, he said, "Behavior like that, miss, will get you—"

Phoenix suppressed her smile as Izri returned with their dinner plates, cutting Max off again.

Izri set the covered plates before them. "Can I bring you anything else?"

"We are fine, Izri. Please tell the kitchen staff everything is wonderful. I think we can manage from here without you," Max said.

Phoenix lifted the cover to her plate with her best deliberately feigned nonchalance. "Oh! Lobster," she exclaimed. "How divine."

"You have everything you need?" Izri asked Phoenix.

"We have everything," Max declared.

"We have everything," Phoenix chimed in with a perky smile.

At last Izri gave a bow and left them alone.

"Whew," Max exclaimed. "After all that, I darn near forgot why we're here."

Phoenix pushed her plate toward him. With the slightest pout, she asked, "Will you do mine?"

Max abruptly gave her a critical eye, a slow grin tugging at the corners of his mouth. He looked behind her, checking for Izri. "If you'll promise to do mine."

She laughed. "Me first."

"I wouldn't have it any other way."

He opened her lobster claws expertly, placing the meat on her plate and the shells in the metal bucket. He pushed her plate gently back in front of her. "Now eat your dinner. You're going to need your strength."

Phoenix didn't wait for him. She pushed her fork aside and rinsed her fingers in the lemon water. With clean hands she tore off a piece of the lobster.

Max opened his claws and picked up his fork. He looked at her just as she dipped the lobster meat in the butter. With his eyes tracking her movements, she tipped her head back and dropped the buttery bite into her mouth. "Mmmmm," she moaned, lips pursed and brow scrunched in bliss as she sucked on the buttered meat.

"You are wicked," he said. He put his fork down and copied her, rinsing his hands and tearing the lobster.

His fingers were tanned and strong, efficient and gentle with the delicate lobster flesh. Phoenix immediately thought of those fingers massaging her breasts, rubbing her thighs, stroking her belly—

"Phoenix?"

In a husky voice that surprised her, she said, "Can we go?"

"If we don't eat this divine lobster, Izri will take offense. We have to do better than one bite."

Phoenix calmed her erotic thoughts and picked dutifully at her lobster. First the piece of lobster was dipped into the butter before taking the perilous journey to her mouth. She dropped the morsel into her lips.

"Stop that," he said. He tipped his head back and dropped a piece in his mouth, grinning.

He carefully pulled apart his lobster and dragged a piece through the butter. He tossed the bite cleanly into his mouth, lapping up the butter with his tongue.

Watching him, Phoenix felt her heart accelerate. She gave him her don't-miss-this look and pulled off a piece of lobster. She dipped it in the butter, slowly dunking it over and over with a soft 'oh' at each stroke. When the lobster was fully drowned, she levered it to her lips, making sure one lone drop of butter hit her cleavage.

"Oh," she declared, lips pursed in surprise. "Look what I've done." She collected the butter from her flesh with a finger and licked her fingertip thoroughly.

Max put his napkin on the table. "I think we've had enough."

"But you said I should eat," she complained. She pulled off another piece and dropped it in the butter. "Uh oh. Now I've done it." She delved into the butter and pulled the lobster out, fingers dripping. His eyes were on her every move. She swallowed the lobster and sucked one finger at a time into her mouth.

"I thought you wanted a brief dinner?"

"I did, didn't I?" she said, feeling they had tortured each other enough. She joined him and stood, dropping her napkin to the table. "Shall we?"

"Whatever you say," he said. He came to her side of the table and leaned in to whisper in her ear. "I can't take any more. I promise, you will be more delicious than the lobster."

A quiver of erotic thrill flooded Phoenix. She turned her face toward him, their buttery breaths mingling. "I have waited long enough." She looked past him, knowing he could hear her soft words. "Don't make me wait any longer."

"Good night," he said. He stepped back to allow her to pass. He winked and added, "I'll see you tomorrow."

Phoenix took her time walking back to her tent. Her pulse joyously raced ahead. While her hips felt fluid, an accentuated swing joined in her step. Heat rose from her core, flushing out through her chest and up to her face. A store of erotic images of her and Max together bubbled up through her mind.

"There will be no turning back," she whispered. A new reality would be born when fantasy made the leap from mind to body.

The future, she thought, *is where I must go. Not the past.*

"Hmm," she mused aloud. "A novel thought for an archaeologist."

In her tent, she prepared her body as if for a ritual. She showered, cleaned her teeth and massaged lotion into her body. Sitting on the bed, she turned out the final light. Soft darkness surrounded her in a cocoon.

Her pulse finally slowed and a calm descended. She eased into the bed and pulled the sheet up to her chin. She didn't know when he could come, but she would be ready.

She closed her eyes and felt the drift to unconsciousness come in spite of her excitement. Soon, a mix of worlds, half familiar, some real, some fantasy, flowed from a deep well in her mind. Memories she didn't recognize flitted, tantalizing and captivating. In this state she could not reason why—nor did she care—that memory came before the act.

The heat of Kedare's gaze touched Byrgamon, alerting her to his presence. She rolled over. He watched her from the darkness. They locked eyes in the pale moonlight. Her arms opened to capture him for all times.

"Come, my love," she called. His clean manly scent made her toes curl with delight as he sat next to her. His hands took her by the arms and held her as his lips traveled down her neck. "My Queen," he exhaled against her flesh, sending ripples of pleasure down her arms.

She wrapped her arms about his strong shoulders and reveled in the thrill of her breasts against his chest. She moved up and down, her hard nipples raking him with her desire, her shifting hips teasing him.

"Argh," he growled, pulling her tight, crushing her with a kiss of possession. Happiness invaded her soul, for she knew she would find heaven this night.

He was on top of her. She felt his hardness probing, seeking that place of heat and desire that served her so well. She opened her legs to guide him nearer. His mouth descended to her breast sucking and gently pulling, causing her to arch her back.

Her passion was a blaze that knew only one culmination. His mouth went to her other breast, sending the wet heat straight to her belly. Rocking her hips back and forth, her body demanded release.

"Now," she commanded. He rose over her. His fingers delved deeply into her, opening her up, pulling her hips into position. She felt the tip of his manhood touch her, and a shudder of relief heartened her begging body.

He kissed and blew on her neck, sending sparkles down her arms. In return, she nibbled at his bulging chest muscles, feeling his flesh ripple in response. She loved this power over him, for he held the same over her. He kissed her, declaring his love in the ancient way, thrusting into her slowly, deeply, reaching—

"Yes," she panted. The flame ignited, sending flares of pleasure shooting out through her limbs as her soaring completion began. She grunted in a most un-queenly fashion and held him tighter. Heaven came as the last spasm consumed her, delivering her to the dark world.

She woke and left him to stare out the tent opening. A full moon shone down on the land, illuminating the plain with a ghostly light. This fertile land and its smell was a part of her, as were her people ... and now this man.

She heard him move and soon felt his warmth at her back. His hands stroked her arms and he pulled her gently into him. "What wakes you, my Queen?"

"Tis the heart of night—when I cannot deny what fills my heart." She dipped her head and kissed his hand.

He hugged her softly, asking, "Tell me, then, what fills your heart tonight?"

"You do, as no other power on heaven or earth can."

"Not even your power?"

She let her head fall back to rest against his chest. He did not understand the relief that would come from giving up her power. She turned to place her arms around him, pressing flesh to flesh from hip to heart, needing his warmth for her confession.

"The power of my magic creates death and destruction," she lamented. "Your magic of love creates pleasure. There is no comparison."

He tilted her chin up from where she nestled into his chest. "Can you give your power up?"

"Give up my power?" she repeated. She smiled, sly and seductive, for she wished to waste no more time in this discussion when they could be making love, creating another power. She drew his head down for a kiss. "Try and stop me."

Phoenix opened her eyes, momentarily groggy as dream images bobbed in her mind. She saw Max in the shadowed doorway of her bedroom and frowned, wanting to know why this moment felt so strangely familiar. The disturbance gave way to warmer thoughts as she rolled over and raised her arms. "Come here."

He walked toward her, bringing his clean, fresh scent to waft ahead of him. She took a deep inhalation and lifted her shoulders in mute delight. The bed sagged and he gently pushed away the covers, exposing her to the night air ... and his gaze. He moved closer, his breath fanning her neck. Light kisses followed and she threw her head back. Her toes curled with childish glee.

He stood and quickly disrobed before slipping into bed beside her. He immediately wrapped his arms around her ribs and hugged her tight. This brought her breasts up against his chest, finally allowing her to slake that one desire. Up and down she shifted, marking him with her nipples, while snaking her legs around his.

"Ah," he moaned into her neck. His mouth moved, scorching a path across her neck and over her jaw. When he reached her lips, she was ready.

"Love me," she demanded. Her hips moved in the dance of seduction, drawing him into her. He returned the action, thrust for thrust. A shot of desire bolted up from her woman's core as the slight friction worked its magic, lighting the fire within. "More," she begged. The passion was a flowing power, sweeping her to the heavens. Her desire to unite with this man seemed to have existed in infinity.

He cupped her breasts and squeezed gently, kissing each tip before running his hands up and down her ribs. "Yes, yes, yes," he cried softly, reverently, worshipping.

Her hips rocked, wanting his attention. Her body was alive in ways she had never known, all a fitting tribute to his claim no one loved her like he did. He rubbed her legs and thighs and stroked her belly, drawing the heat to a peak. "Now!" she demanded, panting.

She didn't have to ask again. Max was on top, his fingers opening her. At the first contact of his engorged head against her swollen lips, she wept, "Yes." When he filled her opening and the angle felt right, she tilted her hips. He drove sweetly into her.

"Phoenix," he gasped into her neck.

She went still, allowing their bodies to become one. Now that he was within her, she was no longer in a hurry. She clenched her muscles and he responded with a thrust. She rubbed her breasts into him, gleeful with the full frontal contact she had wanted for so long.

She was in an erotic place of sweated bodies striving to bring pleasure through friction. He moved and connected with her, sending a shudder of sensual lightning to race down her back. She responded, thrusting at the right moment, opening her hips for better contact, taking him deep.

The beginnings of her orgasm flickered, drawing her sublime intent on that single destination. Exquisite pleasure ignited in her core. She groaned into his neck and tightened her grip as she picked up the pace. He responded in kind, and they slammed into each other with passionate fury.

A flash of constriction fired through her breasts as waves of pleasure raced along her nerves, exploding out though her body. She gave a final thrust and a grunt of release before she jerked with the last spasm and collapsed, unconscious.

Phoenix slowly acknowledged her return. She lay with her face buried in Max's chest and his arms wrapped around her. A glow of absolute satisfaction surrounded her, suffusing her entire being with light-hearted joy. She felt like a teenager discovering love and sex in one powerful moment.

He sensed her return and stroked her hair. She peeked at him through barely opened eyes. He grabbed her hand, she clutched back in response. No words were needed. She understood some connection existed between them. What this was exactly, she had no idea. She would worry over that another time.

Peace returned to their breath, their bodies, their hearts. Phoenix pulled the covers up over her cooling body and snuggled into Max. He rolled over and they lay like spoons, her lips against his back, their legs entwined. Her heart beat inches from his. She was invincible once again as consciousness slipped away, leaving open the door to more memories.

A flame jumped from her fingers, catching the wick of a lamp and blazing brightly. She smiled and nodded at his astonished expression, but there was more. She moved her hands again and was cloaked in the magic particles, making her invisible. When he gasped, she giggled.

"I hear you, yet cannot see you—" he said.

He reached in her direction and she danced around behind him.

"Ah ha! I smell you," he said and reached to grab her.

She laughed and made the move that disbanded the particles, leaving her to appear in his arms. When he squeezed her tightly, she moved her fingers and they immediately appeared outside the tent. His eyes grew huge. She made the move again, whisking them back into the bed.

His expression grew somber. "No wonder you feel invincible. You learned all this from the journal?"

"Yes—the Magic of War is all in the journal."

Phoenix bolted upright in the bed, panting and feeling sweat gather on her forehead. Disoriented, she asked, "Where am I?"

Max stroked her arms and whispered softly. "Ssshh, it's okay now. Go back to sleep. Let the dreams come, Gamon. Dream."

Another world beckoned—no, demanded her attention. She collapsed back onto her pillow ... already floating.

She walked down the Temple, past the spoils of war, so abundant since she became queen. She passed the jewelry and the furniture in exotic woods from lands far to the south. Even the life-like statues of the cheetah and gazelle and the crocodile did not sway her.

"This will be my final and lasting contribution to the art of death and destruction," she said. "I will put the Journal of War out of commission."

At the end of the corridor she stopped and reached out her right hand, waving her fingers in strange contortions. She materialized on the opposite side of the stone in a small chamber she had created with her magic.

The gesture for fire sent flame to hit the wick of a lamp she left on her last trip. The wick ignited immediately, sending a warm glow to drive back the utter darkness of the chamber.

She walked to the far wall and set the lamp on a zebrawood table next to a niche carved in the rock. She picked up the Journal and held it to her forehead. "For a long time, you were all I had."

A tear ran down her cheek. "How lonely I was, with only war and the General to sustain me. But now, I have love—and there is no room for war." She carefully placed the journal in the niche.

"No one shall ever use you again, for I am the last to know your secrets. My hands the last to rouse the power from your symbols. You are forbidden to reveal your presence and knowledge to any soul's hands but mine." She waved her fingers, and the journal disappeared.

A special ironwood panel was carved to fit in grooves cut into the rock, sealing the niche. She poured water from a pitcher into a bowl filled with dried clay and stirred the concoction. A layer was applied, and while the clay was still wet, she collected a handful of small rocks and commanded them to break apart. She tossed the rubble at the wet clay where it stuck and morphed into a seamless wall of rock.

"It is done!" she whispered. In a life without the Magic of War and the General, perhaps she could make up for the death and destruction delivered by her hands. "The journal is laid to rest, never

to see the light of day nor the darkness of man's heart."

The lamp was extinguished. A quick move of her fingers and she was at the rear wall of the Temple. She walked back down the corridor, immensely satisfied with her actions.

Phoenix woke, filled with a deep sense of wellbeing, welcome after so much confusion. She stretched and suddenly realized there wasn't a warm body lying next to her. "Max," she said, sitting upright. She strained to hear any sound of his presence. He was gone.

She rubbed her belly and brought her hands up across her breasts in a hug of delight. Suddenly, the day held a wealth of mysteries and she was glad. Asa was gone, and she and Max had committed carnal acts—and would hopefully commit more. She leaped out of bed and rushed to the shower.

Evidence of their night of sex was all over her—in the tenderness of her lips, her swollen sex, a small bite mark on her shoulder. She blushed and hugged her breasts, enjoying their handled-with-passion tenderness. As quick as possible, she dressed.

Her walk to the galley was filled with a very light step. At the tent opening, she paused to let her eyes adjust. Max was already at the table with Izri.

"Morning, Missy Phoenix," Izri chirped.

"Izri," Phoenix said as she approached. The young Berber turned and departed. Phoenix watched him exit before turning her appreciative gaze to Max. With her mind full of visions of erotica, she felt a blush come over her cheeks.

Max rose. "Good morning," he offered in warm tones and a bright smile.

She thought quickly of how to make the morning even better, and felt her blush deepen. "Good morning," she responded. She went to the buffet table, filled a plate and sat down with him. Contentment came over her.

"You look to have a mouth full of feathers this morning," he said.

Phoenix felt her smile broaden. She picked up a piece of watermelon and declared, "It's a beautiful day. I am a professional doing what I love. I have an incredible lover and a wealth of treasure waits to be inventoried and make me famous. With all that going on, nothing can stop me."

The smile of pleasure froze on Max's face. His eyes crinkled with concern. "What did you say?"

Phoenix read the conflicting emotions and pointed at him. "No, you will not do that to me again. Every time you get that look on your face, you ruin my fun. Today I am queen, and I say no worried faces." She waved her hand in confirmation.

Unrelenting, he peered closely, but she held her ground. "I repeat, no one messes with me today."

Reluctance took the worry from his face with a tentative smile. "You feel that strongly, do you?"

She nodded. "Now, can we get to work?"

The trek up the hill was getting easier and they were quickly to the top. Phoenix followed Max to the artifact tent where they scanned the fruits of yesterday's labor. Tidy row after row displayed a wealth of treasure from a past life.

"This will likely be the highlight of my career," she said, looking back at him. "Your Gamon will make me famous."

A funny smile, not what she was expecting, twitched at the corners of his mouth, but he offered no comment.

"Ready to go inside?" she asked.

"After you."

They left the tent and climbed the stairs to the chamber. Phoenix liked being alone here with Max. He stood beside her as she removed the lock and swung the doors open. She sniffed at the air drawn out through the plastic strips.

"What do you smell?" he asked.

Phoenix shook her head. "There was an odor, but it's not so strong today."

"What, a dead rat?" he asked, looking all too serious.

"No. I can't say what the smell was, but the scent always made me sad. Asa said I smelled the past. When you're with me, there is no sadness." She stepped though the plastic strips, holding them aside for him.

They each carried a lantern, and she took his free hand as they walked through the vacated corridor. Their soft footsteps wrestled echoes from the stone floor.

"I feel good in here," she said. "Asa's 'it's waiting' doesn't threaten me. I believe, however, something here terrifies him greatly."

They stopped three feet from the sarcophagus and set down the lights. Phoenix asked, "How do you feel being this close to her?"

She expected him to look toward the sarcophagus, but he gazed deeply into her eyes, making chills shoot down her back.

"This has been a long time in the making," he said. He took her hands in his, squeezing gently. "But we are far from finished. You must be careful ... around Asa."

His words reminded her of his earlier warning not to drink anything from Asa. A flash of fear prodded her to ask, "Is there something about him I should know?"

He pulled her close, whispering into her ear. "Know he is a very dangerous man."

She nodded, hearing the fear in his voice. "Yes, he's dangerous—but he's not here now." She picked up a lantern and shined it over the sarcophagus. "Look, here's an inscription." She bent on one knee and touched the stone.

"Where is the journal?" Bahk-ir screamed.

My hands, she thought ... my hands will not move.

She reclined on a couch—breathing was getting difficult. A sensation of cold consumed her body and she slid to the floor, half slumped against the couch.

"You will never ... have the power," she gasped.

He grabbed her by the shoulders and shook, flinging her head wildly. "Where did you put the journal? The Temple?"

She struggled to speak these last words while she could, wanting him to know he had lost. "The journal ... is gone. Only my hands ... can find the journal."

Snarling, he pulled her face close. "I take from you all memories of magic. I damn your soul, Byrgamon. Let bitter betrayal follow you, for you do not deserve life, love or magic."

In the chamber, Phoenix screamed and jerked away from the sarcophagus. She flew back into Max's arms, unconscious. When she came to, her head was in his lap. He held one of her hands to his cheek, coaxing her back from her deep level of mind. Her eyes fluttered open.

"Hi."

"What happened?" she asked.

"You screamed and jumped back and then ... blacked out. Do you remember why you did that?"

"No, I—" She closed her eyes and rubbed her temple. "I don't."

Oh, I know this—I know this.

"It's waiting," she blurted. "He's right." She struggled to sit up and took a drink from her water bottle. A pressure was building in her head and she frowned. "I'm getting a headache." She rubbed her temples, but the pressure remained.

Max offered her a hand up. She rose slowly, suddenly not trusting her body.

"Let's take a break," he said. He helped her out through the vertical strips and onto the landing. "Get some fresh air."

She sat on the top stair fanning her face. Silently, Max passed her a semi-frozen Snickers bar. She chuckled drily and took the candy. "Yeah, I might need that."

He sat with her as she silently nibbled the candy and sipped her water. After a while he said, "You're getting a little color back in your cheeks. Can you walk down the hill?"

Phoenix contemplated arguing, but the throbbing in her head left her with little recourse. She stood carefully and shook out her legs. In an attempt to save face, she jutted her chin at the chamber. "We need help to get in," she said, referring to the sarcophagus.

"I know," he replied. He held out his hand and she passed him the keys. He locked up the chamber and gave the keys back before turning her around and pointing her down the stairs. He led her protectively until they reached camp and he brought her to her tent. With gentle hands, he stripped her down and helped her into the shower.

"I can do this, you know," she complained. but his concern was comforting. After a cool rinse that helped greatly, she stepped from the shower into his arms with a towel. He rubbed her down briskly like she was a child and walked her to the bed. The covers were straightened before she was settled in.

"Get some rest," he said. He pushed the hair from her face. "We worked hard last night." A grin pulsed at the corner of his lips.

Suddenly she was grateful for his ministrations, for she was ready to collapse. She tucked her hands under the pillow and whispered, "I love you," before slipping from this world.

Scenes and shadows darted across her unconscious mind in a wild jumble, transferring memories and searing them deep with wrenching emotion. Scenes of victory, loneliness, war and death all poured into her. She experienced each one until the final despair of betrayal.

Tears soaked her pillow.

Never again, her heart vowed. *Never again.*

She woke to darkness, disorientated by sleeping through the day. The air was still—a vacuum seemed to have swallowed the camp. She sat up, groggy and thirsty, and saw the covered dinner plate.

"What time?" She stumbled to her backpack and drank from her water bottle. With no desire to see what was on her dinner plate, she fell back into bed.

She held out her hand, just visible in the darkness. She made the moves and a small spark arced from her fingertip, expiring before hitting the carpet.

"Huh," she grunted, and crawled under her covers.

I knew I could do it.

CHAPTER THIRTEEN

Phoenix woke the next morning, confused as she looked around her tent. "Uh … why am I in bed? What happened—?" The last thing she remembered was being in the chamber with Max.

Frowning, she swung her legs to the floor, unable to remember, feeling disorientation erode her already weak equilibrium. "What day is it? What happened?"

After her shower she dried off, looking for bruises. Beyond the marks left from their recent lovemaking, she found nothing to indicate an injury. She felt around her scalp for a head wound. Again, nothing.

She pulled on work clothes and went straight to Max's tent. He was humming in the vanity area with a towel wrapped around his hips. A razor was lifted mid-air with half his face obscured in lather, the other half scraped clean. The thought of nuzzling up to his fresh shaved cheek was a distraction Phoenix couldn't resist. She paused to admire the view.

"Are you rested?" he asked. He stroked the razor carefully down his face, but his eyes in the mirror were on her.

She wished he'd stop so she could kiss the newly cleaned cheek, but decided it was worth the wait until both cheeks were smooth. Beneath the plowing razor, the beard and lather gave way to the rhythmic, smooth, steady strokes. Mesmerized, she didn't notice when her view eased into a scene from the past.

Oh, how she loved watching him shave. She sat at his elbow, entranced as he lathered his face and drew the long, sharp blade across his cheek. She smiled, knowing she would enjoy that smooth skin when he finished. Her toes curled with delight.

Phoenix blinked and shook her head.

Max stared at her, waiting for her to speak. He had rinsed and was drying his face.

When did he finish shaving? How could I have missed—?

"What happened yesterday?" she asked.

"You passed out in the chamber."

Her jaw dropped. "Why? Was I injured?"

"No. Perhaps you had a touch of heat prostration."

Phoenix thought he knew more, but he was clearly looking at her for an answer. She tried to remember. "I touched the sarcophagus." She looked at her hand and wondered what was so important about her fingers. "I remember a headache."

Not willing to test the boundaries of her mind or body any further, she thrust her hands out in defensive protest. "Whatever happened, I don't want to know. Today is a new day. Obviously, I missed a couple meals in the last twenty-four hours, so I'm going to the galley—

"But before I go, this is too tempting," she said. She went up on her tiptoes and kissed his smooth cheek. "Ooh," she grunted with pleasure. Her thoughts went to the appeal of a quick romp, but her stomach growled loudly. "Oops, gotta go. I'll see you there."

Phoenix skipped to the galley tent. In spite of the mystery of what happened yesterday, she felt good. She started with the coffee urn, drawn by the fresh smell. Her first sip of the strong beverage revved her motor. "Yeah," she said, collecting a breakfast plate of bacon, French toast, and scrambled eggs.

Soon Max came in and joined her. They sat eating quietly when the early morning peace was interrupted by the sound of an approaching helicopter.

Max went to look. "Asa," he called.

Phoenix joined him. The helicopter landed and Asa came out from around the chopper blades. Immediately Phoenix said, "Something's wrong."

Asa came straight for the galley. He sported desert fatigues, two days growth of beard and blood-shot eyes. He went to the coffee urn without speaking and drew a mug, sipping from the cup like it held his salvation. He sighed.

When Max and Phoenix saw Asa move to fill a plate, they returned to their seats. They picked at the remnants of their breakfast while Asa ate like a wolf. Phoenix shot a fleeting glance at Max, but his eyes were on Asa.

Asa finished. He wiped his mouth and took a long drink of water. Phoenix thought the air must have stopped moving, so stifling did it feel in the tent. Another questioning glance at Max gave her no clue. He waited patiently, seeming unperturbed.

She pressed into the edge of the table. Her tense stomach said something is wrong.

"Have you reached the sarcophagus?" Asa asked softly.

Phoenix snapped her lips together. An inquiry about the sarcophagus was the last thing she expected.

"Yes," Max said, eyeing her quickly.

Asa leaned forward. "Have you opened it yet?"

"No, we need manpower to lift the lid."

"Excellent," Asa said, rubbing his hands together. "I hoped to be present for this." He motioned and Irzi jumped forward. "We need—" He looked to Max for the details.

"You, me, and I'd say six others," Max offered.

"Six strong men to help us in the chamber," Asa told Izri.

"I will bring them," Izri said. He darted off.

Phoenix listened to the conversation flow around the sarcophagus until an opportunity opened. "Is there something going on you should tell us?" She nodded to Asa's clothing and appearance.

Asa inhaled sharply, as though he ate something he wanted to spit out.

Phoenix held her breath, fingers crossed that their permit wasn't revoked.

"Libya is at war," Asa said.

"What?" Phoenix frowned and pulled back. "At war with—?"

"Gadhafi. The people are trying to throw the old man out—with NATO's help."

"Are we safe here?" She looked from Max to Asa.

"The fighting," Asa said, lips twisted with anger, "is in the cities along the coast. Rebels are trying to take control of the oil ports and the capitol, but the old man is digging in. While I seriously doubt our little camp is on anyone's radar, I would be remiss if I didn't give you the opportunity to leave."

Ah, that's why he's pissed—he thinks we might give up. She glanced at Max, but he looked down, giving her the decision.

"I have no intention of leaving," she said. "We are going to finish, right?" She looked at the two of them. Her question was rhetorical. She didn't need to hear their response.

"The main corridor is emptied," she rushed to explain. "We will open the sarcophagus today. Then the two side chambers need to be emptied. They contain quite a lot, requiring at least a week, likely two. Then—"

Asa held out his hand, stopping her. "Let's take this one day at a time."

Phoenix saw his interest was in opening the sarcophagus. "Okay," she said, standing. "Let's get going, gentlemen. We have a sarcophagus to open."

By the time they congregated back in the galley to fill their water bottles, Izri had returned with a half dozen strong Berber men. He drew one man forward. "This is Hamzi. He speaks English almost as well as I do. He is happy to translate if you need. I must stay in camp—Mr. Asa's orders."

"Hamzi, we'll definitely need you to translate," Max said. "My Berber is inadequate for this."

"Do we have crow bars and wedges?" Phoenix asked.

"I have everything we need in the artifact tent all ready to go," Max said.

His statement reminded her why she didn't know that. She shook off any lingering trepidation about her mysterious lapse and focused on the day, as Asa had suggested. The sarcophagus waited for them. Perhaps the much bandied about 'it' was in the stone coffin. "Let's go."

At the chamber doors the small group congregated on the landing and spilled down the stairs. Phoenix opened the doors and swung them wide.

Max and Asa flanked her. She shot a look at Asa. He had been rather short on details concerning the Libya war. But what really disturbed her was his single-minded focus on the sarcophagus. "What do you expect to find inside the sarcophagus, Asa?"

Her question took him unprepared. While he visibly worked to come up with an answer, she suggested, "Is 'it' in the sarcophagus? What you believe is waiting?"

His look went from hard to cool with a subtle flash of threat sending a chill down Phoenix's spine. She wanted to step back, but refused to give him the pleasure.

"I have no expectations," he protested. "What I referred to as it's waiting was simply the mystery one expects to encounter when entering a civilization so different from our own."

She didn't buy it. He lied. Obviously there was something in here he wanted. She pushed through the vertical strips and picked up a lantern. The men followed her to the sarcophagus. A chill ran across her arms as she neared the coffin. She hesitated, remembering her experience yesterday. In her lapse, Max spoke up.

"Yesterday I took measurements and made calculations," Max said. He circled the sarcophagus and pointed to the stone lip that jutted over the edge of the lower container. "Three men on each side with Asa and I each on one end. We all lift, and Phoenix puts in the wedges until we build an opening large enough to run in the video cam."

Hamzi gave the men instructions as they put on gloves and took their places.

"On my count," Max called. "One, two—"

"Mr. Asa, Mr. Asa," Izri shouted as he ran into the chamber, breathless. "They say you must come."

Asa did not move from his position at the end of the coffin. He ground out, "Tell whoever I am busy." His tone was adamant, unmovable.

Izri wrung his hands. "No, no, Mr. Asa, not possible. The Colonel's men say you must come—now." He pointed to the sky and moved a finger like a helicopter rotor.

Asa's face slowly turned a deep red. He stepped back, hands clenched, looking at the sarcophagus as though he would gladly take a sledgehammer to it. Without a word he turned and followed Izri with stiff strides. They charged through the chamber opening, scattering the workmen.

Out on the landing, Asa's rage threatened to ignite and vaporize this operation. He looked at the helicopter, forcing himself to speak slowly. "Go. Tell them I am coming."

Izri didn't wait for further instructions.

Asa panted, staring at the fresh wood boards below his feet. He dared not look at Phoenix until he had control. He closed his eyes and massaged his hands, breaking up chemical toxins, literally pulling the anger from his body through his fingertips. Long, slow breaths, and he finally stopped panting. The red haze of murderous desire eased from his mind.

He turned on his heel and walked back into the chamber. The sarcophagus waited, calling him, luring him with the possibility the journal was hidden within its stone, teasing him because he would not be here for the opening.

I want in that coffin.

He shifted his gaze to Phoenix. "I want to know what you find in there."

"Of course," she said. "We'll run in the cam first and examine the video before the top comes off. How long will you be gone?"

"I can't say," he said. He spun on his heel and marched out. Before stepping through the plastic strips, he shouted over his shoulder, "Expect my return."

After his exit, silence descended in the chamber for long seconds. Slowly, everyone let go a breath, pursed lips whistling with relief. The Berbers returned to the sarcophagus, waiting for instructions.

Phoenix turned to Max. "Can we manage the lift being one man short?"

"Sure," Max said. "We'll just do one end first. Hamzi, the same instructions, again on my count."

The men lined up as Hamzi spoke. Phoenix picked up the wedges. Max called out, "Ready on my count. One, two, three."

With a great deal of grunting and shifting of feet and shoulders, they lifted the stone lid. Phoenix ran around, inserting the wedges at quarter intervals.

Hamzi directed one man to take the unmanned end of the sarcophagus. Max nodded and Hamzi called out in Berber. The Berbers grunted and the lid was lifted again.

Phoenix inserted the last wedge. "Where's the camera lead?" she called. She shined her light into the sarcophagus, scanning the interior.

Max brought the lights and camera equipment.

"Ready?" Phoenix asked Max. She thought he would want a moment to collect his thoughts, but he surprised her.

"Go ahead," he said.

Phoenix drew her chin back, seeing a hint of smirk tug at his lips. I'll never understand this man, she thought. She shook her head and fed the camera lead beneath the sarcophagus lid. "Can you see?" she asked.

"Let me get the focus," Max said.

"How are we doing? Can you see anything?" She moved the lead and repeated the process. "Well?" Fearing there was nothing of Gamon here, she couldn't bring herself to look at him. "What do you see?"

"The sarcophagus is empty," he said.

"Really?" she blurted. "I'm so ... uh sorry," she stammered in confusion.

His reaction is all wrong.

She scanned his face, expecting disappointment. What she saw was a complete contradiction. In fact, unbelievably, she saw amusement reflected in his eyes. Her eyebrows shot up in utter bafflement as her mouth gaped open. "What?" she mouthed.

He ignored her and began collecting the camera equipment. A nod to Hamzi and the men moved toward the opening and began filtering outside. Max walked out with them. Phoenix heard in their subdued chatter an eagerness to leave.

She waited as Max and the Berbers disappeared beyond the plastic strips. Alone with the sarcophagus, she stood with her arms crossed at the rear wall, having no desire to touch the coffin.

Max's reaction stumped her completely, but that wasn't news. She refused to let his inconsistencies disturb her work.

With the men gone, she was alone with the coffin, the silence, and the past. A memory teased her mind and, feeling the past beckoning, she closed her eyes.

In the Temple, the energy surrounded Byrgamon, waiting for her command. She moved her fingers. Immediately she was in the hidden chamber.

Phoenix's eyes shot open. Curiosity screaming, she wanted to see if she could duplicate what she just saw. She looked at her hand and recalled the movement from the vision. Oddly, the gesture felt familiar. She repeated the move, thinking *do it.*

Instantly, she was somewhere else, standing in the pitch dark.

"No! Oh no!" she cried in the absolute darkness. Not knowing where she was pulled the strings on her panic. She frantically made the hand move again thinking *return.*

Instantly she was before the sarcophagus.

She screamed. Stunned, she backed up and slapped both hands

over her open mouth to keep from screaming again.

"Did I hear something back here?" Max asked as he came rushing back to her.

Phoenix felt tears gathering. She cried out, "Max!"

A sweeping disconnect washed through her body, making her feel vacant and empty. Vertigo capsized what little stability she retained. She bent over, gagging, knees trembling as a cold sweat broke out across her scalp and ran down her back. She shivered, hanging on to the wall, whispering, "Oh my God. Oh my God."

"You're all right," Max cried, grabbing her. He pulled her close, supporting her limp form. "Shh," he cooed. "You're all right now. I'm here."

Phoenix gulped.

I am not all right. I don't know who I am anymore—

She suddenly felt claustrophobic and pushed her way out of Max's arms. She backed up against the rock wall. The cool surface was soothing as hot confusion flooded through her. She turned and stumbled through the chamber and out into the fresh air, crying.

On the landing, she gave in to hysteria, sobbing and choking, desperately drawing in the fresh air. Tears coursed down her cheeks and her legs refused to support her. She sat heavily on the top step.

Max came behind her and massaged her shoulders. His sympathy made her tears gush even harder and she choked. Silently he handed her his shirt. She wiped her face and blew her nose. "Thanks," she snuffled. "I'm sorry I pushed you back there."

"What happened?"

She couldn't describe what happened, because what happened was impossible. "Don't ask."

He seemed to accept this and sat with her. After a while, he put his arm around her shoulders and gave a squeeze.

"You know what's going on, don't you?" she challenged.

He didn't agree, but neither did he protest. Again he hushed her. "It's okay." He rubbed her arm and whispered, "Everything will be all right."

Phoenix was drained. She couldn't think. "What happens next?" she asked. She looked at him, feeling her misery and confusion bring more tears.

"I think we should take our lunch break," he answered.

Weary, she nodded in agreement. The task of beginning on the other chambers seemed a gargantuan effort. She rubbed her forehead, knowing the two side chambers were not the problem.

What she just experienced was the problem.

"Sorry," she said with a watery smile, feeling like her feet had been knocked out from under her. She wiped her nose on his shirt again and handed it back to him. "Maybe I caught a bug." She stood and shook out her legs. "Maybe it's the Pharaoh's curse." She walked down the steps leaning on the railing. "Maybe I just don't deserve life, love or magic."

She stopped and closed her mouth, feeling the words she just spoke come from someone else.

I would never say magic—

The pressure was back in her head, building. She rubbed her temples and moaned, "Nooo."

Max held her arm. "Can I get you anything?"

"Yeah," she laughed weakly. "Better get a Snickers, I think I'm turning into—"

"Betty White?" he asked.

Too much was happening. She couldn't process and assimilate these experiences. A fresh flood of tears threatened. "Nooo, I'm not Betty," she squealed in answer, scrunching her face. "But I ... I need to lie down."

As they did the day before, Max locked up and gave her the keys. He walked at her side all the way back to camp, his hand at the small of her back. The headache followed.

They had lunch early, but she picked at her chicken salad sandwich. With her hand on her forehead, she said, "I feel a little hot. Maybe I am coming down with something. I'm going to lie down."

He tested her forehead but gave no opinion, simply saying, "Let me help."

They walked to her tent. The trip seemed to take forever. All she wanted was to lie down. He helped her strip and shower, but she pushed away his offer to dry. "No. Too hot," she complained.

She fell into the bed.

"Water is right here," Max said.

He sat on the edge of the bed. The worried look on his face would have made her heart happy if she didn't feel so awful. She wanted to kiss him, but she wanted to fall asleep even more. I love you was on her lips as her mind left this world.

She tossed and turned. A fever burned, not of the body, but of the mind and spirit. Visions and memories spun, churning deep emotions. Everything from the thrill of love to the anguish of betrayal raced through her heart. Her body recalled the terror and numbness of her poisoning—

Phoenix sat up in bed. It was dark. The sheets were soaked, and she was chilled. She went to the shower and let the water soothe her body while her mind felt blank. She dried and sat in front of her vanity mirror. "You look the same," she said, putting a finger on her reflection.

And what about these strange pieces that seem so real—but don't fit.

She rubbed her forehead. It was like piecing together a jigsaw puzzle without a picture to go by.

"Max. Max will know what to do."

She struggled into shorts, a T-shirt, and slipped on her shoes. Without even looking to see the hour or if his light was on, she went to his tent.

"Max," she whispered as she slipped through the front flap.

"Here," he called from the bed.

She sat on the edge of the bed. He was a well of warmth and she dearly wanted to crawl in next to him, but she had to ask a question. Like choosing that last Tarot card, if she didn't seek these answers, she would always wonder about them. She took his hand. "Tell me about Gamon."

Her question should have taken him off guard, but she saw he wasn't surprised. He sat up and made more room for her on the bed. "She was a queen," he said. "She ruled the Amenti people."

"A woman ruling alone? How?" she asked. His answer, she saw, was carefully chosen.

"She possessed a power she called the Magic of War."

Instead of standing up and walking out at the mention of magic, she nodded. "Go on."

"She was a warrior, using her magic to strengthen her people through conquest of adjoining lands. At this, she was very successful."

"And very lonely," Phoenix added. She felt so sad for Gamon, understanding how trapped she felt. "But you saved her, didn't you?" She hugged his arm with possession, feeling a hesitant smile of hope tug at her lips.

"No, I didn't," he admitted.

His admission spoiled her oddly desperate need for a happy ending to this story. "What happened to her?"

Pain creased his brow and drew in the corners of his mouth, making her regret her curiosity. He rose, pulling her from the bed, and seated her before the vanity mirror. The gold sheet came from his backpack. He placed it in her lap. "The truth," he said.

"I can't read this," she protested to his reflection.

"Hold it up facing the mirror."

She propped the gold sheet up on the vanity top and saw the reverse image in the mirror. "Ah, you figured out why the writing wasn't quite right—"

He cut her off. "Here lies Byrgamon, Queen of the Amenti, a great warrior Queen beloved of her people. She was betrayed and killed in treachery by General Omon Bahk-ir. May the truth live to see justice."

Phoenix watched him as he spoke, a slow chill washing down her arms. He stared at her reflection, not reading the document, but quoting it. "Who wrote this?" she asked, even though she knew already.

"Kedare."

Phoenix repeated. "Kedare." The name resonated through her being. "I should know who that is." She rubbed her temples, feeling the pressure return. "Please, no—"

Max set aside the gold sheet. He coaxed her back to the bed, crawled in and held the covers open. She stripped and joined him, feeling dizzy. "Hold me, please," she asked.

He drew her close. Phoenix snuggled, drawing in his scent. "Oh," she sighed with relief. His arms encased her in a cocoon of safety. With him guarding, she could sleep … and be herself.

She closed her eyes as he stroked her head and shoulders. The comfort of his warmth lulled her ragged psyche. She had heard enough for now and needed time for her mind to understand what was happening. Just before she slipped away, she heard him whisper, "Find the journal, Gamon. You must find the journal."

Phoenix slept deeply. She woke slowly, wondering at the warm body next to her, when she suddenly remembered her trek to Max's tent.

"The truth," she said. The story of Queen Byrgamon's betrayal felt terribly close to home, stirring so many emotions. Pain and anguish flooded her mind, sending tears to course down her cheeks. She sobbed, feeling sad for poor Gamon, for herself, and for the lover, Kedare.

Max rolled over and drew her back into his arms. His hands soothed her, stroking away her emotional turmoil, replacing her confusion and grief with empathy and support. His hands brought comfort to her heart, chasing away the chills, warming her insides. She nuzzled close, wrapping her arms around him. He murmured something unintelligible, and his hands reached lower to squeeze her buttocks.

Phoenix grasped his hard length with one hand, stroking in return. His obvious desire made moisture bloom inside her, and she slowly moved her hips. He growled and flipped her over so they lay like spoons.

He kissed her neck, gentle, yet with small aggressive bites that made her nipples harden. His hands stroked her breasts, her ribs, and down her belly. She pushed back into his probing hardness and moved to give him the right angle. He slid between her thighs and entered her.

She gasped. He was quickly demanding. He thrust into her several times before pulling her up on her knees and hands, riding her. He reached around to tease her breasts, squeezing, sending sensuous threads to tighten her interior muscles. He withdrew and turned her over onto her back, kissing her roughly.

She grabbed his hardness and guided him home. "More," she mumbled as they kissed. He glided back in quickly.

Phoenix sobbed, a cry filled with her desperate need to feel another human being close, to anchor her to this world. She tucked her pelvis as he pulled out and returned, bringing quick ecstatic flashes deep inside. She squeezed and quickened the pace, bringing her flash point to ignition, pulling him with her. He bit her lightly on the neck, pushing her over the edge. She cried, "Kedare!" and went rigid with the final wave of her orgasm.

Max found his release with several powerful thrusts before collapsing and rolling off her. Phoenix lay on her side. He came up against her and wrapped around her, stroking her arm. A softly whispered, "Gamon," was the last thing she heard before falling asleep.

When she woke, his arms still held her. She lay there listening to his breath, luxuriating in the warmth he pressed all down the length of her body. In the midst of so much confusion, his calm presence made the chaos less ominous.

"Everything comes back to you," she whispered. She kissed his arm and gently slipped from his grasp. She picked up her clothes and dressed, walking back to her tent.

She showered, dressed, and went to sit on her bed. The fever she had experienced last night seemed to have burned itself out. She felt clear and grounded like she hadn't since before this expedition began. She retrieved the hand mirror from its earlier hiding place in the drawer of her garment closet.

Immediately she noticed the handle's warmth.

Since speaking to artifacts was new to her, she would proceed as a scientist and follow Occam's Razor, which basically says, "Don't ignore the obvious."

"To get the right answer you have to ask the right question," she argued. She looked into the mirror and commanded, "Show me who I am."

The mirror surface moved like water swirling in a vortex. She sucked in her breath and fought the urge to scream and throw the artifact across the tent. Gradually, the mirror's surface settled into the reflection of a face.

My face ... but not me.

A woman, identical to Phoenix, but with long hair and a gold crown on her head. A man leaned into view—

Max!

Phoenix's jaw dropped. A sharp inhalation brought her lips back together. With Max's image came a surge of love and contentment that seemed to flow into her from the mirror, filling her heart.

Phoenix jumped up and shoved the mirror under her pillow. She backed away from the bed. When she bumped into the tent, she held her hands out defensively, but they didn't feel like a part of her body. "What's going on? What's happening to me?"

She moaned with anguish. She pressed her fingers over her eyes.

Fleeting images in bits and pieces raced en masse through her mind, making her dizzy. Her body swayed. "Stop," she whispered, begging, "Stop." But more information streamed, too much for her to comprehend ... and yet she understood.

"I said, stop," she demanded. She opened her eyes. Her hands tingled with energy. She flexed her fingers, feeling warmth dart up her arms. A quick movement with her hand, and a burst of flame manifested off the tip of one finger. She flicked her hand, and the flame expired.

"Yes, I understand," she said. Her right to command this power came from deep within and long ago. She nodded with a tight smile of self-assurance.

Her intellect acknowledged her mastery of the War of Magic. A queenly eyebrow lifted in recognition of the infinite power at her command. Her heart sang for her return to power. Her smile broadened.

"Oh, I will have my day," she murmured. "But first, the journal." She executed a move with her fingers and was—

—In the Temple, just inside the locked doors with her eyes closed. An aurora of scents from the past enveloped her with memory. From her coronation to her assassination, magic controlled her life.

Phoenix snorted. Nothing had changed. The memories simply reminded her why she gave the magic up. She strode down the corridor, past the spoils of war and the trophies of death.

"How often I came here," she whispered, hearing her voice sound small and inconsequential.

This Temple, like the power, was both the seat of her refuge and the source of her torment. She stopped, her limbs shaking. The emotional energy held within the chamber bombarded her like strikes of lightning.

"I am home," she sobbed as tears cascaded down her cheek. She went to her knees in front of the sarcophagus and crossed her arms across her chest. "I have returned," she cried. "I am home. I am back."

She sat on her heels and cradled her face in her hands. Her tears were profuse, washing away the grief of her betrayal by Bahk-ir, a pain her soul had borne through countless lives. Every moment of betrayal she experienced in her lifetimes had originated with Bahk-ir's curse.

"He used my magic against me," she sang with disbelief. A surge of anger drew her up on her knees. She swayed, buffeted by the pain unleashed from her awakened soul. That he would do such a thing to her came throttling into her consciousness, driving her to her feet.

"You bastard," she cried, her voice hoarse and cracking. "You cursed me with my own magic." Her incomprehension echoed through the Temple, returning to feed her outrage. Reeling with full understanding, she shook her head with stupefied shock. "With my own magic—"

How many of my lives did he destroy?

"You bastard," she snorted as fresh tears soaked her face. Her body flashed cold, then hot and trembling. Misery drew her head back and she screeched to the heavens. "You bastard!"

Rage blasted her words around the chamber. She huffed, panting forcibly with the struggle to maintain control. She was an inferno, spewing anger and grief and hatred, her heart and mind on fire. She jerked, maddened with the desire to destroy Omon Bahkir.

Vengeance—

Arms clamped at her sides she swayed, her hands tingling with magic. Unseen energy brought chaos to the chamber, rattling anything loose. Dust swirled, and the hair at her nape lifted as the frenetic energy surged around her. She trembled with power on the brink of explosion.

"I am Queen," she stated.

Instant stillness filled the chamber.

Now that she was aware and empowered, she pulsed with killing desire. The energy rode her emotion with eagerness.

"No, not here, not now." She flicked her fingers. The energy simmered.

"The Journal of War," she said. "He will not have my journal, not ever." She picked up a lantern and made the gestures, materializing on the other side of the wall. In the lantern light, she went straight to the missing zebrawood table. She tapped the front of the niche. "Allow me the journal."

A spider web of cracks shot though the powdered rock and ancient clay plaster. The cracks spread until the plaster fell away piece by piece, revealing the wood panel. She rapped the panel. "Let me in."

Like a sentinel glad to be relieved of duty after all this time, the board squealed. Small ripples flowed across its surface, shaking the remaining fine powdered rock to the floor. Free of the plaster, the wood creaked as it slowly warped, pulling away from the carved grooves with a series of pings. When no longer bound to the wall, it fell to the rock floor.

The niche was empty.

Phoenix smiled. "There you are."

Upon reaching in, her fingers activated the ancient spell. The journal materialized. She withdrew her hand and the journal disappeared again. She smiled in triumph and scooped up the book. With a flash of her hands, she materialized back in the Temple. She walked straight to the sarcophagus and stuck her tongue out.

"Surprise," she taunted.

She put the journal on the coffin. A flick of her fingers and the latch sprang loose and the gold cover flipped open. She scanned the ancient, familiar symbols across each thin gold page, rushing through them until she reached the back cover.

"Just as I thought," she said, rubbing her hands together. She picked up the journal. "Come. Now it is our turn."

CHAPTER FOURTEEN

Phoenix materialized in her tent and set the journal on the bed, giving the book a loving pat. "Yes, today we will serve up a little justice ... justice long overdue."

A quick glance in the mirror and she grimaced. "I look like I rolled in the dirt—not very queenly." She laughed and stripped before turning on the shower.

The water poured over her, rinsing away the pain and anger of Bahk-ir's betrayal. Her grief and its residue from the chamber sluiced away, circled the shower drain and disappeared, leaving her fresh, feeling newborn.

Her body thrummed with excited vitality. Her hands tingled with the power. Her mind delved through possibilities never known, a thousand new thoughts igniting.

But she had only one priority—vengeance on Bahk-ir.

"Oh," she hissed, jaws grinding. "I am coming for you."

She dried in front of the vanity mirror and examined her reflection. Her appearance remained the same, her hair and eyes no different from what she saw yesterday in this same mirror.

And yet there were detectable changes. She saw a straighter spine, recognized that regal glint in her eye, and couldn't deny the aura of power.

"Gamon, you are hard to miss," she said.

It was still dark, hours before breakfast. She dressed, grabbed the journal and set out to find Max.

"Max," she whispered, entering his tent. He looked up, groggy, and smiled when he saw her. He held out his hand in silent welcome.

She sat on the bed, holding the journal out of his sight. With sleepy eyes, he tried to see behind her, but she pushed him back. He sat up against the head of the bed, rubbing his face and slowly coming awake.

Phoenix felt love filling her heart, expanding through her chest. She squeezed his hand, loving the tousle of his morning hair, the deep blue of his eyes, and the strength of his commitment to bring their destiny to fruition.

He was her hero. Because of him, a love greater than her hatred for Bahk-ir was awakened in her heart, saving her soul once again.

"I love you." She stroked the rough morning growth of beard on his cheek and felt the love pour from her heart as it did so long ago. Tears of joy flooded her eyes. "Once again," she said, "you have given me life."

Max's sleepy face brightened and he kissed her hand. "You remember?"

"Yes, I remember … I remember all." Phoenix saw the moisture gather in his eyes as her own tears coursed down her face.

"I have watched your turmoil these last two days," he said. He pressed her hand to his cheek. "I wanted to take you in my arms … to save you from the pain of discovery. I know it wasn't easy for me."

"But I had to meet the past by myself," Phoenix said. "You could not have done that for me."

"It has been hell, watching you, but one I would suffer gladly again and again," he said. "The journal—have you found the journal?"

She pulled her hand forward. The golden book of magic shone in the pale light.

He gasped. "Looks pretty good after being in storage for ten thousand years. Where did you hide it?"

"At the end of the main corridor, in a hidden compartment no one knew about," she said. A smile of satisfaction tugged at her lips. She set the journal on the bed. The book disappeared as soon as she let go. His eyebrows shot up.

"Look." She made a series of gestures and a flame sprouted from the end of her finger.

At his "good girl" look, she giggled. She made another quick combination of moves and the two of them materialized in the chamber. By the time Max realized he was standing there naked and barefoot, she brought them back to his tent.

He grabbed her in a great hug. "Gamon—"

Immediately he stopped and covered his mouth. "No, uh—I mean—"

She put a finger to his lips before he stumbled any further. "I don't know how all this came to be, but I do know you saved my life. Whether I call you Max or Kedare matters not, and if you call me Phoenix or Gamon, who cares? How can I show you what you mean to me?"

"You have only to love me," he said.

She kissed him, her heart overflowing with a depth of emotion she never knew possible. "Love you, dear one, yes. And I will never leave you this time."

Tears glittered in Max's eyes as he recounted his ancient grief as though it were yesterday. "When I was told of your death, I made a vow to the gods I would see justice done. I swore never to rest until you were given another chance."

Phoenix sobbed at this declaration. Her heart was again a well of faith and hope—that this time things will go differently. She grabbed him and hugged him close. She would never let him go. "Never again," she whispered. "Never again."

He took her face in his hands and tenderly kissed her. She reveled in the feel of his magic of love. She was the queen again, and her lover was at her side. She threw her head back, and cried, "I am free. Free to love you—"

Max shook her gently. "This time we will handle Asa together. Promise me you will not attempt to deal with him alone. He is a dangerous man—"

"I have no intention of letting Asa kill me again, or get his hands on my journal. I said I will never leave you and I meant every word. We must rid the world of Bahk-ir, the journal and the Magic of War for all eternity. Come on. We have work to do."

While Max showered and dressed, Phoenix paced. "We have to put the Journal where it will never be found—"

Max mumbled around his toothbrush, "Can't you destroy it?"

She shook her head. "It's complicated. Magic can't be destroyed, but the journal isn't magic. The journal is simply instructions on how to manifest and control energy. The problem is, the journal is protected by the same energy."

"I'm no particle scientist," Max said, wiping his face. "But I think your energy is subatomic particles—quarks and neutrinos, tachyons, that kind of stuff."

"The journal was passed down through my family," Phoenix said. "I have no idea where the magic originated." She paced the short length of his tent. "If I controlled subtle energies, later magic must have de-evolved into management of the larger, coarser aspects of energy—earth, fire, air, and water. All this time, thank God, this knowledge was buried."

"So what can you do?" Max asked.

"I'll have to think on that."

"What about Asa?"

"Oh—we can most certainly destroy him," she said, needing to declare her intentions. She went back to her pacing.

"What do you have in mind?" Max probed.

Phoenix realized she was dealing in death again and stopped, hunching her shoulders with misery. Max stepped up and she went into his arms, placing her face to his chest. His heart beat just beneath her ear, reminding her how precious life was. A fresh flood of tears sprang up as she whispered, "I was with child. We were to have a baby—"

"Shh," he whispered. "I know, I know." He stroked her head, soothing away her pain. "We will have children now."

He held her close, but anger returned, drying her rush of tears. She reached for a tissue, sniffling. "As soon as I figure out how to get the most satisfaction from his demise, I will kill him."

Max went to the small couch and pulled her into his lap. "We will take care of him—together. You weren't the only one harmed by his actions. I, too, have a grievance."

Phoenix opened her mouth to protest.

"No, no ... hear me out," he insisted.

She moved from his lap to sit next to him. "All right. If you have a good plan, let's hear it."

"Asa has one weakness," Max said. "We can use that against him."

His smile inspired a wiggle of excitement in Phoenix. "Go on—tell me more."

"We set a trap and use the journal as bait."

"Isn't that a little risky?" she challenged. "He knows the language, Max. He can read the journal. He's familiar with the moves ... theoretically he could teach himself. I can't chance it falling into his hands."

He held his finger to her lips, silencing her protest. "I have something to show you."

Phoenix waited, listening to him rummage through his bags. He returned with a locked box and a mischievous grin. She scooted over, giving him more room. "I love it when you're sneaky," she said.

"Then you're going to love this," he replied with a wink. He worked the digital combination. There was a hiss of air releasing and the lid on the box swung back.

Phoenix peeked. "Oh!"

He lifted out a duplicate copy of the journal.

Phoenix took the fake journal. She opened the latch on the gold cover and thumbed through the blank pages. A wicked joy for the pain this would cause Asa made her chuckle. "This ought to piss him off."

"We use the duplicate as bait and put your journal in here," Max said. He held up the lockbox. "This is made of titanium and has a pneumatic lock. Without the code, you'd have to destroy the box before it would open.

"I see you've put some thought into this. Go on," she encouraged.

"There's more." He exhaled deeply. "I've been wanting to tell you this since we met at the fortune-teller. This is one of the many lies I hated keeping from you."

"Do I smell a confession?"

"I opened your sarcophagus," he blurted. "Last year."

She sat back, uncertain where he was going. "I saw someone had been in the chamber before us. I figured Asa."

"I exhumed your remains and had them analyzed."

Phoenix arched her eyebrows in curiosity. "And?"

"The venom Bahk-ir killed you with came from a now-extinct species of snake." He reached into a padded interior pocket of the lockbox and lifted a metal vial labeled with an X. "But the chemists were able to make a duplicate venom from the traces they found in your remains. I also have the antidote." He held up a duplicate vial labeled with an A. "I thought you could use these."

Phoenix let her mouth sag open as Max's revelations increased the range of successful possibilities running through her mind. For several moments she hung suspended in thought, fingers drumming. Slowly, her lips came together in a smile.

"I waited ten thousand years for that smile," Max said.

"I love a devious man," she purred.

"I love a vengeful woman," Max replied. He leaned over and kissed her on the nose. "We hide the real journal in the lockbox and use the fake."

"He's expecting to find the journal in the sarcophagus," Phoenix said in a rush.

"With a video of this in the sarcophagus—" He held up the fake. "We lure him to the chamber."

"And I kill the bastard," Phoenix finished. She looked at her fingers, remembering the destructive potential of her magic, along with the loneliness and despair. "Hold me," she said. She stood and pulled Max to his feet.

He drew her into his arms. She sighed, inhaling deeply, absorbing his scent, his strength, his unwavering conviction. "What if something screws up?" she said softly. "I can't lose you."

"You won't. We're a team. We have a plan and we have the tools. Together we rid the world of a terrible, evil man." He lifted her chin and kissed her lightly. "We remembered the past, Phoenix. What transpired long ago will not come again."

She exhaled and pulled her shoulders back. "All right, then," she said. "We go to war."

"First, you take these." He passed her the two vials. "The only thing to remember is this: once exposed to air, the poison is effective for about fifteen minutes. After that it degrades rather quickly."

Phoenix tucked the vials into a pocket of her pants and zipped them secure.

"Now, I take the journal." He held out the lockbox.

"Putting you away again, old friend," Phoenix said. She set the magic book inside.

Max closed the lid. Another hiss of air came as the box pressurized. "I'll just put this out of sight."

"Bring your backpack. We'll put the other journal in there."

He slipped into the bedroom and returned with his backpack. Phoenix passed him the fake journal and he stuffed it into his pack. "Ready?" she asked. "We have to get this done before Asa returns."

At his nod, she wrapped her arms around him and made the moves, transporting them to the chamber. Max went immediately for the lanterns. Phoenix went straight to the sarcophagus.

She stood in the darkness, waiting. A sense of calm suffused her heart, mind and body, giving her clarity.

I always felt like this—before, when going into battle.

This time she fought for her life. And Max. The power tingled in her fingertips, reminding her what she was capable of. For the first time, she felt Bahk-ir's betrayal would at last be avenged.

Lantern light flared and washed over the chamber as Max approached.

She stood off to one side and made a few quick gestures. The sarcophagus lid slowly grated away from the coffin, floating on a layer of energy particles. The wedges she inserted earlier teetered and dropped to the floor.

Max guided the lid sideways.

Phoenix brought the lid down softly. "Hurry," she said. "As soon as we finish here, I need to stop in the galley. I'm famished. Apparently, commanding subatomic particles burns a lot of calories."

Max pulled the duplicate journal from his backpack.

Phoenix made the same gestures that moved the sarcophagus lid. The journal floated from Max's hands over the edge of the coffin and hovered inside. "How's this?" she called.

"Bring it forward a little more, yeah. Right there," he said.

"Get the camera lead. I'll pull the lid back—"

Max opened the camera and scowled. "Damn it, the camera was on—the batteries are dead. We have to go back. I have more in my tent."

"That's okay," Phoenix said. "I can grab something to eat while you get the batteries. Come. Let's go."

•

Asa Ducaine watched the night sky fly beneath him as the helicopter headed back to Gebel and the Temple. "The journal has to be in the sarcophagus," he mused. There was simply nowhere else the damn thing could be. "Maybe the priests packed it with her."

One finger tapped rapidly as he sought this answer. "That's the only solution—she had the journal with her all this time."

He held his hands out, considering the power they would soon hold. "I will be invincible, and the world ... my little oyster."

The helicopter began the descent to camp. Asa peered anxiously even though it was two hours till sunrise. "Drop me off and return to the last fuel stop until I call you," he ordered. When they hovered a few feet from the ground, he jumped. The helicopter lifted immediately. As it flew off, Asa hit the ground and went into a crouch. No lights came on. No footsteps came running out of the night.

He went straight to Phoenix's tent. The archaeological charade no longer served him. He wanted the journal. He barged through the front flap and into the bedroom. He shined a flashlight on the bed.

"What the hell—?" he muttered.

The bed was empty. He spotted the chamber keys on the bedside table and pocketed them. With his flashlight, he started in the clothes closet, systematically tearing through every compartment. He found Byrgamon's silver hand mirror.

"Why does she have this?" he asked. He tossed it aside and kept looking. In a bottom drawer beneath socks, he found an envelope.

"Gamon~Search," he said, frowning. He opened the envelope and read.

With each paragraph of the tale, his rage accelerated, building into a lightning strike explosion. A separate envelope encased a personal card. He opened it.

"Max Parrish. Of course," he spit. "Once again, they collaborate against me, attempting to take what is rightfully mine." A sneer twisted his lips. "So much for Max 'Mister-Doo-caine' the assistant. I'm going to kill him first—just as soon as I find the journal.

"Where are you? Where is the journal?" He looked out the window and saw Max exit the galley in the direction of his tent.

Asa bent down and followed from the opposite side of Max's tent. He tiptoed to the corner, out of sight, waiting.

Max rounded the opposite corner and darted into his tent.

Asa entered right behind him. As Max looked back, startled, Asa brought his fist down on Max's temple.

•

In the galley tent, Phoenix sat in the dark devouring a hastily assembled sandwich.

"Oh no," she whispered, and set the sandwich down. She ran to the tent opening, feeling her insides twist with alarm. Even though she saw no helicopter parked on the pad, she knew Asa was in camp.

"When?"

While we were in the chamber.

She crouched down. The kitchen was cold, not a soul in sight. Her heart accelerated and her palms turned suddenly sweaty. They had managed to change events all right—this time Max was in danger.

"If Bahk-ir wants the journal," she whispered. "Then let him have what he wants." Flexing her hands, she called on the power. She disappeared.

◆

Max sat on the carpet of his tent, gagged and with his hands tied behind him.

"Gamon~Search," Asa snarled. He grabbed Max by the hair and jerked his head back. "Found your little witch, didn't you?" He stepped back and landed a well-placed foot in Max's ribs. "Mr. Doo-caine—" Asa sneered. He kicked Max again and dragged him to his feet. "I'm just getting started on you, Kedare. Where is she? Where's the journal?"

Even though Max was tied up, when he made no response, Asa enjoyed punching him in the face. Max grunted as his head flew back with the impact. Blood spurted from his lip and nose.

"I know where she is," Asa said. He pulled a gun from behind his back and motioned Max out the door. "Come on. We have a date with destiny."

◆

Phoenix walked through the chamber. Here is where their lives and souls would come full circle, where Asa intended to kill her once again.

"Not this time," she said.

She pulled on a pair of latex gloves and set one of the lamps on the lid of the sarcophagus. She clambered up onto the edge of the stone coffin, ignoring the chills across her arms.

"Please, God," she prayed. "Help me bring Bahk-ir what he deserves." She opened the poison vial. Braced on one hand, she carefully poured the liquid onto the fake journal, making sure the poison didn't splash. The fluid pooled in the hammered gold depressions.

Feet stomped loudly outside on the landing.

Phoenix snapped the vial closed and jumped down from the sarcophagus.

"I know you're in there," Asa shouted from beyond the locked doors.

A shiver crawled down her spine. "He's insane," she exclaimed softly. She put the empty vial in her pocket. With her right hand she gestured. The poison on the journal disappeared.

The doors rattled. The lock was being opened. Phoenix made one last flurry of moves with her fingers and stepped away from the sarcophagus.

The chamber doors burst open. Max came through the strips first, blood on his face. A wave of anger flashed through Phoenix. She was tempted to kill Asa that instant—

"Not so fast," Asa called. "I know what you're thinking." He emerged behind Max, holding a gun to Max's head. "Come out, come out. I know you're here." He flicked on the lamp by the door. "Come on out," he sang.

Careful what you wish for, Phoenix thought. She stepped out from behind the sarcophagus. "Asa." She nodded to him as she put distance between herself and the sarcophagus. A quick glance at Max and she saw his hands were bound behind him.

Good.

She also saw the gun held to his head.

Not good.

Asa kept Max in front. The gun moved to a spot behind Max's ear. "You have the journal, don't you?"

"Not yet," she said casually, gradually stepping sideways, bringing Asa closer to the sarcophagus. "But you were right. The journal is in the sarcophagus."

"You expect me to believe you're just going to give me the journal?"

"If you want the journal, come and get it," she replied.

The gun barrel was against Max's skull. She was not faster than a bullet at this distance. She saw Asa's finger on the trigger. "Let Max go. You can have the journal."

"You know it's not that simple," he said. He looked at her hands. "Just possessing the journal is not enough."

Like an animal being stalked, Phoenix felt her hands were already appraised for stuffing and mounting. She wiggled her fingers.

Asa ducked behind Max. "Put your hands where I can see them and keep your fingers still," Asa shouted.

While they talked, Phoenix circled the sarcophagus, keeping the stone coffin between them. She came out into the open with her hands in the air for him to see. He kept the gun barrel pressed behind Max's ear.

Phoenix watched as Asa reached the opened end of the sarcophagus. "Look," she said, "The journal, there it is."

Asa pulled the hammer back on the pistol. "Easy," he instructed. "Lace your fingers together. Put your hands over your head."

Phoenix laced her fingers in a double fist and did as he asked.

Let his desire for the journal be his undoing.

Asa quickly glanced down into the sarcophagus. His eyes bulged.

Phoenix saw greed and desire darken Asa's features. Yes, she thought, you desire the journal above all else—

Come on—clock's ticking. Pick up the journal. Reach in and pick up the journal.

"You think I'm stupid?" he snorted. He drew Max back into the shadows. "Come over here. Get it for me," he demanded.

Phoenix licked her lips, refusing to look at Max.

"That's right," Asa shouted. "You first. You pick it up."

Phoenix clambered up onto the lip of the sarcophagus and reached in. She carefully picked up the journal and held it level as she climbed down. She stepped away from the coffin and held the book out to Asa.

He didn't move.

She thrust the book at him again. When he still didn't move, she snorted with an exhalation of impatience. "If you don't want the journal, I do." One hand lifted toward the latch on the cover.

"No!" Asa screamed. "Put the journal down on the ground." He shoved the gun at Max even harder.

Phoenix knelt and slowly placed the journal on the cavern floor. She raised her hands in the air, fingers clasped together.

"Now, all the way, face down," Asa growled. "Hands out in front where I can see them. Keep those fingers laced together."

Phoenix went to the ground. Asa pushed Max to his knees. "You, too. Down, all the way—that's right."

Side by side, she and Max lay with their faces on the cold stone floor, Phoenix with her arms awkwardly thrust in front of her. She held her breath, straining to keep Asa in her sight.

Time's up. Go for the journal, go for the journal—

Her expression blank, she stared at Asa. He kept one foot on Max's back. Seeing her and Max helpless, Asa bent and picked up the journal. He tried to manipulate the latch, but he needed two hands.

Phoenix's breath refused to move.

Asa backed away, out of reach. He tilted his head back so he could clamp one corner of the heavy book in his teeth while he reached around and shoved the gun in his back waistband.

Phoenix exhaled.

He put it in his mouth—

Asa's face was a grotesque, inhuman caricature, his eyes lit with maniacal satisfaction, his lips drawn back from his teeth. He handled the book reverently, stroking the hard cold surface with trembling hands. His fingers passed through what invisible poison had not already run directly into his mouth.

The latch continued to be uncooperative, even with Asa using two hands. Phoenix knew his fingers were growing unresponsive, defeating his efforts the harder he tried.

Sudden awareness struck as his eyes bulged with terror. "No!" he cried. He stabbed at his lips with the stiff fingers of his free hand. "What did you do?" he gasped.

The fake journal thudded to the stone floor. He stared at his hands, moving his fingers in jerky spasms. "No," he gurgled. Eyes huge, he grabbed his throat with both hands. His knees wobbled in a prelude to collapse.

Phoenix stood. She drew off the invisible latex gloves, quickly motioned them visible again, and dropped them on the floor. She kicked them aside. She pulled a vial from her pocket and waved it. "Antidote, if you want—" She tossed the vial into the sarcophagus and heard it clatter against the dark depths of the cold stone.

"Better hurry," she said. "You don't have a lot of time. Believe me, I know."

Asa lunged after the antidote. Phoenix stepped up behind him and snatched the gun from his waistband.

Max grunted from the floor and struggled to sit.

"Oh, sorry honey," she said. Keeping an eye on the struggling Asa, she pulled the sock out of Max's mouth and loosened the ties binding his hands.

Asa gasped for breath. Phoenix thought his legs didn't seem up to the call and wondered if she might have to give him a knee up into the coffin. He persevered, for his determination was fierce.

Hands rigid, he clawed up the side of the sarcophagus in desperate lunges. Each move came with a barked knee on the unforgiving stone, followed by a determined grunt. He finally collapsed across the sarcophagus lip, his upper body draped inside, his bottom half hanging outside. His gasps came farther and farther apart.

Phoenix walked over and grabbed Asa's feet. With a heave, she hoisted him head first into the coffin.

Max came to her side. They peered over the edge of the coffin as Asa struggled for the antidote. When his stiff fingers almost had the vial, Phoenix flicked her hand and the vial floated out of his reach.

"I don't think so," she said and pocketed the vial. His eyes pleaded to no avail, as she well remembered her own thoughts at this point. She gave him the cold smile of death.

"Bahk-ir, as the one who has killed your body, I curse your immortal soul." His pupils expanded with new fear.

"You will spend all eternity in this box, knowing only darkness forever. I take from you all you have known in this life, the past, and the future. Die, Asa Ducaine, and never resurrect again."

Tears flooded Asa's still attentive eyes. She gazed back, satisfied as he approached death. "Finally," she declared, "fate has delivered you everything you deserve, Bahk-ir."

Max grabbed Phoenix's hand. She turned to him, and they hugged, heart to heart. She buried her face in his neck and let the tears begin to fall. "I thought I was going to lose you."

He pulled back, mocking her fright. "What? After I just found you?" He gave her a that-is-so-not-going-to-happen look.

Phoenix laughed. More tears poured, not from fear, but of gratitude. "I love you ... Max ... Kedare ... Parrish—of Cyrenaica," she stated. Laughter bubbled from her chest, along with fresh tears of joy.

He rubbed the wetness from her face with a gentle thumb. "No more of these. This time, Phoenix Donovan, you deserve love, life, and magic."

A final death rattle squeaked from Asa's chest. They turned to look. A grimace of death split his face.

"Now what?" Max asked.

"Step aside," Phoenix said. When he stood behind her, she commanded the energy to lift the fake journal and steered it into the sarcophagus. She took no chances with the poisoned book. When it was safely inside the sarcophagus, she raised the lid.

Max came forward and nudged the heavy stone back to its seat. She released the energy slowly. The lid settled with a hollow 'thunk' and a puff of dust.

"I guess this changes things a little," Max said.

Phoenix walked around the space vacated by artifacts and gazed at the side chambers. She came to the side Asa didn't touch and clambered up onto the sarcophagus lid. She sat, drumming her heels on the stone. "Yeah," she exhaled. "We have a problem."

Max climbed up next to her and they sat shoulder to shoulder. "What do you want to do?"

She looked down at the sarcophagus. "I rather like him where he is. Seems so apropos."

"If he stays, everything—"

"Has to come back," she finished.

"Do you think we can manage that?" He scrunched his face in a mask of skepticism.

Phoenix looked down, watching her feet bounce off the side of the sarcophagus, enjoying her sense of power. Her eternal enemy lay defeated at her feet. She had Max at her side, and possession of the journal. Nothing could stop her. "I'm the Queen," she said. "I can do anything I want."

Before she could continue, a voice called from the outside stairs. "Hello, are you there?"

Phoenix froze. "Who's that?"

Max jumped down. Before she could stop him, he answered, "Yeah, come on back."

Phoenix felt her mouth fall open. "What?" she hissed at Max as a tall Berber strode in through the plastic strips.

"It's okay," Max said, squeezing her hand.

The Berber walked up to them, a curious smile on his face. "Izri came for me when none of you showed for breakfast." He looked around the chamber. "So, where is the dog?"

Max jerked his head toward the sarcophagus.

"I missed the action? You should have sent for me."

"Uh hum," Phoenix grunted. She looked expectantly at Max as he reached to help her down.

"My dear friend, Amestan," Max began. "This is Phoenix, Queen Byrgamon."

Amestan bowed deeply. Phoenix took the opportunity to mouth silently at Max, "What are you doing?" Before he could respond, Amestan stood up, grinning fiercely.

"Please … uh, call me Phoenix," she said. She relaxed, seeing they both wore the same mischievous grin. She looked at Max. "I believe I smell a plot."

"We attended Brown University together," he confessed. "One night, under the influence of several pitchers of dark beer, he stealthily pried from me our story."

Amestan added, "When I learned of the treachery employed, I dedicated my involvement, realizing he and I spoke of my own distant queen." He turned to the sarcophagus. "He is really in there?"

"And he isn't coming out," Phoenix stated.

Amestan's expression passed from disappointment to satisfaction. "Good. The loss of Asa Ducaine means many innocent lives will be spared. I am sorry to have missed his demise." He gave Max a slanted 'I'll-buy-the-beer-you-tell-the-story' look. "How can you leave him in there?"

"We put everything back and close it up," Phoenix said.

Amestan gave a toothy grin of approval. "My sentiments exactly." He clapped his hands and rubbed them together. "How many men do we need?"

Max rolled his eyes at Phoenix.

"No men. The more who participate, the more have to keep the secret." She brushed off her hands and said, "Stand back." When they hesitated, her eyebrows lifted, challenging their disbelief.

They sprinted back to the chamber opening.

Phoenix followed and took a position just in front of them. She bowed her head. Within her mind was every minute detail of the entire find. Using her heart to communicate her desire, she commanded the power to engage. She moved her hands in multiple commands, attracting the particles needed. With her intention clear in her mind, she stabbed the air with a series of power seals. For the space of a breath, nothing happened. She made a final move with her left hand.

Pressure shifted in her eardrums and she felt her hair move with the air. She lifted her head. The chamber was filled with artifacts, returned to their previous resting place along with their protective boxes.

Max stood by the opening, eyes huge. Amestan held a hand clapped over his mouth.

Phoenix grinned. She would enjoy this power. Thankfully, Max's love would help her keep the power and her ego in check.

"Outside, boys," Phoenix said. "Go on, shoo." She waved her hands and they scurried out the door.

They followed her down the stairs and into the tent, now barren except for the empty tables. "I can make all this … go away—"

"No!" Amestan blurted. "We can either use or sell everything here."

"Can you do that without attracting any curious government officials?"

"With Asa gone, Gadhafi will be so busy hunting a new arms dealer, he'll forget all about this place."

"What if they send the helicopter that collected Asa?" Phoenix protested.

"They will see nothing but a dry mountain top."

Max added softly. "Return the boulders to the opening, and no one will know we were here."

Phoenix stared at the opening to the Temple. She had spent more than enough time in the darkness to last her all eternity. She never wanted to see the Temple again.

She walked from the tent. The men quickly stepped in line behind her. She pointed to the doors covering the opening and moved her fingers. The wood slowly turned dark and buckled, warping away from the rock face. The metal bolts creaked and squealed, stretching as the bucking wood tore at them until the metal snapped. The doors crashed on the landing. The stairs and all the new wood construction moved, writhing, warping, and turning black. Nails stretched and broke, and the darkened boards collapsed to the ground in a jumble.

The exposed opening to the Temple was like a great mouth on

the rock face. She pointed to the loose rocks and boulders on the hillside and closed her hands like gathering up a sack. She threw her fists open and followed with power seals.

The rocks moved slowly, as if objecting to being commanded. But the particles were persistent, and soon the entire hillside was in motion.

Big boulders clustered over the opening, while smaller rocks darted into the remaining holes. Dust rose in a billowing cloud, obscuring the hillside, but the rocks banged and grated in transit as they jockeyed for position. When all was silent, Phoenix spread her hands and flicked her fingers. The dust fell like heavy snow straight to the ground.

The new configuration gave the hill a complete new face.

"It is unbelievable," Amestan said. "I have been coming here since I was a child. I would never recognize this place."

He nodded with conviction. "Your Temple is buried."

They climbed down the dry streambed to the camp. Amestan eyed the first class tents. "I can get good money for these on the market."

"What about Chef Andre?" Phoenix asked. "He—"

"Has no allegiance to Asa," Amestan said. "At least not by what he told Izri. We will see he gets to where he wants."

"The men who helped us open the sarcophagus—"

"Saw a soul released when the lid was moved," Amestan replied. "Even though we are a modern people with good Berber muscle." He stopped to point to his head. "None will want to come back here or discuss what they saw for fear of angering the queen's soul. They expect you to haunt these hills forever."

Phoenix smiled, feeling the bonds of the past slipping from her soul. Tears filled her eyes, but they were tears of relief— and hope.

Max squeezed her hand. "One more stop?"

She nodded in agreement, her heart eager to finally be free. "Yes, one more stop."

CHAPTER FIFTEEN

Phoenix stretched on the bow of their sixty-five foot sailboat, *Magic*, satisfied as a fat cat. The sun warmed her skin, and the ocean glittered impossibly blue under a cloudless sky. Her husband, Captain Max, piloted the luxury sailboat toward the open sea.

After six months sailing the Pacific on their way to the Philippines, passionately loving their way from one small atoll to the next, she don't want this to end.

"We're almost there," Max called over the rushing sound of the wind and the water.

Phoenix sat up, the Journal of War in her hand. She looked fondly at the ancient book, having finally made peace with her part in its destructive path. "It is time, old friend."

She walked back to the stern where a hundred pounds of rock was loaded. Remembering how the astonished dockhands eyed the strange cargo, she quipped, "We must remember to stop by there again—to show them we both came back."

Max climbed down from the pilothouse, laughing. "They thought one of us was getting dumped."

"Are we there?"

"GPS says so."

She set the journal down and walked into his embrace. Chills of pleasure ran down her arms and she pushed her nose into his chest, inhaling his scent. His heartbeat, slow and steady by her ear, always showed her the way.

She stood with him like that, content in her need for him, rocking back and forth with the boat's motion. Halyards slapped and the boat creaked, gradually reminding her life went on.

Tears filled Phoenix's eyes for the incredible turn her life had taken. She understood. And just as Faby predicted, her life was destroyed.

Fortunately, Faby was also correct when she said all that would remain was trust ... and love, of course.

Phoenix hugged Max close. Because the eternal power of justice brought them a second chance, and because she was Byrgamon, as well as Phoenix, she was strong enough to see the journal buried forever. At last, with this man's help, she would finally put the past in the past.

"Ready?" he asked.

She stepped back and dashed her hand across her eyes. "Yes," she said and motioned him to step behind her. He jumped up on the back of the seat, grinning. She blew him a kiss and wiggled her fingers, sending it on the backs of tachyons. His hand shot out, catching the kiss. He pressed it to his heart.

Phoenix held the journal with one hand and made the motions with her other hand that pulverized rock. The one hundred pounds of rock popped like firecrackers and burst into grit and gravel.

She set the journal in the center of the pile. Even though invisible, the heavy book left an indentation in the busted rubble.

Envisioning a rock sarcophagus for the Journal, she made a swirling motion with one hand. The broken bits of rock slowly rose and mimicked her commands, encircling the journal in a vortex. When the moving rock encased the journal, Phoenix commanded the rock to reform, darting through the moves quickly.

The mass of rock particles stopped instantly, solidifying around the journal in a solid lump of new stone. Phoenix held the mass suspended aloft on a layer of energy.

She nodded to Max, who came down from his perch and followed her. They walked to the edge of the stern deck, bringing the entombed journal. Gently, Phoenix elevated the mass and sent it out over the water.

"Go with my blessing. Seek peace in the depths, never to rise again." She flicked her fingers and the rock splashed into the blue sea and sank.

They leaned over the stern and watched the rock fall from sight. "How deep is it here?" Phoenix asked.

"The deepest place on earth," Max replied. They stared at the infinite depths for some time in silence, rocking back and forth with the gentle motion of the water. At last he said, "We passed a nice little atoll a little ways back."

Phoenix nodded. "I saw that. I think she'll like it there." She ducked into the salon and retrieved the container of Gamon's ashes.

Max turned the boat around and sailed away from the journal. The wind gusted, lifting their sails so that *Magic* soared across the water. "Did you do that?" Max asked. He pulled her close.

"Not me," Phoenix protested. She smiled and gave her husband a knowing look. "That's Gamon."

On the starboard side, the small atoll they sought came into view, bearing a ring of palms on brilliant white sand around a small lagoon.

Max pulled *Magic* inside the lagoon and dropped the sails. The boat rocked softly, seeming content in the tiny safe harbor.

Phoenix stood on the bow with Gamon's ashes. A sense of all encompassing peace surrounded her, freeing the final thread from the past. She opened the container and released the ashes into the peaceful lagoon. "Be free, Gamon. Be free, knowing we finally got life, love, and magic."

She looked up and saw Max was smiling at her from the pilot-house. She held her hand out as she walked up to him.

He drew her into his arms and picked up the small gold disk she wore on a chain around her neck. This one reminder—their ancient written names—was all she kept of the past, for it spoke of the eternal power of love. When he offered her the gold jewelry from the sarcophagus, she refused to touch it. "Melt it down and give it to charity," she instructed.

His face held a look full of mischief she couldn't ignore. "What?" she asked.

"I have something for you." He reached into his pants pocket and retrieved a velvet ring box.

"What could you possibly give me that I don't already have?" she asked. She took the box and opened it. "Oh!"

"I give you our future," he said. He took the box and removed the ring. A circle of diamonds caught brilliant fire in the sun. He slipped the band on her ring finger, next to the gold wedding band.

She held her hand out and admired the diamond ring. "Why is this eternity band our future?"

"I saw us on a beach walking in the sand," he said. "You were wearing this ring." He buried his face in her shoulder length hair and inhaled deeply, rousing her curiosity.

"Have you developed a power?" She meant to tease him, but stopped when she saw he was serious.

"On that first trip with Amestan, when I entered the chamber, and realized that magic and past lives existed, I saw a vision of the future. Our future," he whispered.

"And you are just now telling me?"

He smiled and tapped the gold disk she wore so close to her heart. "All things come when the time is right. You know that."

Phoenix peered into the depths of his eyes and saw not only passion and desire, but also peace and a sense of completion.

"I see," she hummed. "On this beach we will repair the circle broken long ago." She turned in his arms as he held her, and gazed across the blue water, so similar to the ocean off North Africa.

"Yes," she said, pulling him close. "At last, the future is ours ... and the heart of night belongs to us."

• • •

DANA LYONS

Dana Lyons lives in the mountains of western North Carolina with her husband, Randy, four cats and two horses. She loves to travel and cook, try new wines, study quantum physics, and discover new mysteries of the heart and mind. Says Lyons, "If you believe enough, if you love enough, you can draw upon a power to create the life and love of your dreams. Love is a force that comes from within, yet steers the course of your life as if from the faraway stars."